POISON

Also by

CHRIS WOODING

The Haunting of Alaizabel Cray

Crashing

Kerosene

The Broken Sky series

CHRIS WOODING

POISON

ORCHARD BOOKS ❦ NEW YORK
An Imprint of Scholastic Inc.

Library of Congress Cataloging-in-Publication Data

Wooding, Chris, 1977–
Poison / Chris Wooding.—1st Orchard Books ed.
p. cm.
Originally pub.: Great Britain : Scholastic, 2003.
Summary: When Poison leaves her home in the marshes of Gull to retrieve
the infant sister who was snatched by the fairies, she and a group of unusual
friends survive encounters with the inhabitants of various Realms, and
Poison herself confronts a surprising destiny.
[1. Fairies—Fiction. 2. Storytelling—Fiction. 3. Fantasy.] I. Title.
PZ7.W860368Poi 2005
[Fic]—dc22
2005002174

ISBN 0-439-75570-0

12 11 10 9 8 7 6 5 4 3 2   05 06 07 08 09

Printed in the U.S.A.
First Orchard Books edition, September 2005

Contents

Soulswatch Eve   1

The Scarecrow and the Changeling   16

The Wraith-Catcher   30

Shieldtown   42

Lamprey   56

The House of the Bone Witch   70

Peppercorn and the Cat   81

Skins and Bones   94

The Fisher Sage   109

Deals and Destinations   122

Spiders   136

The Lady of Cobwebs   150

The Trouble With Phaeries   159

Storytelling   173

An Audience With Melcheron   186

Malaise   198

Assassins   210

The Ur-Lord   222

A Proposition of the Heart   235

Knives   253

To End the Tale   264

The Moving Finger writes; and, having writ,
Moves on: nor all thy Piety nor Wit
Shall lure it back to cancel half a Line,
Nor all thy Tears wash out a Word of it.

—*The Rubáiyát of Omar Khayyám*

SOULSWATCH EVE

〜〜〜

ONCE upon a time there was a young lady who lived in a marsh, and her name was Poison.

She was an odd-looking girl, pale and slender with long black hair that fell symmetrically to either side of her head. Her face was an oval, her forehead high but her chin narrow, her lips thin and her nose perfectly straight, if a fraction too long in the bridge. But it was her eyes that dominated her features, great dark eyes of shocking violet, through which she regarded the world with a sullen and disturbing intensity.

She lived in a village called Gull, deep in the heart of the Black Marshes. It was a whimsical choice of name, since none of the inhabitants had ever seen a gull, much less the sea. Unless you counted old Fleet, who might or might not have travelled the Realm and seen many things, depending on whether or not you believed him. The village was built on stilts, a multitude of interlinked wooden platforms that sprawled over a murky and weed-choked lake, dodging between enormous corkscrew trees and grassy landbars that bulked out of the browny-grey water. Sometimes these landbars were swallowed by the water when it rose up the stilts almost to the level of the houses, and sometimes the lake oozed so low that it was possible to see the dark shapes of the things that swam there, waiting to snatch up the unwary. Here in the Black Marshes, life was a precarious thing, and the only truly solid ground was that which you built yourself.

Poison lived in a round hut near the edge of the lake, where a thick bank of hornbark trees ran up close against the water. She shared the hut with her father, her stepmother, and her baby sister, Azalea. They had a platform all to themselves, with the wall of their hut surrounded by a circular walkway of rickety planks and a banister of crooked branches. A rope bridge linked them to the next platform along, with a gap where one of the slats had rotted through that Poison had been hopping over ever since she could remember. When she was very young she used to sit on the edge of the gap and dangle her feet through. Her mother — her *real* mother — had warned her against it, but she was ever a contrary child and she ignored the advice. Then one day, when the lake had risen particularly high, she had been dangling her feet when a goatfish lunged out of the water. She spotted its horned, looming shadow an instant before it surged out of the murk, its mouth wide like a chasm, trailing a beard of tendrils. She pulled herself up as venomous jaws closed around the spot where her legs had been. It was big enough to have taken them off in one clean bite. She learned her lesson from that.

Her mother, Faraway, had always said that Poison would never take advice, always do the opposite of what she was told. For a time, Poison considered doing the opposite of *that* and following her mother's advice to the letter from then on, but she reasoned that she would only confuse herself and forgot about it. Then her mother died of swamp lung just after giving birth to Azalea, and her father in his grief had married a cold beauty called Snapdragon from the next village west. There was antagonism from the start between stepmother and stepdaughter. Though she was all elegance and lightheartedness in the presence of Poison's father, she hated the violet-eyed girl, and Poison hated her.

It was to spite Snapdragon that she took the name Poison at her nameday. She had not always been called so. What kind of parent would call their newborn Poison? Her name had been Foxglove until her fourteenth birthday, when the whole village gathered on the central platform to hear the name she had chosen for herself. It was tradition among the marsh people. Girls were named after flowers and herbs, boys after animals or features of the landscape. On their nameday, when they were counted as adults, they were allowed to choose their own name. Many, like Snapdragon, kept the one they had been given. Others, like her woodcutter father, Hew, took the traditional names of their profession.

On the morning of her nameday, Foxglove and Snapdragon had argued bitterly.

"You'll never do as I tell you! Never! You'll never be as a good girl should. Always full of questions, never accepting things as they are. Always full of spite for me! You'll never make your father happy, never marry a strong young man. You're poison to this family, poison!"

And so she became. When she announced her new name, there was barely a flicker of surprise among the villagers. She had always been an outcast to them, strange and alien. Only her father and stepmother sucked in their breath in horror, but by then it was too late. Poison she was, and Poison she would be forever.

❧⌣❧

Two years had passed since that day, and Poison was sixteen now, on the awkward cusp of womanhood. Her sixteenth birthday had been entirely forgotten by both her parents this year, and there had been nobody else to celebrate it with her. She didn't care. It was just a day, like any other. Why should she be compelled to feel glad on that one particular day, to dance and drink marshwine and be merry, to commemorate the moment that she was forced moist and bloody from her mother's womb? What was there to celebrate about that? She was happier before, when the world was a hot red warmth and there was only the sound of her mother's heartbeat and the muffled reverberations of her comforting voice. Better that than this — this cold, dreary land of grief and misery.

She envied the villagers her own age, who could forget their cares in the joy of a celebration, who aspired to nothing more than a good husband or a pretty wife, to raise children to perpetuate themselves. She could not think like that. She could not shrug off the fact that one in five of them died of swamp lung by their thirtieth birthday, that every other child was stillborn, that boys and girls disappeared every month and were never seen again, snatched up by marsh creatures or phaeries. The older villagers grieved, and they were full of woe at the harshness of life, but not one of them lifted a finger to do anything about it. People were much happier if they accepted their lot, it seemed; but she could not bring herself to accept hers. To marry a young man of the village, to settle down and idle her life away bearing children and caring for them? She would rather cast herself in among the goatfish. At least that would be a quick death instead of the long, lingering one that staying in Gull would be.

"You have a touch of the Old Blood in you, Poison," Fleet had told her once. "From back in the time when men and women were strong, and they ruled the Realm."

"What happened to them?" she had asked, sitting as she always did on the rug before the fire, with the old man in his battered wicker chair taking puffs from the hookah that stood on the floor next to him.

"They got soft," Fleet replied. "Living was easy, the Realm was at peace. Man doesn't like to be at peace. It goes against his nature. So people began to squabble amongst themselves, and from their squabbles came conflicts, and conflict is such an easy thing to start and a difficult thing to stop. So followed the Many-Sided War, and when it was over, Man had become divided and weak. He took to the swamps and the mountains, and turned his back on his fellows. The old cities are empty and crumbling now, haunted by ghosts of the past, just as we are." Fleet took a draw on his hookah and blew out a jet of aromatic smoke, which feathered in the updraught of the fire and dispersed across the thatched ceiling.

Poison knew all about the Many-Sided War — or at least she knew the legends, for who knew what was fact and what was fiction? — but she liked to hear the old man talk. Fleet was regarded as an oddity, much as she was. Though he kept to himself, he was absent for long periods at a time, and when he returned it was always with new tales to tell. He might have been inoffensive in other ways, but the fact that he wandered at all was enough for parents to warn their children away from him. No good could come of the outside world. Phaeries lived out there, and trolls and ghoblins and things without names. There were not a few in the village who muttered that maybe the old man had a bit of phaerie in him. To be so spry at his age could only mean trouble.

"But you, girl," he creaked at length, "you have some of that ancient spirit in you, as I have. You won't be satisfied with life here. You see beyond what's in front of you."

"Sometimes I wish I could just be ... happy. Happy with what I've got," she confessed. "Like the other girls my age."

"Ach!" he barked, with a wave of his wrinkled and weathered hand. "Don't confuse contentment with happiness, Poison. Besides," he said, staring into the fire, his expression suddenly distant, "some of us are born in the right place, and some of us have to go look for it."

~~~

It was Soulswatch Eve tonight. Poison had spent the day roaming the denser marshes that surrounded the lake where Gull stood, cropping mushrooms and roots with her rusty little sickle. Everything metal rusted within a year in this place, with all the moisture in the air, yet they could never seem to get wood or stone sharp enough to serve as decent blades — another aspect of life that was accepted with a weary shrug by the people of the marsh. She cursed as she hacked through her hundredth foilscap stem and wished for a sharper edge.

When she returned, night was falling and the soul cages were already being hung in the trees. She carried a basket brimming with tiny mushrooms. Snapdragon would be angry, of course; she had specifically told Poison to gather the biggest ones for the pot. But Poison preferred the smaller ones, for their taste was sharper and not so bland, and in the end, who was doing all the work anyway?

She idled past a couple of children monkeying their way through the upper branches of the dense trees to secure another soul cage. They chattered amongst themselves as they affixed it, an orb of wooden bars cradling a candle in the middle. The candle was set in a bulb of rare coloured glass. When the candle was lit, it would glow a soft purple-pink. Poison glanced a little farther upward, and saw the muscular flank of a murksnake hanging in lazy loops and coils around a higher branch, watching the morsels beneath it uninterestedly. It was too late in the day for murksnakes to feed, and for that the children would have been thankful, if they had even known it was there. Had it been a few hours earlier, with the snake's metabolism powered by the faint heat of the sun, it would have bitten them both and coiled around them to crush their bones to jelly while they were paralysed. Poison wondered how many more times they might brush by death like that before it caught up with them.

She navigated her way around the platforms of Gull to get back to her hut. The air was chill and full of the pirriping of insects and the slovenly rustle of the larger marsh animals. Fireflies swung back and forth like pendulums in the shadowy recesses of the trees. A soupy white mist obscured the water of the lake. Because of the way the town was laid out, it was necessary to pass by several huts on the way back home. Most platforms had three or four huts clustered together with their doors facing inward and a plank walkway around the back of them. Murky, circular windows, divided into quarters by their frames, ran around the outsides of the round huts. Tar torches blazed on long poles around the edges of each platform, adding their light to the glow from within the huts. Smoke wisped through stone chimneys in the thatched roofs.

On the last platform before home, Poison heard an excited chatter ahead of her. Automatically, she considered avoiding it; she was not fond of the village children, and they were not fond of her. Unfortunately, there was no way to pass it by unseen. She had to skirt the platform to get to the bridge that linked to her hut. With a sigh, she forged stoically onward.

She had guessed what the disturbance was before she rounded her neighbour's hut and it came into sight. A man was striding across one of the rope bridges that linked this platform to others, dogged by a gaggle of children who darted about behind him and before him. He seemed oblivious to them all, loping along under the burden of a vast array of metal jars that clanked and clattered as he walked. He was clad all in furs, with thick hide gloves and a broad, battered hat, and his face was grizzled with whiskers and a great white moustache. A wraith-catcher.

Poison stopped to watch him, less out of interest and more because she wanted to pique Snapdragon by being as late as possible. A wraith-catcher came to the village every Soulswatch Eve, to buy up all the marshwraiths that the villagers had caught in their soul cages. Poison reflected that he himself did not do any actual catching on this night, just bartering and haggling; but she supposed that he spent enough time during the rest of the year hunting the poor things down to justify his title. It was only on Soulswatch Eve that catching marsh-wraiths became a public spectacle.

On this night in the year, when the moon was right, the marshwraiths came out to dance and swirl. Poison found it beautiful to watch them, softly fizzing balls of ethereal light trailing phantom sparks as they looped and curled around each other. Nobody knew why they emerged on the same night each year, or why they danced and flashed their colours, gliding through breathtaking hues that went beyond the spec-trum of human vision. Some speculated it was a kind of mating ritual; others said it was the souls of the dead, the chil-dren whom the marsh had taken from them, come back to visit their relatives.

If that was so, Poison found it faintly strange that the vil-lagers lured them like moths to the soul cages and trapped them. For the coloured glow of the candles drew the marsh-wraiths in, and they would stay there as long as the candle burned. Each cage had a dangling cord that could be pulled to cinch the flexible bars tight, squeezing the orb closed so that the marshwraith could not escape. Then they would be brought to the wraith-catcher.

Her neighbour opened the door of their hut just as the

wraith-catcher raised one gloved hand to knock. Poison knew well enough the sickly grin on Bluff's face; he didn't want the wraith-catcher any more than anybody else did, but this was Soulswatch Eve, and nobody could refuse him. He would stay at Bluff's hut tonight, eat his food and take his bed, and in the morning he would buy up all the marshwraiths that the villagers had caught and put them in those metal jars he carried. Then he would take them elsewhere, where they would be imprisoned in glass lamps and sold to those rich enough to afford such luxuries.

He went inside, leaving a disappointed crowd of urchins milling about on the platform or trying to get a glimpse through the windows. Poison went on her way. What excitement the appearance of a stranger provoked, when it was really such a little thing. There was more attention given to that wraith-catcher than when someone was found half-eaten by mud-spiders. She supposed the latter was more common, so people were less interested.

Snapdragon was at the stove when Poison returned, her strawberry-blonde hair tied back from her face. Poison's father sat nearby, with Azalea in her pen next to him.

"You certainly took your time gathering the mushrooms," Snapdragon said, without looking up from where she was stirring a pot. When she did glance over, she added, "And you got the small kind, as I asked you not to."

Poison regarded her silently with her disturbing violet eyes. She could see by the pulse at her stepmother's temple that she was angry, but she was restraining herself in front of her husband. Hew was watching them with that expression he always wore when his daughter and his wife were together — the sort of expression a man might wear if he was balancing a stack of valuable plates that might totter at any moment.

"Set them down there," Snapdragon said with a sigh, indicating the table behind her. "Now the soup will taste wrong." She returned her attention to the pot. Poison was about to go to her room when Snapdragon spoke again. "I try with you, Foxglove, I really try. Why must you go out of your way to hinder me?"

"My name is Poison," she reminded her stepmother. Snapdragon had always refused to call her by that name, for she knew why Poison had taken it. "And don't feel hard done by, Snapdragon. I go out of my way to hinder everyone."

"Poison, don't speak to your mother so," Hew said wearily. "Come and see Azalea."

Poison did not deign to make the obvious response. She had corrected her father every time for months: *step*mother! Yet he never stopped referring to Snapdragon as Poison's mother, and Poison would never call her anything other than Snapdragon, and *she* would never call Poison anything other than Foxglove. *How idiotic,* Poison thought.

She did not blame her father, or even Snapdragon. She believed that Snapdragon truly did love Hew, in her own way; that was why she made such an effort not to berate his daughter in front of him. And Hew loved Snapdragon, though Poison suspected he still saw his first wife, Faraway, when he looked at his daughter. He was caught between two enemies, and he loved them both in different ways.

Poison did not begrudge him his happiness, even when he forgot her birthday because he was too wrapped up in Snapdragon's affairs; but she could not help being a thorn in Snapdragon's foot.

If Snapdragon had simply been *herself,* then everything might have been all right. It was just this ridiculous charade that she insisted on playing out. On the one hand, she protested that she was not trying to replace Faraway, while on the other she made every effort to do exactly that. She tried hard to be homely, to cook and clean and ask how Poison's day had gone; she did everything she could to be an attentive wife and mother. But it was all fake. Poison could see that.

The real Snapdragon did not have a homely bone in her body. She wanted to be carefree, wanted to live the life she had heard about in stories, stories of glass slippers and three wishes and magick rings. Poison had watched her as she sat rapt at the storytellings that Fleet gave on the central platform, during those occasional days when he was in the village. She had seen the stars shining in Snapdragon's eyes. Snapdragon was beautiful, and she knew it, and in her heart she wanted to be a princess. But when the tales were done, she would come home and protest that she had never heard such fancy and nonsense.

Snapdragon was a wife and a stepmother because she thought she ought to be. She was just another person floating down the river of life who had grabbed on to a spar and was hanging on — hanging on because she dared not let go. Like everyone else here, she lacked the strength to swim.

Poison was doing her a favour by making her life awkward. At least it made things a fraction more interesting for her.

She sat by Azalea's pen. Her father gave her a smile. He had a kindly, simple face, creased with lines of care. Brown hair and a brown moustache, and eyes that seemed to have gone a few shades bleaker since Faraway had died. Poison loved him for the same reason she loved Azalea: she could not help herself.

Azalea was two years old now, almost three. She was old enough to scamper about the place on her own, but not unsupervised. Children in the village were not let outside the house on their own until they were wise enough not to totter off the edge of the platforms into the water, and certainly not before they were taught to swim in one of the safer pools to the north, where goatfish did not lurk. She reached up as Poison came over.

"Poy-zun!" she cried happily.

Poison scooped her out of the pen and dandled her on her lap. Azalea, believing that freedom was within her grasp, tried to squirm out of her grip and onto the floor, but Poison foiled her. Snapdragon cast an irate look over her shoulder at the child. She half-expected Poison to let her go, knowing how Azalea was forbidden to run about while Snapdragon was cooking. It was as much for the child's sake as Snapdragon's; she was terribly clumsy with kitchenware, and was forever sloshing boiling water about or dropping hot pans.

Poison got up, carrying Azalea into their room where they could play in relative freedom behind a closed door. Snapdragon, who had begun washing the mushrooms, said, "Careful now," as Poison picked up the girl.

"If I can carry a basket of mushrooms, I can carry my own sister," Poison replied and shut the door of the bedroom behind her.

The hut was divided into four sections. It was single-storey, for the stilts of the platform could not take the weight of anything more than that. The main living-area took up almost all of the hut, with a fire and a stove and some chairs and a table. Everything was made of wood except the stone fireplace and the rusty iron stove. They took their baths there, too; there was not much room for modesty in the Black Marshes. The remaining strip of space, which ran up against the back wall of the circular hut, was divided into three sections. The two biggest ones were the bedrooms: one for the girls, and one for the adults. A third one was the toilet, which was little more than a hole that emptied out into the lake beneath.

Poison's room — she thought of it as hers, at least until Azalea was old enough to start asserting her personal space — was cramped and dim, but it was her refuge and she treasured it. A tatty single bed lay against one wall, and a crib was placed against another, with high bars to prevent Azalea from escaping it in the night. In between was a low table on which a candle burned and a few shelves crowded with little ornaments and a few books, all of which had either been given to her or borrowed from Fleet. Snapdragon predictably disapproved of her friendship with the old man, but Poison could tell her heart was not in it; she was merely parroting the rest of the villagers because she thought it was the right thing to do.

Fleet brought her such wonderful objects from his travels: strange carvings, a feather he swore came from a gryphon, a petrified egg from a bird that flew upside down. She suspected this last one was a fancy, for she had been very young and more gullible when he had given it to her. The books were legends and tales, stories from all over the Realm. These she had devoured voraciously — so voraciously, in fact, that she started to become fatigued by them. It was possible to have too much of a good thing, she reflected.

"They're all the same," she complained to Fleet one night. "The soldier rescues the maiden and they fall in love. The fool outwits the wicked king. There are always three brothers or sisters, and it's always the youngest who succeeds after the first two fail. Always be kind to beggars, for they always have a secret; never trust a unicorn. If you answer somebody's riddle they always either kill themselves or have to do what you say. They're all the same, and they're all ridiculous! That isn't what life is like!"

Fleet had nodded sagely and puffed on his hookah. "Well, of course that's not what life is like. Except the bit about unicorns — they'll eat your guts as soon as look at you. Those things in there" — he tapped the book she was carrying — "they're simple stories. Real life is a story, too, only much more complicated. It's still got a beginning, a middle, and an end. Everyone follows the same rules, you know.... It's just that there are more of them. Everyone has chapters and cliffhangers. Everyone has their journey to make. Some go far and wide and come back empty-handed; some don't go anywhere and their journey makes them richest of all. Some tales have a moral and some don't make any sense. Some will make you laugh, others make you cry. The world is a library, young Poison, and you'll never get to read the same book twice."

Poison snorted derisively, even though she loved it when the old man talked this way. "What kind of stories do the folk of Gull have to tell? They're as boring and predictable as these legends are. Once you've read a few, you've read them all."

"Do you really think so?" Fleet asked, his spine cracking like fireworks as he leaned nearer. "I think you don't know the half of what goes on in this village, because you've already decided it's not worth reading past the cover."

Poison gave an insouciant shrug. "I don't care," she replied. "I'm not interested."

"Well, let me leave you with this, then," said Fleet. "Every story has its twists and turns, and you never know when the next one is coming. Don't forget that, Poison."

"I won't," she replied sarcastically, instantly dismissing it from her thoughts. But she took with her the books that she had been meaning to give back to him.

For some reason, Fleet's words came back to her when she went to bed that night. Snapdragon's soup had been the best she had ever tasted — a fact she attributed to her mushrooms — and then Snapdragon and Hew had gone out to watch the marshwraiths. Poison did not have the heart to watch the display tonight; she was unaccountably depressed. Instead, she tucked in Azalea, crawled under her moth-eaten covers, and went to sleep with the sound of faint laughs in her ears, of children chasing the twinkling wraiths, and the distant chiming of a small silver bell. The chime seemed to follow her down, down into sleep, and she remembered thinking it strangely out of place in the sounds of the marsh. Then Azalea gurgled in the midst of a dream, and Poison opened her eyes muzzily and looked fondly on the child in her crib before oblivion claimed her.

It was the last time she ever did so.

THE SCARECROW AND
THE CHANGELING

～⌒～⌒～⌒～

I T WAS Snapdragon's scream that jerked Poison awake. She half-rose out of her blankets, sloughing off a thin dusting of sparkling flakes that covered her. Strangely, despite the circumstances of her waking, she immediately felt the warm hand of sleep enfolding her again, making her eyes droop. She shook herself in puzzlement, looking down at the stuff on her blanket and in her hair. It was like unmelted snow, yet it glimmered in the cloudy light of the morning sun that came in through the round window.

She felt herself drowsing again, against her will, and this time she flung her blankets aside and pulled herself out of the tattered old bed. The flakes . . . it was something to do with the flakes. . . . She did not understand how or why, but some instinct had made the connection between the mysterious stuff that covered the bed and the weight of slumber that pressed down on her. She tousled and shook her hair and patted down her hemp nightdress frantically, as if trying to beat out flames, and she felt her tiredness lift from her as the flakes fell free. She stared at them in alarmed wonder for a moment.

"What have you *done?*" Snapdragon shrieked at her from the

other side of the small room, and Poison suddenly remembered why it was she had been awoken. Snapdragon was standing at Azalea's cradle, her face a rictus of horror, her eyes needling accusation at Poison.

Poison rubbed a hand across her face to smear the last remnants of sleep from her eyes and came over to the crib, ignoring Snapdragon completely. There was a terrible sinking in her chest, a spreading void of premonition.

She looked into the crib. Whatever it was that lay in there, it was not Azalea.

"Why didn't you wake?" Snapdragon hissed. "You were right there! You terrible thing! Why didn't you wake?"

Poison was not listening. The world seemed to have shrunk to the size of the crib and what was inside it. Sounds had become faint, even Snapdragon's shrill voice in her ear. She could hear the slow whoosh of blood as it swept round her body, the inrush and release of her breath. She put her hands on the side of the crib to steady herself. Somewhere in her memory, a small silver bell was chiming.

She pushed herself away from the crib and snatched down the thickest tome on her bookshelf. She had borrowed it from Fleet a long time ago and never thought to give it back. Its dusty leather cover creaked as she opened it, and the pages flickered under her fingers.

"Reading? Reading at a time like this?" Snapdragon howled. Poison spared her an annoyed glance before resuming her search. Her stepmother began to weep. "Poor Hew. What'll I tell him? What'll I say? His heart will break."

The page that Poison was looking for flipped flat, and she felt her head go light. There it was. The leftmost page was dominated by a black-and-white woodcut print of a hunched figure dressed in a long, ragged coat, its face shadowed under a wide-brimmed hat. Its eyes were two slits in the darkness. It

held out before it one long, thin arm, and its scrawny, emaciated hand held a tiny bell delicately between thumb and
forefinger. With its other hand, it was scattering something
that looked like dust. In the picture, it was in a wooded glade,
surrounded by sleeping people.

"The Scarecrow," Poison whispered.

She heard the chime again in her head. She frowned, puzzled, and stared hard at the page. Had she seen something *move*
there, just a moment ago? She peered closer.

The picture suddenly seemed to grow under her gaze, as if
she was falling into it or it was rising from the page to swallow
her. The black-and-white leaves of the trees seemed to stir. She
felt dizzy, her violet eyes going wide.

The Scarecrow turned its head to look at her, staring out
from the page, and her throat tightened in terror. She wanted
to close the book suddenly, but she could not will her muscles to move. She felt herself pinned there, unable to even blink.
Disbelief and panic clawed their way upwards from her chest.

The Scarecrow began to walk towards her. Its movements
were curiously jerky, as if she was watching a flicker-book, but
it was definitely moving. Coming closer in short, hobbling
steps, its tiny bell held out before it.

Impossible, she told herself. *Impossible.*

But she could not draw back, could not look away. The
chime sounded again as the Scarecrow twitched the bell, a
pure and unutterably sinister note, quiet and yet clearer than
anything else she could hear. It had loomed until its upper
body almost filled the page now, as if she was looking at it
through a window and it was almost at the sill. The bell
chimed again, dominating her consciousness. The white slits
of the Scarecrow's eyes burned into her from within the inky
darkness of its face.

Poison could barely breathe. What air she could force into

her lungs came in shudders. Everything she knew was telling her that this could not be happening, that it was only a picture on a page she was looking at; yet the Scarecrow grew, shuffling closer and closer until it seemed that there was only the thickness of the page separating them.

It put one hand on the edge of the picture, and its fingers folded over the bottom of the page and scraped against her wrist.

The slam of the outside door jolted her out of her trance, and she flung the book away with a cry. It tumbled to the floor and landed shut with a heavy thump on the planks. Trembling, she stared at it from her bed, ready to run if it should do anything other than lie where it was.

Nothing happened.

Poison felt her heartbeat decelerate slowly, and she began to breathe again. She clasped her hands in her lap to try and stop them from shaking, stealing glances at the book now and again. There must be an explanation, there must be. . . .

It was then that she noticed that Snapdragon was gone, and married that realization to the slam of the hut door she had heard a moment ago. The crib was empty, too.

In a flash, she saw what Snapdragon was going to do. Poison scrambled off her bed and fled out of the door to try to stop her.

~~~

It was a cold and dank morning, the sun clambering up through the faintly greenish miasma that hung over the Black Marshes. A little early still for the flies to be out, for the waters of the marsh had not yet warmed to the day's heat. Poison emerged from her hut into the chill, clad only in her hemp nightdress. It did not bother her overly. Most of the village was still abed after the excitement of Soulswatch Eve, and though she looked faintly ridiculous, her nightdress was thicker and warmer than her daywear and she did not care what the villagers thought anyway. She had the sense to pause to put on some boots though, for it was virtually suicide to walk barefoot in the mud of the marsh, where insects and snakes, venomous spiders and spiny snails, could kill with a bite or a scratch.

Snapdragon was nowhere to be seen, but there was only one bridge from their platform to the next, so Poison hurried over it to her neighbours' platform, where the wraith-catcher snored in Bluff's house while Bluff and his wife made do with the floor. Two rope bridges branched off from there; one of them was still swinging slightly in the wake of Snapdragon's passage. Poison took it, already knowing where Snapdragon was going.

She caught sight of her stepmother just as she was disappearing into the trees that crowded up against the lake in which Gull stood. The thing that had been in the crib was wrapped up tight in a blanket, held against her chest. Poison called out to her as she ran onto the rope bridge that spanned the murky water from shore to village. Snapdragon paused momentarily and looked back, a kind of madness in her expression. Then she plunged on into the trees. Poison rushed after her and slipped on the moist planking of the bridge, but she caught the ropes at either side with her armpits before she could fall, and she suffered only sore burns on her skin. Cursing herself, she ran on and into the marsh.

The ground squelched beneath Poison's boots as she followed Snapdragon. This was relatively solid ground as far as the Black Marshes went, and she knew it to be mercifully free of bogs and sinkholes. She caught a glimpse of her stepmother's blonde braid swinging ahead of her through the trees. Something crunched under her boot, but she did not stop to see what unfortunate creature she had stepped on. The trees had been chopped back a little way here, forming a bumpy trail that had been flattened down by innumerable feet. She put on speed and began catching up with Snapdragon, who was slowing as she ran out of breath, until by the time they got to the well Poison was almost close enough to touch her.

The well sat in the middle of a roughly hewn clearing, a stone-lined shaft with square walls that rose out of the ground to waist-height. A tight, rusty grille lay over the shaft and a roof above that. The roof was sloped inward to a funnel, so that any rainwater it caught was spouted down into the shaft. Rainwater was fine, and so was the clear water from the underground spring that the well fed off; they did not want any of the murky surface pollution of the marsh to get into their precious drinking supply, nor any slimy marsh creatures to fall in, hence the wall and the grille.

Snapdragon stumbled to her knees as she entered the clearing, dropping her burden to the soft earth. It made not a sound. When Poison reached her, Snapdragon was hyperventilating great whoops of air.

"Here, here, do this," Poison said, her impatient tone masking real concern. She pulled Snapdragon's sleeve over her hand and put it to her stepmother's mouth. "Hold that."

Snapdragon did so with her free hand while Poison pulled the sleeve tight at her elbow, cutting off the air and making a reasonable cloth bag for Snapdragon to breathe into. She gasped a little more, but soon she was breathing normally again, and finally Poison let her go.

"You shouldn't get so excited," Poison advised.

Snapdragon sagged, her eyes falling to the bundle on the ground before her. "It's so heavy," she said.

Poison looked at where it lay, eerily still. Snapdragon had wrapped it up like a loaf of bread. Poison wondered whether it was breathing or not. Then she wondered if it needed to.

"You were going to put it in the well?" she asked.

"I can't let Hew see it! It would kill him!"

"Don't be an idiot!" Poison snapped back. "For one thing, you'd pollute the water supply if you left it rotting down there; hadn't you thought of that? Besides, you can't drown it. Don't you know what that thing is?"

Snapdragon gave her a furious glare. She hated being made to feel ignorant. "I suppose *you* do?"

"It's a changeling," Poison said. "A changeling. And if you put it down that well, we'll never get Azalea back."

Snapdragon looked at her in disbelief. "How do you know? How do you *know*, you little witch? Did you do it to her? Did you?"

Poison did not bother to answer that. Instead, she scooped up the bundle — and it *was* heavy, like carrying stone rather than flesh — and looked down on where Snapdragon had begun to sob in the mud, her dress slimed and ruined.

"Say nothing of this. I will deal with it."

"Where has Azalea gone? What are you going to do?" Snapdragon called after her as she walked away.

"Say nothing of this," Poison called back, partly because she wanted Snapdragon to understand how important that was, partly because she did not know the answer to either of her questions.

But one man would.

❦

"All right, all right, just hold your knocking there!" Fleet griped as he pulled open the door to his hut. It was early in the morning and he liked to sleep in, but his annoyance dissipated as he saw the expression on Poison's face.

"The Scarecrow came last night," she said with a tremor in her voice. "It took Azalea. It left us this."

Fleet took a moment to process this; it was too large a thing to face so soon after getting out of bed. Then his brows raised in surprise and alarm, and he quickly ushered her inside. He paused a moment at the door, glancing about to see if Poison's presence had been witnessed. Luckily, the village was asleep. Fleet's hut resided with two others on a platform braced between two towering corkscrew trees, and his neighbours were worse slugabeds than he was. With a final, suspicious grimace, he shut the door.

"Does anyone else know?" Fleet asked Poison as she laid the bundle on the kitchen table with a grunt. Fleet was a man of mysterious wealth, and he could afford a hut big enough for several rooms, including a separate space for eating and cooking, and a room for his bath, too.

"Snapdragon knows," Poison replied. "She won't say anything."

"Are you sure? It's important," Fleet said.

"She won't...." Poison said, and she was suddenly ashamed to find tears rushing up inside her. She tried to swallow them down, but they were relentless. "Better she was just gone.... She..." She gave up trying to speak, for her voice betrayed her. She felt Fleet's leathery hand on her shoulder, his voice a comforting rumble.

"Come on, Poison," he said. "All is not lost yet. Let's see what we have here."

Fleet moved around the table and unwrapped the bundle. Inside was Azalea, dressed in roughly embroidered woollen pyjamas, lying still with her eyes closed. She looked as if she were asleep, a little pale but chubby-faced as always, with a crop of blonde hair.

"Is it dead?" Fleet asked, tugging one leg.

The changeling's eyes flickered open, and they were pupilless orbs of black. The temperature seemed to drop a little under their cold regard. Though it did not move a muscle from where it lay on its side, it glared at Fleet balefully.

"Oh, my," said Fleet. "It really is a changeling."

"I told you it was," Poison said truculently. She was not yet too grief-stricken to snap at him.

Fleet scratched his stubbled cheek with his knuckle. "Better come in by the fire," he said. He picked up the changeling and carried it with him into the next room, his reading room, where a pair of battered old chairs sat in front of the embers of last night's hearth. The room was stiflingly warm and dim, with thin, threadbare curtains pulled across the window. A bookcase that put Poison's to shame dominated the shadowy back wall.

"Sit down, sit down," he said, laying the changeling aside like it was a parcel. Poison settled herself, only now realizing that her feet were freezing inside her boots, as she had no socks on. She watched Fleet potter about behind her. He was a tall, rangy thing, without much flesh on his bones, with a large, solid nose and whiskery ears. His hair was a mix of grey and white, and still surprisingly thick for an old man, flopping about this way and that as he moved. He wore a faded old waistcoat and trousers; in fact, Poison had never seen him in anything else. A thought occurred to her suddenly.

"Did I wake you?" she asked.

"Hmm?" Fleet said over his shoulder as he ran his fingers over the spines of his books, searching for something.

"Just now? Did I wake you when I knocked?"

"I should say so," Fleet replied with mock grumpiness. "You'd have raised the dead."

"Do you *sleep* in those clothes as well?"

Fleet paused in his rummaging for a beat too long. "I was asleep in that chair, if you must know. I'm an old man; I can sleep anywhere." He sighed and turned away from the bookshelf. "I can't find it."

"Find what?"

"*Machmus's Bestiary*," he replied. "I was sure I had it."

A sudden, chilling flash; the Scarecrow's fingers curling over the edge of the page, touching the skin of her wrist.

"It's at my house," Poison replied. "And I'm not going near it again."

"Ah," said Fleet, seeming to understand. It was not quite the reaction Poison had expected.

"What do you mean, '*Ah*'?" she said, her voice rising.

"Books are dangerous things sometimes, Poison," he replied. "They feed your imagination. Soup?"

"Soup?"

"Soup. Do you want some? You haven't had breakfast yet, I'd guess."

"Fleet, what am I going to do about *this*?" she demanded, flinging a hand out at the changeling, which lay silently and immobile where Fleet had put it.

"Let me get you some soup," said Fleet, "and I'll tell you."

⌒⌒⌒

Fleet stoked up the fire and threw on some wood while the soup heated in the kitchen. As he did so, Poison explained to him all that had happened that morning. When the soup was ready he gave a bowl to Poison and took one for himself, furnishing them both with a pair of crusty rolls — real *wheat* bread and not the tasteless mush made from the local marsh reeds. Then he sat in his usual chair, and Poison sat cross-legged before the fire in her thick hemp nightdress, and the old man began to talk.

"Phaeries are evil things, Poison," he said. "Evil and magickal. The changeling and the Scarecrow — they are creatures of phaerie. They leave strangeness and illusion in their wake. They lie with their tongues and deceive your senses. What you saw in my book was an aftereffect of the Scarecrow's sleep-dust. A trick of the mind." He smiled grimly. "Most often their kind stay out of our affairs, for they already have enough of our Realm to roam without having to bother finding us in the marshes and the mountains. But the phaeries can't resist their mischief now and again."

Poison glanced at where the changeling lay in the shadows on a low table at the back of the room, watching them with its black eyes. It had not moved a muscle from where it was put, and its stillness was as unsettling as its gaze.

"What have they done with her?" she asked quietly.

"They have taken her back to the Realm of Phaerie," Fleet said, biting into a hunk of soup-soaked bread.

"But why?" Poison asked, her violet eyes tearing again. She forced her sorrow away. Now was not the time.

"That, I can't say," Fleet replied. "Sometimes the child is returned. It could be a day, a week, a year, twenty years. Sometimes they come back the same age as when they were taken, when their parents are old and grey; sometimes they come back fully grown. None of them remember anything."

"How many . . . how many times has this happened?" Poison asked, staring furiously into the mounting flames to dry her eyes.

"More than you know, Poison," he said. "And it's happened in this very village more than once. But you did the right thing, you know. I see you learned from those books I gave you. If Snapdragon had killed it, the phaeries would never swap it back. Azalea would be gone for good."

"Does . . . can't anyone *do* anything?"

"It's like the mud-spiders and the murksnakes, like the goat-fish and swamp lung and everything else here," Fleet said, chewing. "It's part of life. You were unlucky, Poison, and they came for your sister."

"Unlucky . . ." Poison repeated softly.

"You couldn't have stopped the Scarecrow, you know," Fleet said. "Don't blame yourself. It puts that dust on you to keep you asleep. Then it takes the child and puts a changeling in its place. You have to keep it fed — oh, they eat a *lot*, and many a back's been broken by working hard to try and keep a changeling — but if you ever want to see that child again, you'll do it. Some folks believe that the changeling is still their child, that it's just sick. I suppose it's easier if you let yourself believe that. Then one day, if you're one of the lucky ones, you'll find your child back in its crib and the changeling gone forever. But some people never do." He shrugged. "It's the way of things."

But as he spoke, Poison felt a burning inside her that grew with every word he said. Her tears had dried now, and in their place was something darker. Anger.

"I refuse to believe I'm hearing this!" she shouted suddenly, standing up and knocking her soup aside, untouched. "Not from you!"

"Ah, now you've spilled your —" Fleet began.

"Fleet!" she barked. "Listen! This is not part of the *way of things*, it is not part of *life*. Someone came and kidnapped my sister! Do you understand? Day after day I watch everyone around me put up with misery and death and squalor, and all of them justify it by those same words. It's only part of life because we *let* it be!" She was shouting now, red-faced in her anger, but Fleet seemed uncowed. "I'll not wait until the phaeries decide to return my sister; I'll not work myself to death to feed that black-eyed monster over there!"

"Then what will you do, Poison?" Fleet asked softly.

"I'll go and get her back!"

The words fell into silence. She glared at Fleet, and Fleet met her gaze unwaveringly. The fire snapped behind her in the dim room, sending shadows jumping across the old man's face.

"You do not know what you are saying, Poison," he warned, his voice gone suddenly cold. "The world is much bigger than Gull, and far crueler."

"Then I'll be crueler still," she replied.

"Where will you go? And what will you do when you get there?"

"I'll go to the Phaerie Lord," she said, deadly serious. "And I'll ask him for my sister back."

"You don't even know he exists!"

"The Scarecrow exists," she replied. "That changeling exists. Why not him?"

"And what about your father and Snapdragon?"

"I don't care about Snapdragon," Poison replied. "And my father will grieve, I know; but better that than give up as you'd have me do."

"And the changeling?"

Poison was silent, glaring at him.

"You know your father will have to be told," Fleet said. "This is not something that can be swept under the rug. You can't hide it from them. He and Snapdragon will have to look after that thing. And if you go, your father will be losing two daughters instead of one."

"Can't you look after it? Keep it secret?" Poison begged.

"Oh, no," said Fleet, warding off the suggestion. "I have other obligations outside Gull. I can't tend to that phaerie monster."

Poison went silent again, her jaw set stubbornly.

"You have not thought about this in the slightest, have you?" Fleet prompted.

"No."

"And you're going anyway."

"I am."

For a time, Fleet searched her face. She was always wilful,

but *this*. . . . He had never seen her so determined upon anything. A slow grin spread across his face.

"You really do have the Old Blood in you," he said.

"Fleet, time is short. I want to be gone before my father wakes. Are you going to help me or not?"

"Of course I'll help you, Poison," he said. "You only had to ask."

THE WRAITH-CATCHER

THE wraith-catcher returned to his cart in the afternoon, his morning's business done. He came labouring through the trees, clanking and clattering as the metal pots that hung from a webbing over his heavy coat bashed against each other. Not a bad Soulswatch Eve, and not a good one. There were plenty of better spots to catch marshwraiths, but Gull was his territory, and he liked the way the villagers threw themselves into their work. Some wraith-catchers had to go out and hang the traps personally, work from dusk till dawn. All he had to do was set the villagers to it and give them a pittance in the morning for their trouble, one copper mark for each marshwraith they brought him. They were too ignorant to know that copper marks were not even used in currency anymore beyond the Black Marshes. Not that it mattered, he supposed; none of them was ever liable to go far enough to find out.

His cart had wide wheels with studded rims and chains wrapped around them for better purchase in the mud. It was a low, flat thing, dirty but sturdy, and pulled by a grint. Grints were the only beasts of burden who were adapted well enough to get around the Black Marshes; with their spatulate, webbed feet and flat, beaver-like tails, they never sank into the mud even when the cart did, and they had the muscle to pull it out when it got mired. They were lizardine things with dark green scales, five feet at the shoulder with blunt muzzles and incurious yellow eyes on either side of their heads. Granted, they were stubborn and slow, but they were also strong and docile, and they needed very little looking after. Unlike the lizards they resembled, they were vegetarian, and they could digest almost anything that grew in the swamp, poisonous or not.

Huffing, he pulled back the tarpaulin on the cart and dumped the metal jars with their bright prisoners inside, crashing them against the jars that were already there. He had almost a full load now, as he had expected; it was time to go and sell them. He wrinkled his nose as he clambered around to the front of the cart and up onto the driver's bench there. It would be a relief to get out of this stinking place.

It was then that he noticed the girl standing in the trees nearby. She had an odd face, a strange sullen intensity about her, and she was watching him with her large, violet eyes. He brushed his thick white moustache with the back of his hand and looked her over. She was wearing a ragged dress, a simple, long-sleeved thing made of thin hide and scabbed with dirt at the hem. There were sturdy boots on her feet, a heavy pack on her back.

"You can't come with me, girl," he said, guessing her intention. Nobody from the village had need of a pack like that unless they were going far.

"I can pay," she replied.

"Ha! And what can you pay with?"

She walked up to the side of the cart and held up a shiny silver sovereign. "This."

"That?" the wraith-catcher harrumphed. "I'll need more."

The girl's gaze did not flicker. "This is more than enough," she said.

The wraith-catcher's shaggy white brows came together in a frown. "And where did you get a silver sovereign, girl? Stole it, did you?"

"None of your concern. Do you want it or not?"

He weighed it up for a moment, then reached out to take it from her. She snatched it away. "After we get there."

"Where are you going?" he replied, indignant. For a girl one-third his age, she certainly possessed an uncanny amount of front.

"Shieldtown," she replied, testing out the unfamiliar name. Just the act of speaking it aloud seemed to her breathlessly exotic.

"I see," he replied, studying her. "And what if someone comes after you, hmm? A boy, perhaps? Or your parents?"

"Nobody will come," she said levelly.

The wraith-catcher sucked on his lower lip and looked at the grint, thinking it over. Eventually, he looked back at her and nodded. "Come on then, girl. But don't you try to cheat me, or so help me I'll show you what sorrow is."

"I know what sorrow is," she assured him, clambering up onto the driver's bench with him. "My name is Poison."

"Choose it yourself, did you?"

It was supposed to be a joke, but Poison replied earnestly, "Yes."

The wraith-catcher frowned again, already wondering if he had made a mistake in agreeing to take her with him. "Bram," he said by way of introduction.

"That's not a marsh name," she observed.

"I'm not a marsh person," he replied. "Shieldtown, you said? You're in luck. I'm on my way there now."

Poison nodded. Of course he was.

∽∾∾

There was a certain tree that grew in the marshes called the clubroot tree, whose leaves were famed for their elastic quality. Poison had got hold of some as a child, nailed one end to the planking of a platform, and pulled it out to see how far it would go. She was fascinated by how the leaf thinned as it became longer and longer, and finally, when she had pulled it too far, it snapped and sent her tumbling.

It was as good an analogy as any for the sensation that had been growing in her all afternoon. Within an hour, the wraith-catcher's slow-moving cart had carried her as far away from her home as she had ever been; by the time evening set in, the world had become unfamiliar. She felt her connection with Gull, like that leaf of the clubroot tree, stretching thinner and thinner, straining harder and harder to pull her back as she got farther away. She began to think of never seeing Fleet again, or her father, or even Snapdragon. She became acutely aware that she was utterly, totally alone now. If the wraith-catcher chose to throw her off his cart here, she had no bearing or direction. Home was behind her, and in her heart there was a sudden and terrible ache, a longing that she had never imagined she could feel.

Then, as dusk fell, the link snapped. Her grief and sorrow upended and became excitement. With the realization that there was no way back came the knowledge that the only way was forward. Wasn't she free now? Hadn't she begun what she had always dreamed of beginning? Wasn't this the first step on the road out of Gull and into the world of Fleet's legends?

"What are you grinning about?" Bram asked her. It was the first thing he had said for hours.

Poison, who had not realized that she *was* grinning, shrugged. "Why shouldn't I grin?"

"People who grin usually have something to hide," Bram grumped.

"Oh, I most definitely have *that*," she replied, widening her grin just to annoy him.

As night came on, Bram brought them to a low hill where the soil was rocky and miraculously dry. The trees held back from the bald top of the hill, straggling round it in a circle, enough to obscure their view of the marshes but not enough to crowd them in.

"Here's where we stop for the night," Bram said, drawing on the reins to bring the grint to a halt. It murmured some kind of purring chuckle low in its throat, obviously unhappy about the lack of greenery for it to crop.

Bram made a fire from the wood that he had in his cart. Poison waited about nervously. She had never slept outside before. There were too many things that crawled and slithered, too many dangers in the marsh. Bram cast a glance at her from under his bushy white brows, then motioned with the stick he was prodding the fire with.

"Sit down, girl, and stop acting like a squirrel. There's nothing to be afraid of. The fire keeps them away."

Her fears were little eased, but she felt piqued that her nerves had shown through. She slung her pack before the fire and sat on it, wondering what a squirrel was but unwilling to admit her ignorance. The warmth on her face and hands seemed to have a new edge out here, in contrast to the fire in the hearth at home. Here, without walls to keep them safe, it was the only source of comfort against the night, and all the more precious for it.

"I found this spot a while back," Bram said, making a vague gesture with one gloved hand at the bare hilltop. "Something in the soil, don't know what. Keeps it dry, keeps some of the slimier things away. I always stop here on my way from Gull. It's one of the only habitable places in this disgusting marsh."

Poison didn't know what to say to that.

"Why is it that people live here?" he asked. She could not tell if he was talking to her or to himself.

"I was born here," Poison said simply. She reached into her pack and brought out a string of sausages, from which she snapped off four and then stuffed the others back.

"Are they *pork* sausages?" Bram asked, peering across the fire at her.

Poison shrugged. "Could be," she replied. "I don't know."

"Where did you get them?"

"A friend gave them to me," she replied. The same friend who had supplied her with everything in her pack: food, blankets, a knife, even a battered old map. The same friend who had told her that the wraith-catcher's next port of call would be Shieldtown and had given her the name of a man who could help her there. The same friend who had promised to shoulder the burden of taking the changeling back to her grieving father, of explaining what had happened and where Poison had gone, because Poison knew that if she had to break Hew's heart that way, to tell him that he had lost one daughter and was now losing another, then she would never have had the courage to leave. If ever she had doubts about Fleet's stories before, she had shed them now. He was a genuine adventurer and a true friend. The only one she had.

"I have an eyefish that I caught only the day before yesterday," Bram said. "I'd be happy to trade you the whole thing for those four sausages."

Poison gave him a look. "I've never tried pork."

"But you like eyefish, hmm? Everyone in the marsh likes eyefish."

"But I've never *tried* pork," Poison said, more emphatically this time. Bram's obvious hunger for the sausages only made her more determined to keep them.

"I am taking you all the way to Shieldtown, you know," he reminded her.

"And I'm paying you more than the trip is worth," she replied implacably. At least, that was what Fleet had assured her when he gave her the coin, and many more besides.

Bram grumped for a while as they cooked their food. He had produced a blackened metal grill that stood on thin legs over the flames, and cut strips of eyefish to put on it. Poison put her sausages on as well. She had no idea how long to cook them for, but she had a reasonably keen instinct for that sort of thing and was not overly worried.

"Is it a good life, being a wraith-catcher?" she asked suddenly.

"Good as any, I suppose," he replied. He shifted his bulk in the firelight and was silent for a time before deciding to continue. "Lonely, though. Always going from one place to the next, never staying long. I see other wraith-catchers from time to time . . . we cross paths . . . but we're a pretty solitary breed. You have to be."

Poison nodded. She understood that. She glanced over at the cart, where the grint was asleep, still tethered to his load of metal jars.

"Do you suppose they're alive? The marshwraiths?"

"Hmm?"

"Do they think and feel like we do?"

Bram peeled a strip of eyefish off the grill and laid it down on its uncooked side. "You ask a lot of questions, girl."

"Only about things I don't know," she replied.

Bram barked a laugh. "I've never thought about it," he mused. "Maybe they're just mindless flashes of light. Maybe they're like fireflies. Or maybe they're phaerie things. It's all the same to me."

"You think they might be phaeries?" Poison asked.

"Here, you'll burn them," Bram said, rolling her sausages

over with the end of a stick to expose the browning undersides. "If they're phaeries, then so much the better. I'd feel less guilt about caging a phaerie than I ever would an insect. You know, of all the things crawling around in the Realms, they're the worst."

"What's it like? Out there?"

"You mean beyond the marsh?" Bram asked. "Better than here, anyway."

Poison felt a strange thrill. She had never heard anyone say that about the world beyond the marsh. Not even Fleet, who spoke of all kinds of wonders and dangers, ever said that the world outside was *better*.

"There are places you don't go, of course," he said. "The old cities . . . the phaeries are all over them. And there's ghoblin tribes here and there, up in the mountains, and trolls and dwarrow in the deep places. You know, this used to be *Man's* Realm, so they say. The other things kept to their own Realms. Not been that way for a long time, though. One thing you can say about us humans, we never did know how to stick together." He looked out at the dark wall of the marsh, which was alive with insect noises. "But we weren't meant to live in places like this. Man was meant to rule the plains and the hills and the valleys, not skulk in the forests and marshes and hide in the mountains." His eyes returned to the fire. "That's the way it is, I suppose."

Poison did not reply to that. Instead, she said, "Do you want a sausage? I think four is too many for me anyway."

❧❧❧

She lay awake for a long time by the fire, listening to Bram snore inside his blankets and jumping at every sound in the night. Small insects flitted around the glow of the blaze, and things shuffled and cracked twigs in the trees that surrounded the bare clearing. The discomfort of the ground did not bother her; it was the fear of the small, venomous things that infested the marsh that kept her awake. She marvelled at how Bram could be so careless.

She cried a little, after she was sure Bram was asleep. She could not help imagining her father's face as Fleet broke the tragic news to him. He had not been up when she returned from Fleet's hut to gather her belongings, nor had she seen Snapdragon. She suspected, knowing her stepmother, that she had slipped back into bed with him and would pretend she had slept soundly all night. Hew was always a deep sleeper; if he had slept through Snapdragon's hysterical scream on discovering the changeling, he would not have woken when she slid under the blanket with him.

More than anything, she regretted not leaving her father a note or a message. The guilt she felt at the cowardly way she had slipped out of the village was bad enough; even though she was afraid that seeing him might change her mind and make her stay, he deserved better than to hear about his daughters' fate from a virtual stranger. But if only she had thought to leave him some words of comfort, something to let him know she was not deserting him, only leaving him for a time.

Too late now. She could see him weeping, trying to find meaning in what had happened as Fleet stood glumly by. Taken why? Gone where? Coming back when? She pictured Snapdragon trying to comfort him, all the while knowing that she could not tell him the truth just as Poison could not, secretly glad that the violet-eyed girl was out of their lives. Hew had lost his two daughters at a stroke; but worse was the knowledge that the phaeries had one of them, that they had left a monstrosity in her place, and now he and his wife would have to care for it if they wanted to keep alive any hope of seeing their daughters again.

But that was the way of things in the Black Marshes.

Eventually, Poison got up from the fire and went to the cart. Beneath the tarpaulin was a space where Bram kept travelling supplies and food. She lifted them out and dumped them by the fire, then crawled with her blanket into the gap where they had been and pulled the tarpaulin over her. The metal jars clanked about as she wrapped herself up, but soon she had fashioned herself a warm, cramped cocoon, and she fell asleep to the soughing of the grint's breath and the faint whispering of the marshwraiths as they darted about inside their prisons.

⟳∼∼⟳

Poison lost count of the days remarkably fast as she travelled with Bram. It was only by the most intense calculation that she worked out that it had been a week since Azalea had been taken by the Scarecrow. A week that had passed at the plodding tempo of the grint's webbed feet slapping in the mud, broken only occasionally by stops to camp or when the cart became stuck and they had to lever it out. She thought about Azalea, what she must be going through, but she found that she could not even speculate. She knew nothing of the ways of the phaeries. All the legends and stories of changelings made no mention of what happened to the children that were taken.

And though it gave her a guilty feeling to think it, she was enjoying herself.

Oh, it was hard and uncomfortable, that was for sure. The midges and flies bit them during the day, and every morning she woke up stiff from another cramped night curled up in the cart. Bram never made any mention of the way he found his travelling gear in a neat pile on the ground every day, but he never stopped putting it back in the same place, and Poison never stopped unpacking it to make space for herself under the tarpaulin. Last night it had rained hard, and she had heard him cursing as he flailed around the campsite, trying to find shelter for the packs and blankets she had displaced; he had pulled back the tarp that she lay under and glowered down on her, water drooling from the brim of his hat.

"My supplies are getting wet!" he blustered.

"So am I, now," she said sleepily. "How's the floor, by the way?"

He huffed indignantly and threw the tarp back over her. She never did find out how he kept them dry, but she heard him rummaging around at the other end of the cart and presumed he'd taken out his tent and replaced it with the supplies. She didn't care; at least she was dry. One for the marsh folk, she thought mischievously as she fell asleep.

And yet all the discomfort could not sour the pride and excitement in her breast, for she was really away: away from Gull, away from Snapdragon and the villagers who disdained her, and soon, away from the Black Marshes. She tried to keep her feet on the ground, but she could not resist spinning off into heady fantasies of witches and trolls, strong heroes and quick-witted heroines.

Silly girl, she told herself. *They're just stories.* But somehow, she never quite believed it.

And Bram was good company for her as well. He was a taciturn fellow, but he was perfectly willing to answer questions that Poison asked him. Her interest in what she called the "outside world" was insatiable, and she listened attentively to even his most mundane anecdotes. But while he talked long about places he'd been and people he'd met, he never asked questions of her — perhaps because he wasn't interested, perhaps because he was being polite — and that suited her fine. He was a good man, she decided. Gruff and solitary, but honest and decent. She was not so naive that she had never thought what might happen between a man of his size and a young girl, in the depths of the marshes where nobody could help her. Bram had never made her feel threatened that way.

It was midday and uncharacteristically sunny when Bram announced they would be coming into sight of Shieldtown any moment. Poison felt her heart leap and craned forward in the seat, peering at the trees ahead. They had been thinning out all day, and the ground was firm enough to be almost called a road now. She waited eagerly, with Bram stealing amused glances at her out of the corner of his eye. The cart wheels creaked on.

Finally, Bram could stand it no longer. "You'll fall off your seat if you lean any more, girl."

"Where is it?" she demanded, still staring furiously at the unyielding trees ahead.

He tapped her shoulder and she glared at him irritably. He gave her a wink and then pointed with a stubby, gloved finger.

"You didn't look *up*," he said.

She did so, raising her gaze to the canopy where the trees meshed their branches overhead. She took a sharp breath in amazement as she laid eyes for the first time on Shieldtown.

SHIELDTOWN

~~~✦~~~

IT **WAS** at that moment, more than any, that Poison realized the true scale of things.

Her entire life had been spent below the canopy of the Black Marshes, her vision hemmed in by the dank leaves overhead so that she never got to witness the full expanse of the sky. The marshes were flat, too, and hills such as the one that she and Bram had camped on that first night were rare. There were few vantage points from which an observer could gaze out over the tops of the trees and see the sprawling immensity of their surroundings, and Poison had not been to any of them.

And now, suddenly, she saw this.

The trees peeled back, cut away in a wide semicircular clearing. Towering above them was the most immense wall that Poison had ever seen. It stretched up so high that Poison had to tip her head back to the point of dizziness just to see the top. To either side it seemed to go on forever until it was lost behind a curve or a fold in its vast length. Its surface was dark rock, jagged and pleated by the ravages of millennia of weathering, pocked and scabbed with bumps and ruts. This was no man-made wall but the implacable strength of nature. The land — *all* the land — rose by a thousand feet or more. It was as if she had lived her whole life on one stair of a stairway and had just come to the base of the next one up.

To say that she was staggered was an understatement.

"Something of a wake-up, eh, girl?" Bram grinned, unable to conceal the relish in his voice at the sight of his precocious companion stunned to silence.

She could see very little of Shieldtown itself, for the angle was too steep. What she could see were the enormous elevators that winched up and down the wall, disappearing into steaming buildings of metal as they reached the ground before emerging again to ascend up to the dizzying heights. There she could see a fringe of exotic buildings crowding over the edge of the precipice, some of them leaning dangerously or projecting cranes out into the air: tantalizing glimpses of the wonders of the town to come.

Bram nudged her. "Put your jaw back together," he said. "You look like a snake trying to swallow an egg."

She cast him an irritated glance, embarrassed at being caught gawping. They were heading across the clearing now, towards the cluster of buildings at the base of the wall. Other carts were there, as well as foot-travellers in all kinds of attire, watched over by helmeted guards with long, hooked swords hanging from their belts.

Poison gathered herself a little, annoyed that she had betrayed her naivete by her reaction. If the world was as frightening and cruel as Fleet had warned her, then she could not afford to let anyone know how little she knew of it. She suddenly felt like a small child again, consumed by wonder and frightened of the unknown.

Bram brushed his bushy moustache with one gloved finger and harrumphed. "They call it Shieldtown because of that great big wall there. It's called a shield wall, when the land rises sheer like that. You know, the Black Marshes are completely surrounded by this wall. It's like a great big section of the world, hundreds of miles wide, just suddenly dropped a thousand feet. The marshes are below sea level now; that's why they're always wet."

Poison digested this without showing anything on her face. She had been mistaken in her perspective. It was not that Shieldtown was higher than the marshes; it was that the marshes were lower than Shieldtown. Shieldtown was the same height as the rest of the land. And that meant that her entire life she had been living in one vast, immense pit.

"Does anyone know why it happened?" Poison asked. Bram looked across at her with a questioning murmur. "Why the land fell like that?"

Bram turned his eyes back to the plodding grint that was hauling them ever closer to the outbuildings of Shieldtown. "There's legends and stories. There always are. I don't pay much attention to them."

Poison felt vaguely disappointed, but the feeling lasted only a moment, for by that time they were near enough to the base of the wall for a guard to come striding over to them. He was wearing a half-head helmet that left only his mouth and chin visible, and his uniform was a scuffed assemblage of metal greaves, hide, and leather. It was not exactly the shining armour that Poison had envisaged a guard wearing.

"State your business," he said.

"Bram of Oilskin, wraith-catcher," Bram announced. "And this is Poison, my daughter."

Poison did not so much as twitch an eyebrow at the lie. The guard looked up at her with calculated suspicion. She met his scrutiny with her disconcerting violet gaze.

"Poison," he said, deadpan. "That's an unusual name to give your child. You must love her very much."

"She's a treasure," Bram agreed, blithely ignoring the sarcasm.

The guard gave a long-suffering sigh and went to the back of the cart, pulling open the tarpaulin and looking inside. He picked up one of the metal jars within and held it to his ear. Then, apparently satisfied, he tossed it back in with the others.

"You can go," he said, dismissing them rudely as he walked away. Bram snapped the reins and the grint squawked before ambling into motion again. They went a few dozen feet in silence, until they were out of earshot of the guard.

"*She's a treasure,*" Poison mimicked, and Bram burst out laughing.

⌘

The interior of the wheelhouse was a noisy roar of machinery, hot and dark. They had to queue for a short while behind other carts, waiting while the lifts were loaded up each time one arrived. When it was their turn, Poison watched as their ride clunked down from above. She was glad for the darkness, for it concealed her trepidation. The lift seemed such a fragile thing, merely a cradle of metal with a flat floor and a few pitifully inadequate railings running all around it. Bram urged the reluctant grint onto it as a team of sweat-streaked attendants held it steady. Two more carts, both pulled by horses, were crammed onto the same lift as Bram and Poison dismounted. For some reason, it seemed safer to be standing on the metal floor than sitting atop a cart. Poison felt a slight nausea as the gates of the lift were clanged shut, and then there was a great lurch as the mighty cogs in the wheelhouse bit together and they were carried upwards.

For the first few moments, they were surrounded by the darkness and the din of the wheelhouse; then suddenly all noises ceased as they rose through the roof and out into the sunlight and open air. Poison saw the buildings dropping away beneath her at a terrifying rate, the trees that had previously seemed so high bowing forward as perspective made them tiny, and for the first time in her life she was above the canopy of the Black Marshes. Her breath was stolen anew.

It was vast. Every moment of her life, every beat of her heart, had been played out beneath that awesome, never-ending eternity of green, an undulating blanket of dank marsh-trees cut through by sludgy rivers that she did not even know existed. The flat plane of the marshes seemed to tilt downwards as she rose higher, exposing more and more of its back, disappearing into a swampy haze in the distance. She could not even see to the other side, where Bram had told her the shield wall rose as high as this one. It was swallowed by the curve of the horizon.

"I feel so small," she said aloud.

"We *are* small, girl," Bram said, leaning on the railing of the lift, apparently heedless of the inconceivable drop below.

Poison shuffled warily to the edge of the lift and looked down. "I wish you'd stop calling me *girl*," she said, more to distract herself from the strange terror she felt than because it bothered her.

Bram grunted. "Better than Poison," he said. "What possessed you to come up with a name like that?"

"What do you care?" she replied. "You were happy enough to tell it to that guard."

Bram frowned. "Just couldn't think of anything better on short notice, that's all. Didn't want him getting suspicious. If I'd have said you were from the marsh . . . well, not many folks come from the marsh, they don't like to leave their villages. And if you were anything other than my daughter . . . and us travelling together . . . hmm . . ." He blushed beetroot behind his white moustache and tugged his hat rim down a little more. "Don't like awkward questions."

Poison had been looking over the edge at the ground below;

she was surprised to find that the initial fear had died and she was not in the least bit scared, though they still clanked and clattered and swayed higher and higher and the world fell farther and farther away. She glanced at Bram and gave him a quick smile. "I think I'm enjoying this," she said.

"Ha!" he barked. "I can tell *you* weren't made for the swamp. Never met a marsh-dweller who wouldn't have fair soiled themselves if they ever got up this near the sky." He blushed again, suddenly. "Pardon my language."

Poison looked at him in frank surprise. "Why, Bram, I do believe there's a gentleman hiding behind that moustache!"

Bram went a deeper shade of red and then excused himself and made a great show of seeing to the grint.

೧౾

Poison did the best she could to hide her amazement at Shieldtown and its inhabitants, but she suspected she was not particularly successful. Bram seemed to be greatly pleased with himself, casting sneaky glances at her and then chuckling into his collar when she scowled at him. They rode their cart down the main thoroughfare, jostling with traffic. Poison had never seen so many people, nor heard such a noise as they made when they were all together, gabbling and shouting amid the bray of horses and the growl and squawk of grints. She was accustomed to the drab fashions of the marsh folk, where fabrics were made from the rough resources they had at hand and bright colours attracted flies and wasps and other, more deadly creatures. Here there were no such restrictions, and the outfits that she saw were dazzlingly gaudy. Billowing dresses with puffed sleeves, open-throated shirts with pleated hems, tall hats and soft leather shoes. Poison thought they looked ridiculous.

She was much more awed by the town itself. Metal, a rare

and frankly half-useless commodity in the marshes, was all around her. Great towering spires of iron jutted out towards the sky. Domes of tarnished bronze were surrounded by steaming pistons that pumped up and down, making them seem like the dancing legs of a bloated metallic spider. Streets seemed to crowd in haphazardly, houses overlapping each other as if parts of the town had melted and flowed like wax into other sections before rehardening. There was nothing like the uniform huts of the marsh here — the dwellings were each and all different, some rounded and lumpy like a heap of mudballs in a pile, some rigid and tall and triangular, some flat and low and unassuming. Signs outside the shops on the thoroughfare fizzed and blinked with a strange energy, flashing bright and then dim even in the daylight.

"Is it what you expected?" Bram asked.

"I didn't know what to expect," Poison replied. "Not this, though."

"Do you know where you're going?" he asked. "Want me to take you anywhere?"

"I need to find a man called Lamprey."

"Ah," Bram said. Then, surprisingly, he asked, "And what do you need to find him for?"

Poison gave him a strange look. "We've been in the same cart together for a week now, and that's the first time you've ever asked me why I was going to Shieldtown."

Bram shrugged his massive shoulders. "Not my business."

"That's right, it's not," Poison said.

They were silent for a short time, Bram nudging the grint through the sluggish flow of the traffic.

"Do you think you might know where he is?" Poison asked at length.

"Maybe," Bram said. "I thought it wasn't my business."

"It's not," Poison replied. "I can find him on my own."

"I'm sure you can. You don't need me." Bram nodded as if at his own wisdom and shook the reins idly.

More silence passed.

"So you *do* know where he is?" Poison prompted.

"I never said that," he replied.

"But if you did, you'd tell me?" she queried.

"If you asked," he replied.

"Well?"

"Well what?"

"Well, where is he?"

"How should I know? I've never heard of him."

Poison gritted her teeth and swallowed down a retort. Bram gave her a sidelong glance and pulled his hat brim down over his bushy eyebrows.

"I'll do you a deal," he said.

Poison studiously looked the other way, pretending that she didn't care. "What kind of deal?"

"I'll help you find him. You give me *two* silver sovereigns when we do."

"What kind of deal is that?" she snapped, amazed at his audacity. "I can find him on my own."

"You could," he agreed. "But you don't know this town, you don't know these people, you don't know their ways. Now maybe you'd do fine; you're tough, and you've got a quick head on you. But likely you'd end up facedown in an alley, and for a lot less than the silver sovereign you offered me, or the other coins I hear jangling in your pack."

"You stay off them!" she hissed.

"How much is a meal at a bar in Shieldtown?" he fired at her.

The question put her off-guard. She took a wild stab, guessing it would be expensive compared to the marsh. "Three copper marks," she declared.

"Ha! You'd be dead before you got your money out! Copper marks aren't even currency here."

"Then I won't buy food in a bar," Poison declared.

"It doesn't matter. This city can spot a stranger, and strangers are easy pickings. Especially rich ones. You have no idea how much a silver sovereign is worth, do you?"

"More than your company for a week," she replied acerbically.

"Well, you owe me that one already," he pointed out, unfazed. "But I know this city, and I can help you find this man you're looking for. But it'll cost you another sovereign."

"Don't you have wraiths to catch?" she snapped.

"Soulswatch Eve is the end of the season," he replied steadily. "That's why I'm up here. Can't catch marshwraiths if you're not in the marsh."

Poison glared at him. She hated being put in this position. She knew he was right, and yet to agree to his deal would be to cave in. She was not a person accustomed to relying on anyone. Perversely, the only reason she even considered his offer of help was because she knew with certainty that he was swindling her. If a silver sovereign was too much for a week-long cart ride, it was far, far too much for a bit of simple assistance.

"All right," she replied, glowering sullenly out at the traffic-choked street. "Two silver sovereigns. When we find Lamprey."

"There, I knew you'd see sense," Bram said with uncharacteristic cheeriness. "You're tough, but you're not stupid."

⤫

By the end of the day, Poison could not help feeling a little relieved that she had agreed to Bram's deal. She was exhausted and bewildered by the sights and sounds of the day, and by the effort of maintaining an uninterested manner in the face of it all. She had to admit to herself he had been right — when she was with him, she could at least pretend that she was not a complete stranger to the city, but without him she would have been lost.

They went first to an enormous indoor market, which was bigger than Gull and crammed with all manner of stalls, booths, and stands. The constant cry of hawkers and the gabble of store-tenders and customers echoed off the low, tarnished dome of the roof and came back as reflected nonsense. It was dim beneath the dome, for the only light came from outside where the sun glared in around the edges, forcing its way through the short brass columns that held the dome up. Hot wafts of cooking meat brushed past them, and shadowy faces lunged out of the gloom with sickly grins to catch their attention and show them some wares. Bram led the grint on foot through the byways of the market, and Poison sat on the back of the cart as he had asked her to do. "They'll snatch the jars from under the tarp unless someone keeps watch," he told her, and she decided to oblige him.

Bram led them to a stall laden with exotic lamps, curling tubes of glass fashioned in all shapes and designs, each one lit by the soft, gently fluctuating light of a marshwraith. Poison watched the little balls of light as they roamed around their prisons, sometimes chasing each other about — often there was more than one in a lamp — and sometimes lying still at the bottom. Use of coloured glass, combined with the marshwraiths' own tints, created different moods in the lamps. Some were restful, casting dappled blues and greens, while others were fiery red and purple. They were beautiful things, works of art, but somehow Poison could not help but feel a touch of sadness that such wondrous things as the marshwraiths were trapped inside for the entertainment of the rich. She wondered if the folk of Gull ever considered for a moment what they were condemning these strange creatures to, when they set their eager traps on Soulswatch Eve.

She watched over the cart, listening with half an ear while Bram and the short, wizened storekeeper haggled. Bram showed him some of the wraiths he had in his cart. The metal jars were cleverly designed so that the lid could pop up with a twist, allowing a small space to see inside but not enough so that the wraith could squeeze out. By the end, Bram had sold five jars, and he seemed grudgingly satisfied with the price. He then climbed back aboard the cart and urged the grint onwards.

Much of the day was spent this way. There were six more places to visit in different parts of the town, which Bram explained were wholesalers, who would buy the wraiths from him and sell them in other parts of the Realm. There was not enough demand for such a luxury as wraith-lamps in Shieldtown to support more than one store. Poison was content to wait until he was done, drinking in the sights and sounds all around her, observing everything with her disconcerting gaze.

It was late evening when Bram returned to the cart with a girl of about Poison's age in tow. Poison appraised her cynically. She looked waifish and tired, dressed in tough, battered travel clothes, her dark-blonde hair straggly. Probably she would have been pretty if she had not looked so worn, and her eyes had a strangely haunted, distant cast to them.

"Here's a thing," he announced. "Until I found you I'd hardly met one marsh-dweller who'd step outside of their hometown, and now I've found the only person misguided enough to *want* to go there. And to Gull, no less."

"You're going to Gull?" Poison asked the girl.

"One of my wholesalers was arranging a ride there for her," Bram explained. "When I mentioned you, he pointed her out. Thought you two might want to meet, in case you had ... umm ... second thoughts. About leaving."

Poison was faintly touched by his unexpected consideration. The girl was watching her incuriously.

"Why are you heading there?" Poison asked.

"That's my business," the girl replied bluntly, casting an irate glance at Bram. She was obviously not pleased to be dragged over here.

Poison considered for a moment, and was surprised to find that she was not in the least tempted to take up Bram's suggestion. Turning back would be worse than never having set off at all. But there was one thing . . .

"Could you take a message for me?" she asked.

"Who's it for?"

"Hew and Snapdragon."

The girl watched her coolly. She had terrifically dark eyes.

"What's the message?"

"Tell them . . ." Poison began, and then suddenly realized that she had no idea what she wanted to say, no words that would make them understand. They had never understood her up until now; she was as alien to them as to the rest of the village. What message could she really give them that would ease their burden? It was only at that moment that she comprehended how vast the chasm yawned between her and her parents.

"Why don't I just tell them you're sorry?" the girl said levelly.

Poison was surprised. She opened her mouth to ask how she knew, and then shut it again.

"It's written all over you," the stranger said.

Poison felt faintly abashed that this girl had seen through her so easily. Usually her emotions were impenetrable even to people who knew her well.

"That would be best," she said. "Thank you."

The girl nodded and then, without a goodbye, she turned

away and drifted back towards the wholesalers, where she was waiting for her ride to Gull.

Bram scratched the back of his neck as he watched her go. "She was a strange one," he commented.

Poison squinted in the evening sun, her eyes on the departing traveller. "I forgot to tell her my name," she said absently.

"I'm sure they'll figure it out when they get the message," Bram said.

Poison made a distracted noise of agreement.

⌁

"You've been very patient, *girl*," Bram remarked as they rode through the streets at dusk. It was quiet now, and Bram had exhausted himself of clients. There were still a few jars left, but he was not worried. They would go to private buyers sooner or later. He was always one of the first wraith-catchers to get back from the marsh after the season ended, and he always sold his stock.

"I told you not to call me *girl*," Poison replied. She rubbed the back of her neck, which was aching from slouching on the cart all day. "What happens now?"

"Well, when the season begins again, I collect all my jars once more, and it's back into the marsh," Bram replied with a note of faint resignation in his voice.

"I mean, what happens *now*?" she replied. "I seem to recall hiring you for a purpose."

He laughed heartily, his moustache trembling. "How could I forget? Let's get something to eat first. I owe you that much for guarding my cart all day."

"What about Lamprey?" Poison prompted.

"Ah," Bram said with a twinkle. "He doesn't get up until dark."

"You know him?" she asked, pouncing on Bram's words.

"I know where he is," Bram replied. "I wasn't only selling my wraiths today, you know. Though I suspect I owe one of my wholesalers a favour for the information."

Poison felt a grin spread across her face. "Bram, if you weren't swindling me as we speak, I'd hug you."

Bram harrumphed, colouring a little. "You may want to rethink that after you've met Lamprey," he said. "I have a few things to teach you while we eat. Like how not to get killed after dark in Shieldtown."

LAMPREY

IT WAS terribly quiet at night.

Poison had never noticed how loud the marsh insects were until they were not there. Every night of her life she had fallen asleep to the raucous sawing of marsh crickets, jipiriris, and reedweavers. A full moon brought the distant booming of krarl as they swung their hairy, starfish-shaped bodies through the trees. At home, there was the lapping of water, the creak of the hut supports, the soft breathing of Azalea in the crib.

In Shieldtown, the quiet seemed louder than anything she had ever heard. The squeak of the cart wheel, the snuffle of the grint as it plodded along, even the rustle of Bram's hide coat seemed deafening. Instead of the cacophony of insects there was only a dull, heavy drone of some nearby machinery, and the occasional rattle of a gate or incoherent cry from another street. The rest was silence.

They travelled slowly, glancing furtively about as they went. Knots of people turned to watch them, eyeing the cart menacingly. Brightly lit signs above dark dens crackled and popped, sparking as they passed by. Poison and Bram sat up at the front of the cart, their hide cloaks bunched around their shoulders, trying to ignore the stares from all around.

"Don't look afraid," Bram had told her. "Don't avoid their eyes, but don't meet them for long either. When you break the look — and you'd better be the first to break it, because *they* won't — you turn your eyes forward, got me? Not down, but forward. Look down, that's submission, that's weakness. You make it look like you've every right to be there, but you don't challenge them. See?"

Poison didn't see, but she nodded anyway. Now she realized what he meant. She did not dare ignore the surly eyes that followed them, but nor did she dare meet them in case it was interpreted as a challenge. She was reminded of an old story Fleet had once read her, about a prince of an exotic land who had to walk through a cage of hungry tigers. She remembered how she had made Fleet describe over and over the wondrous animals, with their striped fur and lethal grace. Now she thought she knew how the prince must have felt.

The streets seemed to close in around them, and the lights became few and far between. Bram appeared to know where he was going, but she could tell he was edgy by the way his hand clenched and unclenched on the club hidden inside his cloak. They were in the slum districts now, where the haphazard dwellings of Shieldtown had begun to collapse in on themselves. Steam hissed from gratings as they passed by, and rats scurried along the gutters. The cart creaked on, the grint oblivious to it all, but Poison's skin prickled with the presence of danger.

"... must have been a fool to come here in the first place ..." Bram was muttering to himself, hunched over in his seat.

"You do know where this Lamprey is?" Poison asked.

"I know what I was told," said Bram. "And you'd better have a good reason for seeing him. I'll thank my lucky stars if we drive out of this place alive."

"Then why did you come?" Poison asked, more to hear the sound of her own voice than because she really wanted to know.

They turned down an alley that bumped and dipped beneath them, making the cart rattle loudly and shaking them on their bench. "I'm a simple man, Poison," Bram said. "And I think you're an honest girl, and you'll keep a bargain once you've made it. A silver sovereign is what I earn in a *year*. You understand?"

Poison did. A year of work. She had a little coin in her pocket that represented a year of work to this man. A swift mental calculation of how much Fleet had given her made her stagger. Either Bram was very poor or Fleet was very rich.

"Now *two* silver sovereigns," Bram was saying in a low, quiet voice. "Two silver sovereigns, and the money I made today . . . that means a lot to a man like me. Maybe I can buy a house with that. Maybe a farm. Sell up this old cart and this stubborn grint and get out before it's too late. The marsh isn't a place for people, and I'm getting old, you know. Every year I go back in there, I take a gamble with swamp lung or black rot or any of the other things a man can catch in that place. Every year the odds get a little worse."

He looked over at Poison, and his eyes were tender and wistful beneath the brim of his hat. "A place of my own, in the mountains where the grass grows and there's nobody around for miles. That's a risk worth taking."

Poison could hear the yearning in his voice. She was always good at reading people, and Bram wore his heart on his sleeve anyway. Now she realized the true weight of their relationship so far. He had known all along that the coins she carried in her pack were enough to make him a rich man, enough that he could live the rest of his life in wealth and comfort. He could have simply taken them off her at any point; she was defenceless against a man his size. But he was a man who believed in earning what he gained, and so here he was, taking her into the darkest alleys of Shieldtown because he had made a deal with her. Even faced with the greatest of temptation, he was no thief.

However, the man who jumped up next to her was.

She yelped in surprise, but he was quick. She had not even seen him slip from the shadows of a cross-alley and duck alongside the wheels of the cart. In one smooth motion, he had vaulted up on the bench alongside Poison, and before she had time to react, she felt the cold steel of a blade at her throat.

"Get away from her, you —" Bram blustered, letting go of the grint's reins and reaching for his club. The grint ambled to a halt.

"Ah! Ah!" the man cried, pressing the knife harder so that Poison's head was forced back. "I wouldn't, if I were you. I'll give her a bloody smile."

Her violet eyes were wide with terror, her heart thundering in her ears. She was paralysed, both in body and mind, panic taking her in an ambush. For a few seconds that seemed like minutes, she could do nothing but suck in shuddering breaths and try to lean herself away from the cruel edge that pressed mercilessly into her skin.

Another man clambered up alongside Bram, putting a blade to his ribs. "You behave now," he said. "Wouldn't want your little girl getting hurt."

"Take the cart!" Bram said, clearly as scared as Poison was. "Take the cart and the grint. Don't hurt us. Just take it."

The first thief leaned over Poison to lift up the tarpaulin and look in the back. She could smell his sour breath on her face.

There was hardly anything there, just a few unsold jars with wraiths humming inside and their packs and travel supplies. Poison's pack, of course, had her money in it; but she did not even think of that then. All she could think of was the story of the prince and the tigers, and Fleet's face in the firelight as he recounted it.

"What do we want with a grint and a cart?" the first thief sneered. "Got anything in those packs? Maybe we won't cut your throats if you've got something worth taking."

"Yes! Yes. Just don't hurt us," Bram said without hesitation.

"I'll say who gets hurt here," the thief hissed.

"You'll . . ." Poison began, and as soon as the noise had left her lips she regretted it and stopped. But it was too late. The thief turned his attention onto her.

"I'll *what?*" he snarled.

She had started now. To retreat would be a weakness she could not afford. "You'll be the ones who get hurt," she said.

"Really?" the thief leered, pressing closer to her. "And who's going to hurt us? You?"

She was set on her course now, and she had to follow it through. "Lamprey," she said.

The thief was not fast enough to hide the flicker of fear in his eyes, nor did Poison miss the way he withdrew his knife for a moment.

"Never heard of him," he said.

"You're a liar," Poison replied, with as much conviction as she could muster. "Everyone's heard of him here."

The thief drew back with a wild menace in his eyes. Poison quailed inwardly, but she forced herself to meet him with a steady gaze. What she was doing went against every instinct she had; if she was wrong, she had very probably just signed her own death warrant. But to back out of her bluff now would certainly mean that neither she nor Bram would live to see another sunrise. Fleet had professed to know very little about Lamprey beyond his name and that he would know the way that Poison should go if she wanted to get to the Phaerie Lord's palace; but he had also warned her to be very, very careful. The things he had heard about Lamprey were enough to make him afraid for her. She was gambling that Lamprey's reputation was even stronger this close to his home.

He glared at her for what seemed like an age, a vein pulsing at his temple. Had she gone too far in calling him a liar?

"Talk fast, little witch," he said. "Before I scoop out those eyes of yours with the point of my knife."

Bram was watching her with a combination of disbelief and terror on his face. She could feel her scalp prickle with dread, but she forced herself to speak with a mouth gone suddenly desert-dry.

"This is Bram, best wraith-hunter in the Realms. In the back, in those jars, are his finest marshwraiths. Lamprey wants to buy some for his lanterns, and he trusts me to find the best."

"He trusts you?" the thief sneered. "And who are you?"

Poison steeled herself. "I'm his niece."

The thief did not laugh, as she had expected. Instead, he looked uncertain. He glanced at the other one, who gave a barely perceptible shrug.

"Lamprey doesn't have a niece," he said, but it was too late to be convincing. Poison seized the advantage.

"And you would know, is that it? You're a close friend of Lamprey's? You're just another gutter thief, not even worth my uncle's notice."

The man's eyes blazed and his blackened teeth bared in a snarl. "You should watch what you say," he growled. But the knife was no longer at her throat.

"If these wraiths don't get to my uncle soon, I assure you he'll be *very* angry," Poison said, her voice calm though her insides were a mass of thrashing butterflies. "I'll be sure to describe the two of you to him."

The first thief muttered something foul under his breath and reached over her to snatch up one of the metal jars from the cart behind her. "In here, are they?" he said. "Wraiths? Well, let me just have a look. We'll see if you're telling the truth."

He twisted the cap of the jar, but he turned it too hard. Instead of springing up a little way to allow him to see inside, it came right off. The marshwraith was out in an instant, a sparkling trail of blue and purple that arced into the sky and disappeared over the rooftops, headed unerringly back towards the Black Marshes.

The thief looked for a moment like a boy who had just smashed his father's favourite plate.

"Are you satisfied?" Poison challenged. "By all means, open them all. Lamprey will take the compensation out of your hide."

"You've got a mouth on you, witch," the thief warned, but all the strength had gone from his voice. "One day it'll get you killed."

With that, he motioned to his companion, and they jumped down from the cart and were gone.

Bram whuffed out a huge breath that he had been holding throughout the conversation. He looked over his shoulder, then at Poison, then shook his head and picked up the reins. The grint, who had been patiently waiting the whole time, took up the strain again.

"That was a stupid risk," he said angrily.

Poison brushed her long hair back behind one ear and felt her throat, where the knife had left a mark. "You were willing to let them walk off with all my money. And all of *yours*. What about your dream being 'a risk worth taking'?"

Bram scowled darkly, hunching his broad shoulders forward. "What possessed you to try something like that anyway?"

"The prince and the tigers," she replied. "An old story Fleet used to tell me back in Gull. The prince had to walk through a room full of hungry tigers. He did it by pretending to be a bigger tiger."

Bram snorted. "That's just a story," he said. "He'd have been tiger food."

Poison shrugged. "Story or not, the point is the same. People don't know how to react if you don't do what they expect. It doesn't matter what you are, it's how you *appear*."

Bram's expression made it clear what he thought of that idea. "Well, we know one thing about Lamprey, at least," he said. "People are afraid of him. So we should be, too."

❧

The encounter with the thieves seemed to have taken the sting out of the streets, and they reached Lamprey's den unchallenged after that. It was an innocuous door in the middle of a dimly lit terrace, hunkered beneath enormous lintels and buried under a mass of balconies. Bram recognized it by the insignia on the door, a mark with two circles interlinked by a slash. There seemed to be nobody outside. The street was eerily quiet.

"Here it is," Bram said uncertainly, drawing the grint to a halt. He felt terribly exposed out here on the street.

"You should stay by the cart," Poison said, picking up her pack. "We can't leave it here unattended."

"You can't go in there on your own!" he protested.

"And you can't afford to lose your cart and your grint," she said. "I don't think anyone will bother you outside this Lamprey's place." When Bram still looked doubtful, she said, "You've earned your second sovereign. You don't need to do any more." Then she smiled wanly at him. "I would appreciate it if you'd give me a ride out of here when I'm done, though."

She was clambering down from the cart when she felt him lay his massive, gloved hand on her shoulder. "Be careful," he said.

She put her fingers over his in thanks, and then she went to the door of Lamprey's den and knocked on it.

The door was unlocked and unlatched. It swung ajar on the first rap. Poison looked back at Bram, who was watching her from beneath the brim of his hat. Then she pushed the door open and looked inside.

A long set of wooden stairs led downward, with soft lanterns illuminating framed paintings all the way along. The paintings were of underwater coral, or fish, or storm-lashed seascapes. Poison voiced a cautious "Hello?" down the stairs, but there was no response. There was a curtain of beads and glass crystals at the bottom of the stairs.

Well, she had come this far; she could not very well turn back now. Slipping inside, she shut the door behind her and went softly down the stairs. She called again midway down, but once again she was met with nothing. Not knowing what else to do, she pushed aside the bead curtain and looked through.

The room inside was surprisingly plush, rich with reds and purples and golds. Stuffed sea creatures were mounted on plaques high up against the lacquered walls, squids and sharks and other creatures that were too outlandish for Poison to recognize from Fleet's descriptions. A great bulb-shaped, brass-coloured stove had a fire glowing in the grate, and an exquisite armchair was placed before it with its back to her.

"Ah," said a voice, soft as a whisper and yet seeming as loud as if the speaker were right next to her ear. "Poison."

Poison jumped involuntarily, looking around the room. A slight movement in the armchair, and she saw an elbow robed in deep purple shift into view.

She was about to ask how he knew her name, but she knew from stories that the question was always met with some vague and enigmatic response, and she was determined not to be predictable.

"Lamprey," she said evenly. "If you know who I am, I assume you know why I've come?"

"Of course," Lamprey replied. "Do sit down."

Poison noticed an armchair next to the one that Lamprey sat in. She wondered how she could possibly have failed to see it before.

She moved closer to him. The eyes of the stuffed sea creatures seemed to follow her disconcertingly. There was something wrong about this, she thought — something very wrong. She halted a few steps behind him. Apart from his elbow, he was entirely obscured by the back of the armchair.

"I prefer to stand," she said.

Lamprey wheezed in what might have been a laugh or a cat-like hiss of anger. "I insist," he whispered.

She walked over to the chair, glancing up at the squid on the wall above the stove. She could swear its hourglass eye was following her. The skin on the back of her neck crawled.

"I have a question," she said as she put her hand on the back of her armchair and passed around it. The wide wings of Lamprey's chair obscured him from view still, but she could now see the end of his robed arm, and she halted. His hand was pale and rotted with the nibbles of a thousand tiny fish. The nails were blackened and cracked.

"Come closer," Lamprey whispered.

Poison took a breath. She was suddenly terribly afraid of what she might see when Lamprey's face was turned upon her. She looked into the stove, to the fire behind the grate. At least that was a real thing, something she could trust. She kept her eyes upon it as she slid around the chair and sat herself in it.

"Won't you look at me, child?" the voice at her left whispered. She could not resist a glance at that hand, that drowned hand, but her gaze flicked quickly back to the fire.

"I . . ." she began, sensing that a response was needed but unable to think of one. Eventually, she said the only thing that came to her. "I fear you."

"Very wise. As well you should," came the soft hiss. "*They* did not fear me enough."

"Who?" Poison asked, almost turning to face him and then catching herself at the last moment.

"Them," he said, making a small motion with his hand. She caught the movement and looked up. The squid was looking down on her. She felt a crawling dread trickle down her breastbone. The shark, the seal, the ray, the other creatures that she had no name for . . . they were all looking at her. It was no trick of her imagination.

"What happened to them?" she asked, her voice tiny.

"They did not answer my riddle."

Poison felt a strange sense of unreality settle on her. Had he really said what she thought he had?

"A riddle?"

She heard the rustle of Lamprey's robes as he nodded. "If you answer incorrectly, you will join them on my wall. If you solve my riddle —"

"You have to answer my question," Poison finished, but the words seemed to come as if in a dream. This surely could not be happening to her. Hadn't she read it a dozen times in Fleet's phaerie tales? It seemed that every epic quest had a riddle in it somewhere, a knot to be unravelled that would let them past a guardian or defeat an enemy that could not be beaten any other way. But it was fiction! An artifice, a cliché, no more part of real life than the wicked king or the happy ending.

"Why?" she asked.

"Why?" Lamprey echoed. "You are in no position for *whys*, child."

She frowned, staring harder into the fire. "I only want to understand," she said. "Why ask a riddle? If you will help me, then help me; I'm sure you already know what my question is. If you want me for your wall, I don't think I can stop you. I have money; can't I pay you instead? Then we both profit. What do you gain from a riddle?"

Lamprey was silent for a time. When he replied, he seemed less certain than before. "Will you hear my riddle or not? You are free to leave if you wish, but once the riddle is asked, there is no turning back."

Poison felt a twinge of frustration at his answer, but it was his game she was playing. "I've always been good at riddles," she said.

"We shall see," Lamprey replied, and then spoke his riddle:

"Mistress of the sea, the waves flock to her call.
She floats in rippled pools, to rise and never fall."

"The moon," Poison replied instantly. "There, that was easy."

"*Do not take me so lightly!*" Lamprey howled, and his cold, dead hand snatched up her wrist as he pulled her around to face him. She screamed as she looked into the mouldering sockets of his eyes. His skin was white as bone and withered on his skull, and his jaw hung at a slant as if broken. His nose was a bridge of gristle with a few tattered strings of muscle anchoring it to his cheeks and eyebrows, and what hair straggled from beneath his hood was matted and filthy. She fought to pull away from him, but his grip was like iron. He smelt of damp and rot, and the reek was so strong that she wanted to gag.

"Look at me," he hissed, but Poison would not. "I was like you once. Young, arrogant . . . I thought I knew how the world worked. I see into your mind, Poison, I see that you *think* you are very smart. I thought so, too. I thought I was so clever that I could outwit a kelpie. You know how to catch a kelpie, Poison?"

Poison was sobbing with fright, but she managed to reply. "Riddles . . ." she said.

"Riddles, yes. You can lure them with riddles, you know. I thought that I could swim in her river and when she came to me, I could fox her with riddles long enough to get her ashore, and then she'd have to be my wife and do as I said for the rest of her days. Wouldn't that have been a fine thing?"

"She drowned you. . . ."

"I got a riddle wrong," Lamprey said, his voice a soft exhalation of hate. "All the tales, all the stories, but they never said anything about that! She was beautiful, so beautiful . . . but I had so many riddles to remember, and she answered them so fast, and I forgot one of the lines. . . ." Lamprey released her, and she drew back her hand and clutched it to her body. But the hood of his robe had fallen over his face as he bowed his head in despair. "She turned fearful then, turned to her true form: a thing of teeth and claws. Curse all phaeries! She drowned me, yes, but that was not the end. It was a phaerie river, and death is not so final there. I escaped from her after many long weeks, when another poor fool came to try his luck. So I came here, and here I stay, asking my riddles. A phaerie river does things to you, child. I thought I knew it all, but like you I know nothing."

Poison was trembling, but he seemed to have diminished now, and she was not so afraid of him anymore. She wanted desperately to be gone from that place, but there was one thing left to do.

"I answered your riddle," she said. "You have to answer my question."

Lamprey seemed to sag and wither, becoming small and frail. "Follow the road north for three days until you see a great tower on a hill. From there, travel west for a day. There you will find the passing-place."

"Passing-place?" Poison asked.

"There are many spots in the Realms where they touch upon one another. At these points, when the circumstances are right, a person can slip from one Realm into another."

"And I'll get to the Realm of Phaerie through this passing-place?" Poison asked.

"That depends," he said with a foul chuckle. "On whether *she* catches you or not."

THE HOUSE OF THE BONE WITCH

"**HERE**," said Poison, holding out the coins. "Two silver sovereigns for past services, and a third for bringing me here from Shieldtown. You've earned them."

Bram let her put the coins into the broad palm of his glove, looking doubtfully over her shoulder at the tumbledown house at the top of the hill. In the light of a bright, cool evening, it stood out like a scab against the surrounding countryside.

Poison closed his fingers over the coins with her own and looked back, following his gaze to the house. A light wind stirred her dark hair against her upper arm.

"I don't suppose I could tempt you with a fourth sovereign?" she said, only half-joking.

"Not all the money in the Realm would get me in there," he said, dropping the coins into a pouch at his belt. He patted the head of his grint absently, adjusting the tilt of his wide-brimmed hat and frowning. "I'd try and change your mind, but I know you too well."

Poison gave him an apologetic look.

"At least tell me why," he said. "Since we'll never meet again, at least tell me why."

"The phaeries stole my sister," Poison said. "I'm going to get her back."

"Ah," said Bram. She knew by the way he voiced the syllable that he understood.

They stood in silence for a time, looking at the house. It was massive, seeming to creak under its own weight, a crooked heap of uneven spires and balconies, sooty windows and blackened gables. The whole thing appeared to *loom*, becoming larger at the top than it was at its base, and even in the daylight it gave the impression that it was waiting, patiently and hungrily, for the next morsel to step inside. A badly constructed fence surrounded it, silhouetted against the blue sky, and though it was too far away to see it did not appear to be made out of wood, but rather some other material that Poison did not recognize. So this was the passing-place then — a bridge between the Realm of Man and the Realm of Phaerie.

And inside waited Maeb, the Bone Witch.

"Maeb is the guardian of the gateway." The voice of Lamprey came back to her. "She is blind and deaf, but do not be fooled. She can smell you. And she has two hounds, two hounds that can tear you limb from limb if they get hold of you. Be warned, child — she is always looking for intruders. She wants your bones."

"What must I do?" she had asked.

"You must enter the house while the moon is full, and leave the night after, at midnight," Lamprey had whispered. "That will take you to the Phaerie Realm. All you have to do is stay alive until then. But don't try to get out before your time is up. There are . . . *things* that live in the space between the Realms. You wouldn't want to meet them." He had given her a rotted grimace that was meant to be a smile. "You won't have to worry about Maeb while the sun is in the sky, but the dogs never sleep. They are ever watchful."

She had pressed him for more details, but Lamprey would say no more and she had retreated, not wishing to spend another moment in that rotted thing's presence. Once back with Bram, she had offered him a third silver sovereign if he would take her as far as the passing-place. There they would have to bid their farewells, for she would be entering the Realm of Phaerie, leaving Bram behind.

And now the moment had come, and Poison felt a queer sadness at the thought that she would never set eyes on this cantankerous old man again. She had grown strangely fond of him during the time they had travelled together, more so even than Fleet. He had shared her first adventure, been there with her as she set out into the world that she had only heard about in stories. Even though she had paid him every step of the way, she had an intuition that he had only taken the last two coins because he knew she would not accept charity. He had not wanted to leave her to the mercies of Shieldtown, so he had struck her a deal that would allow her to accept his aid without denting her pride. And she was certain that if she had asked he would have taken her this far for nothing; but again, she offered a coin to ameliorate her sense of independence. In an odd way, he was her friend, and she would miss him.

"Well," she said with a glance at the sun as it slid towards evening, "I suppose I must go in." The moon was already up in the west, a perfect circle hanging like a ghost in the blue sky. Bram took her pack out of the cart and handed it to her, his face set in an unfamiliar expression between sorrow and frustration. She knew how much he hated phaeries, and that he believed Poison was marching to her death. She knew he thought he could protect her, and it grieved him to watch her go. She took the pack and slid it over her shoulders, then gave him a hug. Her slender frame was dwarfed inside his huge embrace, and just for a moment she considered how it might be to stay like this, to be content as she was and not to face the terror she knew lay ahead. But that was not her way.

"I'll come and find you when I return," she said.

"Don't make promises you can't keep, Poison," he replied, his voice a rumble in his chest. "You're going to the Realm of Phaerie. Time is not the same there as here. You might be back tomorrow or a hundred years from now." He did not need to add the third option: *or you might not come back at all.*

"Then I promise I'll try," she said. "I'll look for an old man with a farm on a grassy mountainside, keeping himself to himself."

Bram laughed mirthlessly. "Sounds like me, all right." He let her go, and she stepped back from him. He looked her over with tenderness in his eyes. "You've given me a second chance, Poison. I won't forget that."

"See that you don't," she said, with a wink to indicate she was joking. She looked up at the house, then back to him. "Farewell then, Bram of Oilskin."

"Farewell, Poison of Gull. Good luck. I think I'll camp here tonight and set off in the morning." He scratched the back of his neck and harrumphed in embarrassment. "In case you change your mind."

"You're a good man, Bram," she said as she walked away up the hill towards the house. "You deserve a wife!"

Bram stood by his cart and watched her go, but she did not look back. If she had, her resolve might have crumbled completely.

❧❧❧

The fence, unsurprisingly, was made of bones. What was more disturbing was the scale of it. If the house had appeared oddly proportioned from a distance, up close it was even more evident. From the base of the hill, the fence had seemed to be built to be waist-high, coming up only to the sills of the lowest windows; but now that Poison stood next to it, it was as high as her head, and she could easily duck through it into the thick, untended scrub of weeds and thistles beyond. Even the plants seemed huge, with thorns big enough to open a vein if she brushed against them and blades of grass as long as her arm. Everything within the perimeter of the fence was at least twice the size of things outside.

This house was half in the Realm of Phaerie, half in the Realm of Man, she reminded herself. In the liminal places of the world, there was no telling what was possible and what was not.

The structure towered over her as she picked her way carefully through the forest of weeds. She was approaching the side of the house rather than the front. If she wanted her presence to go unnoticed, she thought that knocking on the door was not the best way to go. Cautiously, she crept up to one of the grimy windows, grabbed the sill, and pulled herself up to peer through.

Inside it was dim, and the lack of light and smeared glass combined to foil her. She could only make out an impression of size, and nothing more. There was no movement within. Had she not known better, she would have assumed it was empty.

She dropped back into the weeds and began to make her way around the rear of the house. Her palms were already cold and moist with nervousness; she wiped them against her coarse dress. The windows she had seen so far had been nailed shut, and they could not be opened unless she smashed them. She would not do that unless it was a last resort. There had to be another way in.

She found it, eventually, when she almost fell down it.

Around the back of the house was a coal chute, hidden under the thick grass. It was covered over by planking, but rain and woodworm had made it brittle. She stepped on it before she saw it and it gave instantly. The feel of wood rather than turf beneath her feet had forewarned her, and she managed to shift her weight so that it was only her ankle that went through the flimsy covering and not her whole body.

She crouched on the edge of the rectangular shaft, massaging her bruised ankle while she peered into the darkness. The chute was slanted and wide enough to crawl down. She regarded it dubiously before getting up and making a full circuit of the house. As she suspected, there were no other ways in besides the front door or the windows. Climbing was not an option; the scale of the house was simply too big. She returned to the coal chute, glanced at the westering sun, and shrugged to herself. The moon was up, so that meant she could go inside, daylight or no daylight. At least she would only have the dogs to deal with until night fell. Considering that everything else about the house of the Bone Witch was twice normal size, she was not looking forward to meeting them.

She pulled away the rest of the planking and eased her head and shoulders over the edge of the shaft. Cold air blew up from within, smelling stale and rancid. She took her pack from where she had laid it by her side and dropped it into the shaft ahead of her. It slid down with an ascending hiss and was swallowed by the darkness. She turned around, braced herself against the shaft sides with her boots and began to crawl down feet-first after it, her dress bunching up around her knees.

The descent itself was not so difficult; the shaft was just the right width for her arms and legs, and the slant was shallow enough so that she would not plunge to her death if she slipped. Nevertheless, she was frightened, and it was only by not thinking about what was ahead that she managed to force herself to continue down. The shaft was entirely lightless; only the rectangle of sky above her gave any indication that she was not completely blind, and that was moving farther and farther away with each step downwards. She felt like she was crawling backwards down the house's throat, into its cold belly. In the absence of anything else to occupy it, her imagination began conjuring pictures of the Bone Witch and her dogs waiting at the bottom of the shaft, the Bone Witch sharpening her knives in anticipation of the morsel that was clambering into her lair.

Then her feet touched something lumpy, and she realized it was her pack. She cursed under her breath. Was the chute bricked up? Certainly, this did not seem to be the coal chamber she had expected. She worked her booted foot around the edge of her pack and pressed it against the obstruction. It creaked. Wood. Not brittle, but weak and thin.

I hope she really is deaf, Poison thought to herself, and kicked downwards. The wood splintered and broke away with a clatter that made her shudder; now there was faint light coming through from beneath her, and she knew that beyond was the cellar of the house. She held herself still and quiet, listening. Her heart thudded in her chest. But if the dogs had heard her, there was no sign.

She had to kick through two more planks before she could drop her pack through and squeeze after it. Each time was followed by a terrible silence, as she strained her ears for a noise in the house above; each time there was nothing, not even a creak.

Whatever the coal had once emptied into had long been removed, and she dropped onto a flagstone floor in a cavernous cellar. Once again she was struck by the size of the place; here, she was a midget, and even the bricks of the cellar walls seemed massive to her. Dim light struggled in through thin slots of murky glass around the upper edges of the cellar.

It was cold and heaped with sacks of coal, and other sacks of what might have been grain or oatmeal. A stone staircase led up to a shadowy door high above.

She took a few moments to listen. She was inside now; whatever happened, at least she would be here when night fell. She estimated she had at least an hour before dusk in which she could change her mind and get out. But after that, escape was not an option. She remembered Lamprey's warning about the things that lived in the space between the Realms, and wondered if they would be worse than the Bone Witch. She thought of Bram, waiting out there for her.

Part of her counselled staying in the cellar, simply burrowing into a corner and hiding there till her time was done and she could escape through the coal chute. But there was very little cover down here apart from a few piles of sacks, and she did not want to trap herself like that; if it came to it, she could probably clamber up the chute again and hide halfway, but not fast enough to prevent the dogs from reaching her in time if they came bursting in. No, there had to be a better hiding place than this.

I'll just have a look about, she thought, to placate her urge to escape. *Then I'll decide.*

She crept up the stairs, taking giant steps. At the top, she listened again, but once more there was nothing. A faded brass handle was set into the door at the height of her eyes; she heaved it down and the door popped ajar, opening inward. She peered out through the gap.

The hallway beyond was massive, with its dirty walls of rough stone cast in a smeared light from outside. Skulls were set in sconces high up, with half-melted candles waiting unlit within their jaws. Their eye sockets and teeth were blackened by smoke, making them look strangely daemonic. Poison stared. She was not particularly scared; it was just that there was something odd about them, and it took her a few moments to work out what it was. Of course: the skulls were normal size, and in this house that made them look unnaturally small.

The angle of the sun through the window at the end of the corridor seemed lower than Poison expected; perhaps she had spent longer in the coal shaft than she had imagined.

Fear making her cautious, she stopped and listened again, but the house was eerily silent. A chill wind seemed to breathe through it, blowing gently one way and sucking back the next into the grimy lungs of the building.

She was about to step out when she heard a heavy thump from the wooden ceiling.

She shied back, ready to close the cellar door if anything should appear. But nothing did. Instead, she heard the loping of something massive overhead — the languid stride of a dog. Having never lived in a house with more than one storey, she was unaccustomed to deciphering the sounds of movement on the floor above, and it took her a long moment to realize that the thump had been the dog jumping down from whatever perch it had been lying on. She listened hard, her heart fluttering from the fright, but the dog seemed to have stopped moving.

At least that's one of them accounted for, she thought to herself, eking what positive thoughts she could out of her predicament. She determined to herself that she would stay on the first floor for the moment.

Finally mustering her courage, she slipped out of the relative safety of the cellar and into the corridor. She felt terribly exposed here, like a mouse scuttling along the skirting-board, but scuttle she did, as silently as her boots would allow.

The corridor ended in a great, stone room, in which a vast black cauldron was bubbling over a fire and an iron stove sat against one wall. It was spacious in proportion to the dimensions of the house, so it seemed unnaturally huge to her, and the cauldron was far taller than she was. Above the stove was a shelf, on which an assortment of clay pots stood. Poison presumed they were spices or some kind of witch's ingredients, but there were no labels on them.

Of course there aren't, she thought to herself. *She's blind, isn't she?*

There were no windows here, and the only light came from the blaze beneath the cauldron, making the room stiflingly hot and painting everything in shades of sullen red. A set of stairs ran up to her right to a balcony that overlooked the room, and a door beyond that led on to the second storey of the house. The balcony's railings were made of smoke-blackened bones, as was the chandelier that hung from the centre of the ceiling. It was this that snared her attention: a great cartwheel of human femurs, with skulls at each spoke, and in each skull an unlit candle. So entranced was Poison by this macabre sight that it took her a while before the most obvious thought occurred to her.

Who's tending the fire?

She felt a sudden alarm. The fire had certainly not been burning since last night; it would have been embers by now. That meant somebody had been feeding it coal. And it wasn't the dogs.

Was there somebody else here, someone Lamprey hadn't warned her about?

She cursed under her breath. She should not have been so naive, to trust a bitter and dangerous thing like Lamprey. If half of what he told her about this place was true, then that was more than enough to deal with. What if he had been lying to her about the house being a passing-place? What if he had meant to send her to her death?

A soft mewl from above made her jump out of her skin. She was halfway to running back out of the room before she processed the sound in her mind and determined that it was a cat. She looked up and saw it on the edge of the balcony, a black tom watching her with eyes that glinted green in the firelight. Furthermore, it was of *normal* size, which meant . . . which meant . . . well, she didn't know what it meant. It was gazing at her with an unsettling singularity of interest, and as she held its gaze, she felt curiously like it was sizing her up. After a moment, it wandered away and began gently scratching at the door on the balcony, wanting to be let through.

"Sorry, cat," Poison said under her breath. "I'm not going up *there* for anything." She wouldn't give much for the cat's chances, either, if it came across the dog that she had heard earlier. Better that it stayed on this side of the door.

There was nothing more she could see in this room, and she didn't dare to linger for long. She turned to head back down the corridor and go the other way. The second dog was still unaccounted for, and she had to find a good place to hide before . . .

night . . .

fell. . . .

Her blood ran cold. The window at the end of the corridor was dark. The sun had set. She could have sworn she had not been in the house more than a quarter of an hour, yet in that time the day had worn from evening to dusk and beyond.

The cellar! She had to get back to the cellar!

But it was too late. From the far end of the corridor, where it turned the corner, she heard the heavy creak of stairs, and a thin, cracked voice floated through the house.

"*I can smell you, my dear! I'll have your bones!*"

The Bone Witch was awake.

PEPPERCORN AND THE CAT

~~~~~~~~~~

POISON was frozen to the spot, terrified. A wild plan hatched in her head: could she make it to the cellar door before the Bone Witch got there? Could she clamber up the coal chute and get out before it was too late? She was caught between her fear of going farther into the house and her fear of the thing creaking down the stairs, somewhere out of sight. She heard the dogs thumping about above, excited by their mistress's voice. Trapped by indecision, she wasted precious seconds in the doorway of the room with the cauldron.

"Don't hide away, little one. I'll make dice from your knuckles! I'll suck your marrow dry!"

The cat mewed, scratching at the door.

Poison made her choice. Rather anything than come face-to-face with the owner of that horrible voice. She clambered up the stairs, climbing each step with a giant stride that hitched her dress up to her thighs. When she got to the balcony, she looked down into the cauldron below and saw what was in it. Boiling bones. She should have known.

The cat backed away as she neared, alarmed. She ignored it, heaving on the handle and pulling the door ajar. The cat darted around her legs and through the gap like a flash. Poison took just enough of a look down the corridor beyond to see that it was empty, and then she went through and pulled the door shut behind her.

She fled, the hideous promises of the Bone Witch receding behind her. Somewhere ahead, she heard a deep barking, and it was taken up elsewhere by another canine throat. It was almost too dark to see; skulls lined the walls as they had downstairs, but their candles had not been lit for a long while. What did the blind care for light?

The cat had stopped up ahead by a side door and was looking back at her expectantly. The nearby barking was a frenzy now, and she heard the sound of another door at the end of the corridor rattling in its frame as one of the dogs launched itself at it with a snarl. She yelped in fright. Only a few inches of wood stood between her and the slavering creature on the other side.

"I'll hunt you down, my pretty dear! I'll sniff you out!" came Maeb's voice from below.

Reasoning that the cat would only go where the dogs weren't, she opened the side door for the cat and went through herself. It led onto a short, narrow set of stairs that went steeply up to a second door at the top. She had almost reached it when it was opened for her — and there, holding a candle in a metal tallowcatcher, stood a girl of about her age in a nightdress.

"Come inside! Hurry!" she urged, her eyes wide and fearful. Poison did not hesitate more than a moment. She scurried into the room and let the girl shut the oversize door behind her.

The room was tiny by the standards of the house, and the furniture inside it was of usual, human size. A bed stood just beneath one curtained window; a chest of carved drawers rested against one wall, scattered with combs and bone hairgrips and with a mirror standing on it. There was a wardrobe, a little wicker basket for the cat, and a fireplace in which coal and branches were waiting for the flame to light them. It was an entirely normal girl's bedroom, though exceedingly dark, for the only light came from the candle that its owner now put next to the mirror.

The girl herself was a frail-looking, pretty thing, with golden hair in ringlets and wide, watery blue eyes. Poison had barely come into the room before the girl had snatched up a perfume bulb and was spraying her head to foot in it. Poison flinched automatically, but did not protest. The perfume was foul, an overwhelming and sickly violet reek; it was obvious that it was meant to cloak her from the Bone Witch's sensitive nostrils.

"Get under the bed!" the girl said, casting frantic glances at the door. "Go on, get under the bed!" she repeated, when Poison did not immediately react.

This time, she did as she was told. The girl sprayed herself liberally with the perfume as well, and then covered the room with it. Poison scrunched herself under the bed and found the cat already occupying the space. It gave her a grudging glance and moved over so that she could slide in.

"*Come out, come out, my dear,*" the Bone Witch cooed from below, and she heard the sound of her footsteps coming up the stairs, just outside the door. "*You can't run forever!*"

Poison watched as the girl composed herself breathlessly in front of the door, straightening her nightdress and folding her hands before her as if waiting to receive royalty. Then the door creaked open, and Maeb loomed in.

Poison's heart shrank. The Bone Witch filled the room, her hunched back almost touching the ceiling. She was enormous, eleven feet high even with a stoop. She wore a moth-eaten black dress and a grimy apron, and a filthy headscarf was tied at her chin. The skin of her hands was wrinkled and disgustingly warty; her fingers were long and thin and tipped with broken nails. But it was her face that was worst of all. She seemed to have been *twisted* somehow, pulled out of proportion so that she resembled a child's drawing of a witch rather than any natural thing. Her eyes were merely blanks, skin grown over the sockets, and grey hair straggled out from beneath her headscarf and over them. Her nose was enormous and pointed, more like a beak, with massive elliptical nostrils that twitched as she sniffed the air. She had no chin to speak of, and her mouth was a wrinkled slash; when she opened it Poison saw it was full of dozens of overlapping triangular teeth, like the shark she had seen in Lamprey's house.

Maeb's gargantuan nose wrinkled in disgust and she recoiled slightly.

"*Oh! Oh, you foul thing!*" she screeched. "*You've been wearing your perfume again! Didn't I tell you never to wear it? Didn't I?*"

The girl stamped twice on the floor.

"*No? Well, never again, do you hear?*"

One stamp.

The Bone Witch reached down and ran her hands over the girl's head and body. The girl's face tightened in disgust, but she remained still.

"*You're hiding someone, aren't you?*" the witch crowed.

Two stamps. Maeb leaned closer, until her nose was almost touching the girl's.

"*Don't lie to me, little one. I smelled her all the way here.*"

The girl stamped twice again.

Maeb sniffed the air again, questing this way and that. "*You're such a disobedient child. Always lying. If I find her, you'll be for the pot. The pot, I say!*"

The girl glanced down at where Poison hid under the bed.

"Stay still," she whispered. "She can feel it if you move. Through the floor."

Poison felt a shock of alarm, thinking for an instant that the girl had given her away. But Maeb was deaf, of course, and she heard nothing.

"*Come out, dear,*" the Bone Witch crooned, coming farther into the room. "*Maeb needs her fresh bones, and you smell young and strong.*" She began to pat around with her warty hands, knocking brushes off the chest of drawers. The girl made a snatch to save both the candle and the mirror. Maeb did not notice, beginning to pat along the floor instead, shuffling closer to the bed. She was blocking the door with her bulk. Poison unconsciously tried to huddle herself smaller. In the flickering light of the single candle, she saw those long fingers brushing closer and closer, feeling along the floor, up the bedposts, on to the mattress. She cringed as she felt hands patting along above her, the Bone Witch cooing and moaning softly to herself.

"*Not here, then? Perhaps she's under the bed, eh?*"

Poison went still as stone.

Maeb's hands spidered blindly around to the underside of the mattress. Poison drew back, not daring to breathe, the Bone Witch's cracked nails passing within an inch of her cheek.

"*Yes, under here. . . .*"

In the candlelight, Maeb's face suddenly came into view, as she stooped all the way down to sniff under the bed. Poison barely managed to suppress a cry of horror as the leathery, veined beak of a nose poked into her hiding place, twitching.

"*I can smell you,*" she singsonged.

The cat burst out with a feline yowl, scratching the Bone Witch's sensitive nose and darting through her legs with a thunder of paws. She howled in surprise, flailing at the air, retreating back to the doorway with one hand clutching her nose protectively.

"*Oh! Oh, that vicious little thing! My nose! My nose! I'll catch it, so I will! That cat's for the pot!*"

But the cat was already gone, down the stairs and away. The Bone Witch moaned in anguish and stumbled out of the room.

"*I'll be back, you spiteful little child!*" she promised as she stamped down the stairs. "*I'll have you for the pot, too! You and your cursed cat!*"

Then the door slammed, and she was gone.

Poison was still trembling when the girl came over to the bed and crouched down next to it, peering underneath with her candle.

"Don't worry," she said. "She's got a terrible memory. By the morning, she won't even remember what she said."

Poison crawled out from under the bed and allowed herself to be helped up.

"I'm Peppercorn," the girl said timidly.

"Poison," came the reply as she sat down on the bed.

"That's your name?" Peppercorn said uncertainly. "How nice."

"I chose it myself."

Peppercorn brightened. "So did I! Mine, I mean. Maeb never calls me anything." She put the candle down on the floor and sat down next to Poison. "You have lovely hair. I wish mine was straight."

Poison didn't quite know what to say to that, so she changed tack. "What are you doing here?"

"I live here," Peppercorn said proudly. "This is my room!" She got up and began picking up some of the things that the Bone Witch had scattered. "It's a bit of a mess, though," she said apologetically.

Poison watched her in amazement. The girl seemed to have forgotten that Poison had come within inches of the Bone Witch's grasp. She carried on chattering as she tidied up.

"I've always been here, I think. I can't remember anything before, anyway. I clean up and keep the fires going, things like that. You have to cook bones all day before they're soft enough for Maeb to eat nowadays. And she likes the soup you get from boiling the marrow out into the water."

"You look after the house?" Poison asked numbly.

"She'd eat me if I didn't," Peppercorn replied, as if that was the most obvious thing in the world. Again Poison could not think of what to say in response.

"Is that cat going to be all right?" Poison asked at length, listening for further sounds of the Bone Witch. She was lumbering about downstairs and shrieking faintly, with her dogs bellowing and barking.

"Andersen? He'll be fine," Peppercorn replied confidently. "So why are *you* here?"

"I'm trying to get to the Realm of Phaerie. I have to rescue my sister."

"Really? How exciting!"

Poison gave her a look that was meant to convey the seriousness of her task, but Peppercorn merely smiled sweetly, uncomprehending. A moment later, the black tomcat slunk back into the room and wound itself around Peppercorn's legs.

"Andersen!" she cried, squatting down and making a fuss over him. The cat threw a reproachful glance at Poison before surrendering himself to pleasure, as if to say: *There, I saved your neck, the things I have to do for some people. . . .*

Poison allowed herself to calm down for a few minutes, making small chat while she got over the shock of her brush with the Bone Witch and the bizarre meeting with this happy young girl and her cat in the midst of a house of horrors.

"Can I hide here?" she asked at length.

"Ooh, better not," said Peppercorn, straightening. Andersen, disappointed at no longer being stroked, slid up onto the chest of drawers and began to lick his forepaw, with an occasional glance up to see if anyone was paying attention to him.

"Why not?"

"She'll come back eventually. She's very sly. If she thinks you're in here, a bit of perfume won't keep her away for long. And she'll bring the dogs. They can't smell a thing, but they can see and hear."

Poison cursed under her breath. "Is there somewhere else I can hide?"

"Oh, the house is full of hidey-holes," Peppercorn said brightly. "But once she's on your trail, you'd better be a good hider! Most of the people who get out of here are the ones Maeb doesn't know about. She's after you now."

"She caught me out after dark," Poison replied.

Peppercorn nodded in sympathy. "The days go very fast here, but the nights are very slow. That's why I only burn one candle at a time. Can't waste candles, you see."

Poison thought for a moment. "How many people have come through here?"

Peppercorn resumed her tidying. "A few. I've got a calendar over there." She pointed vaguely. Poison went over to where a calendar hung on the wall, but with the candle on the other side of the room it was too dark to see anything. She decided not to bother, and sat back down on the bed.

"Maeb says this is one of the only bridges between the Realm of Man and the Realm of Phaerie," Peppercorn chattered. "That's why the phaeries put her here to guard it. Some people are trying to escape the Phaerie Realm, some people are trying to get into it. Either way she's supposed to stop them. Phaeries don't like humans, you know. Except to eat."

"Do many make it out?"

"One or two," she replied. "Andersen comes and tells me if they do. It's not good if Maeb catches me with them; she gets really mad."

"The cat tells you?"

Peppercorn gave her an odd look. "Yes, the cat," she said, clearly unable to see why Poison was surprised.

Poison shrugged inwardly. "Doesn't it . . ." She paused, then decided she would finish for the sake of curiosity. "Doesn't it concern you that you're the housemaid for a creature that eats people like you and me?"

Peppercorn looked back over her shoulder, and her face in the candlelight was one of terrible sorrow. "There isn't anything else," she said. "Do you think I like living here, with only Andersen for company? Everyone I meet only stays for a night or two, then they're eaten or they go. There isn't anything else."

"No, that's not right," Poison said, getting to her feet. "I was like that, before. I lived in a tiny village, and I never left it. I dreamed of faraway places, and I scorned everybody for being stuck in that horrible swamp and never wanting to leave. But I was trapped, just like them, and for all that I talked about it, I might never have gone away if it weren't for my sister being kidnapped. I might have stayed there, always meaning to go but always putting it off, and every year something would come along that made it harder for me to leave until one day I would realize that I was old, and I *couldn't* leave anymore."

Peppercorn came over to her, bringing the candle closer. "Weren't you scared?"

"Terrified," Poison said. "And I'm still terrified. But I wouldn't go back home now for a thousand sovereigns. I've seen a glimpse of what's out here, and I can never again be content with that tiny world."

"Oh, you're lucky," Peppercorn said, her eyes shining. "I would love to go and see the world! The people who come through here tell me such stories. . . ."

"Then what's stopping you? You can just walk out of here!"

"I'm not strong enough," Peppercorn said. "I'm only a girl."

"So am I," Poison pointed out.

"What would I do? Where would I go?" Peppercorn bleated.

"That you can decide as you go along," Poison replied. "That's the beauty of it. Now I have to leave. I don't want to be here if *she* comes back."

"Good luck!" Peppercorn said, brightening again. "Come back in the daytime; I can fix you something to eat when Maeb's asleep."

Poison bade her farewell and left, going down the short staircase to where another door led onto the corridor. She listened, but she could hear nothing now. Half of her wanted to go back and beg the girl to let her stay, to hide under her bed till morning, but what Peppercorn had said made sense. The Bone Witch would not be gone for long, and when she came back there would be nowhere to hide. Besides, there was something faintly disturbing about the cheery way Peppercorn went about her business, living by candlelight in a house of death with a monstrous bone-gnawing witch as a mother figure. Poison would not have been surprised if she was more than a little mad. She certainly seemed to believe her cat could talk to her.

Poison peered out into the corridor, but it was empty. The fear began to grow in her again, made worse now that she knew what it was that hunted her. The Bone Witch was either too far away to be heard, or she had stopped her screeching. The dogs, similarly, were silent. That was perhaps worse than when she could hear them; at least she knew where they were then.

She crept down the corridor, back towards the room with the cauldron. After listening once again, she slipped out onto the balcony. Waves of heat washed up to her, and the room seemed to shift in the light of the fire beneath the great iron cauldron. She looked over with horror at the bone broth that bubbled away below, and at the macabre chandelier that hung above it; they only served to remind her of what might happen if she was caught, and she dismissed them from her thoughts. There was no sign of witch or dog. She slipped down the wooden stairs to the floor of the room and peered down the corridor that stood between her and the cellar.

Nobody was there. The house seemed to breathe quietly.

She had already decided that it was far too dangerous to go looking for new hiding places while the witch was on the prowl, so she had determined to head back to the cellar. True enough, the sacks of flour and coal were not good places to hide, but she still had the coal chute. She could climb into it and wedge a few boards back into place. The slant was shallow enough for her to sit there until morning, and even through to the next night, when she could escape. She could smear herself in coal or flour to mask her scent.

She wished she had thought of that before she decided to go exploring.

It took her a while to build up the courage to make the dash from the cauldron room to the cellar door, but though she feared that something would spring out at any moment, nothing did. She raced down the shadowy corridor, her way lit by the feeble moonlight from the window at the end of the corridor. She peeped down into the cellar, and her heart sank.

There was one thing she had forgotten. The sun had set. It was pitch dark down there.

She gazed down into the blackness. The thin slots of grimed glass high up on the cellar walls were barely adequate in full sunlight; by night, they let in next to no illumination. She could hardly even make out the heaps of sacks that lay down there.

There was a growl from the end of the corridor, accompanied by a rhythmic thumping. Her eyes widened in terror. One of the dogs was coming downstairs and would turn into the corridor at any moment.

There was no time to deliberate. She slipped into the cellar and closed the door quietly, leaning her back against it. Her breath came in trembling shudders. Somewhere ahead of her, massive steps plunged down to the stone floor, but she could see nothing of them. Her vision had been extinguished. Everything was dark.

She heard the dog as it loped into the corridor. The absence of light seemed to sharpen her hearing — or perhaps it was the size of the thing that prowled nearer, for she could hear the heavy panting of its breath, the click of its claws as it walked. She dared not move, in case it heard her; it seemed that her heart was hammering loud enough to shake the door she leaned against.

It loped up to the cellar door, and there it stopped.

Poison held her breath. She waited for what seemed like forever, and then breathed out again. It still had not moved.

Suddenly, there came a lurch that almost sent her tumbling down the stairs. She pushed back against the door instinctively, enough to stop it coming open. The dog had butted it with its head. She got her foot under a crack in the stone and wedged herself against the door, feeling chill sweat prickle under her hairline. The dog butted again, harder this time, but she was ready for it, and the door did not give.

Go away, there's nothing here, she thought, willing the words into the dog's head.

Again, harder still. But Poison was well braced now.

There was a puzzled whine from outside, and then silence. Poison squeezed her eyes shut, praying that the dog would give up and move on.

Amazingly, it did. She could barely credit her luck as she heard the receding click of the dog's claws, heading towards the cauldron room. She waited for a few minutes to see if it came back, but silence had fallen on the house once again. Finally, she allowed herself to believe the danger had passed.

By now her eyes had adjusted somewhat to the darkness, and while it was little better than being totally blind, she could almost make out vague shapes in the room. Gingerly, she felt her way down the stairs, into the deep black of the cellar. It was chill down here, and she began to shiver a little, though whether out of fear or the cold she could not tell. Nobody liked the dark, and in a place like this it was awful. She edged out across the cellar, heading for where she imagined the coal chute would be. If she could just make it there, she could feel a little safer. Taking tiny steps across the room, without a wall at her back, she felt like something would grab hold of her at any moment. The sensation of being watched was overwhelming, so much so that she had to stop for a moment to calm herself. She listened to the silence, to the soft, sinister breath of the house all around her.

No, not all around her. *Behind* her.

"*I can smell you, little pretty,*" the Bone Witch crooned softly from the dark, and Poison screamed as a sack went over her head and she was bundled up like a rabbit.

SKINS AND BONES

DAWN came to the house of the Bone Witch, but it was a strange dawn, the sky an odd clash of amber and purple that did not look quite natural. A mist seemed to have come down, cloaking everything outside the bone fence but not straying inside its perimeter. Shadows shifted within, beneath the dull bruise of the sun, but whether they were the movements of the mist or something altogether worse, Poison could not tell.

She sat in a rusting iron cage, her head hanging and her long black hair falling over her face. The cage was suspended by a chain from the ceiling of the cauldron room, high above the stove. Beneath her were Maeb's collection of mysterious ingredients, great clay pots full of all sorts of powders, leaves, and pastes. The chandelier of skulls grinned at her from across the room. Through the doorway, she could see down the corridor to a single window by which she marked the time. The cauldron was still bubbling as ever, a fresh collection of bones boiling within. The room was sweltering, even more so up near the ceiling where the heat gathered.

Poison sat in the midst of despair.

She had tried everything: squeezing through the bars, picking the lock with a flake of metal, even calling for help. It was all useless. She could not break out of the cage. And even if she could, there was still the matter of the dog that was the size of a horse, curled up on the floor and gnawing noisily on a shinbone in the firelight.

She watched it for a time, studying its long, lean grey body and wide-muzzled face. It looked remarkably normal apart from its size; so did its twin, whom she had also seen in the latter hours of the night while hanging in her cage. Yet when she observed its lips skinning back, exposing yellowed fangs as it crunched and chewed on the bone in its jaws, she reminded herself of what Lamprey had said: that they could tear her limb from limb if they got hold of her.

The night had been an ordeal of fraying nerves. She had watched as Maeb fished bones out of the cauldron and chewed on them herself or fed them to the dogs. Mostly she had been left alone, ignored, wondering at her fate. The Bone Witch had stuffed her in the cage without a word, and left her hanging in sight of the bubbling cauldron until just before dawn, when she came back and prodded Poison through the bars.

"*We'll have all that nasty flesh off you, my dear,*" she said. "*Come tonight, you'll be for the pot.*" She smacked her lips and grinned her shark-tooth grin. "*You'll make a tasty nibble.*"

With that, she hobbled off to bed and left Poison there to contemplate the following night, which would come all too soon. What Peppercorn had told her was right. Here, the nights were long, but the days were awfully short.

The morning was brightening distressingly fast, the light growing at the end of the corridor, when she heard the sound of the balcony door opening and in came Peppercorn. Poison had lapsed into a drowse, for she had not slept since the night before last, but she sprang awake at the noise. The dog looked up, too, though once it established that it was Peppercorn it lost interest and went back to its bone.

"Have you seen my cat?" Peppercorn called to Poison.

"Your *cat?*" Poison cried. "Help me out of here!"

Peppercorn twiddled her blonde curls, anxiously looking around the room. "I haven't seen him since last night," she said. "He disappeared just after you left."

"Peppercorn, *please!* You have to let me down from here!" Poison urged. "There's a chain over there, see? See where it's hooked through that big iron eyelet? Just unhook it and run it through slowly. You can do it!"

Peppercorn's gaze went to the chain. It ran from the top of the cage through three similar eyelets: on the ceiling, the wall, and one on the floor where it was secured. "But I can't find my cat!" she wailed.

"I'll help you find your cat!" Poison lied, putting on her most encouraging tone. "We can find him together!"

Peppercorn chewed her lip, thinking this over. "I can't," she said uncertainly.

Poison wanted to scream. "You can!" she said. "If you leave me here, Maeb will eat me! Is that what you want?"

"No," Peppercorn said, shuffling her feet and evidently wishing she were somewhere else. "But I can't let you out. Maeb would know. Then she'd be really mad. She might eat *me!*"

"Then we'll get out together! I know a way!"

"I can't leave!" Peppercorn said. "I've never left this house!"

"I'll look after you," said Poison. "Didn't you say you wanted to go and see the world? Don't you want to see the Realm of Phaerie?"

"Well, I do, but —"

"Do you want to spend the rest of your days looking after

that old witch, living in fear of being put in the pot, watching new friends come and get eaten or leave and never return?"

"No, but —"

"Then let me down!"

"What about the dog?"

"I'll worry about the dog!" Poison said, though she really had no idea how she would deal with it. Just to get out of the cage would be a start, and it was more hope than she had a few minutes ago.

Peppercorn seemed caught in indecision; and making decisions, as Poison had ascertained by now, was not her strong suit.

"I daren't!" she bleated at length. "We can't leave the house until midnight! Otherwise the things in the mist will get us. She'll be awake by then, and she'll see you've gone. She'll catch us and eat us both!"

"We can hide!" Poison cried desperately. "Please!"

But whether Peppercorn might have been persuaded or not, Poison never got to find out. For at that moment, they heard a loud meow from the doorway to the corridor, and there was Andersen. The dog leaped up in an instant with a deafening bark, and the cat turned tail and ran with the dog thundering after it.

"Andersen!" Peppercorn squeaked, running down the stairs from the balcony and off in pursuit, ignoring Poison's cries for help. The sounds of the chase faded, and Poison was left alone.

She slumped down to the floor of her cage and wanted to cry.

"Poison?" called a voice softly. "Are you up there?"

A smile of disbelief spread across Poison's face, and she sprang up and grabbed the bars of the cage.

"*Bram?*" she cried.

Her ears had not deceived her. There he stood by the doorway, in his heavy hide coat with his thick gloves and wide-brimmed hat. He grunted at her and waved a meaty hand.

"What are you *doing* here?" she asked.

"Saving your neck, apparently," he said. "I must be mad."

"There's a chain over there," she urged. "Untie it and let me down. Slowly!"

He did so. The iron eyelets took some of the weight of the cage, so he was able to play the chain through gradually; but even so, it was a strain. The chain clanked noisily through the eyelets, each link scraping so loudly that Poison was sure it would bring one of the awful guardians of this place. Agonizing minutes passed, punctuated by the periodic sound of clattering metal, until with a thump the cage was down. Bram hurried over to her.

She gripped his gloved hands through the bars. "Bram, you're a wonder! I've never been so glad to see anybody as you right now. How did you know?"

He flushed to the roots of his great white moustache and harrumphed, letting her hands go. "That cursed cat, that's how. I swear it's not a natural thing. Anyway, all that's for later. Let's see about getting you out of here." He grabbed the bars and gave them an experimental rattle, peering up at the point where they joined the top of the cage. "Rusted, see? Can't have done them much good hanging about over that boiling cauldron for ages. Step back."

Poison did so, wondering what he had in mind. He answered her question soon enough, by putting his boot into one of the bars with a resounding clang. Another kick, and it broke away from the top of the cage. One more, and it had been bent inward enough to almost come away from the bottom. Bram reached in and wrenched it a few times, and it snapped off, making a gap big enough for Poison to fit her willowy frame through.

Poison slid out and hugged Bram around his broad chest for the sheer relief of being free. She could almost feel the heat of his blush as he awkwardly patted her back.

"Thank you," she said, meaning it as deeply as she had ever meant anything. "I know what it must have taken to come in after me."

"Let's just get out of here," he said. "I suppose you have a place to hide?"

Poison was about to reply in the negative, for the Bone Witch had already caught her once that way, but another notion struck her instead. Buoyed by the presence of an ally, she felt a little of the fear that this place engendered fall away.

"Forget that," she said. "I need your help. I've got an idea."

Bram groaned an oath. "I was afraid you'd say something like that."

"That's the spirit!" Poison grinned and slapped him on the shoulder.

It was no easy task, to manhandle the clay pots from the shelf above the stove up to the balcony. The stove came up to Bram's shoulders, and the pots were on a shelf that was another shoulder-height above that, so he had to stand on the stovetop while Poison tipped them gingerly into his grasp, and then repeat the process standing on the floor. After that, the two of them hauled the pots up the stairs and dragged them across the balcony. Each was about the size of a barrel and packed full. Poison kept half an eye on the corridor, in case either of the dogs should return; she was careful to take note of the angle of the sun as it sped across the misty sky.

"So tell me . . ." she panted, "about the cat. . . ."

Bram's face was red from straining, and he put the pot down for a moment and wiped his brow. "Came last night," he said. "I was in my camp, and I could hear the voice of that witch-woman on the breeze. I'd half made up my mind to leave — couldn't stand to hear her any longer — when that cat appeared. I swear it was actually biting my trouser leg and tugging me towards the house. Never seen a cat do that." He shrugged. "Well, I wasn't coming anywhere near this place. I guessed it was sent by the witch to snare me in. But then it just let me go and meowed, and . . . well. Never thought I'd see a cat ask for help, but . . . that thing. I can't say how I knew, but I *knew*, just as clear as if it had spoken to me."

"Really?" Poison exclaimed, thinking about how Peppercorn had claimed that she could communicate with Andersen.

Bram grunted. "I came in through the coal chute. Not easy for somebody my size. But I knew I had to get in before sunrise, because that mist was coming down, and I reckoned when it lifted the house would be gone. I hid down in the cellar until morning, waiting until that cat decided it was safe to go. You know, it's luring the dogs away on purpose. You know that? That's not any natural cat."

"But you came in here to rescue me," Poison said, catching her breath. "Why? You could have just taken the money you had and lived out the rest of your life happy."

"Couldn't leave you like that," he said with a shrug, turning away to pick up the pot again. "What kind of man would I be then?"

Poison smiled to herself in amazement at the way he downplayed his decision. He knew as well as she what it meant. Quite aside from anything else, he had trapped himself in this place with her, with the Bone Witch and her dogs, and the next stop was the Realm of Phaerie. Anyone but him would have turned away and kept what they had; she had already made him rich. But not Bram. His selflessness staggered her. She wondered what she had done to deserve a friend like him, and whether she would have done the same if their positions were reversed.

It took them almost an hour to assemble five pots on the balcony, and by that time the misted sun outside was heading into mid-afternoon. The dogs, mercifully, were nowhere to be seen; only an occasional thump from upstairs reminded Poison and Bram that they were still pursuing Andersen.

"Do you even know what's *in* these?" Bram said, taking off his hat to blot his brow with the back of his glove. The heat of the fire had made the work doubly hard.

Poison looked down at the pots of powder and herbs at her feet. "She's a witch," she said. "I doubt they're very nice."

Bram shrugged. "I hope you know what you're doing."

"No," Poison said truthfully, tipping the first of the pots over the balcony, into the bubbling cauldron below. The water — which had been a sludgy yellow-brown — turned pink immediately.

"I wouldn't like to drink that," Bram commented, eyeing the foul hue.

"That's the idea," said Poison, and between them they pushed all the pots into the mix.

It took them some time to fish out a couple of bones from the cauldron. They found an enormous ladle, and it took two of them to steady it, lying on the balcony and dipping down into the hybrid broth they had created. It was now a putrid brown colour, and the stench was frankly abominable. Their eyes teared as they cast around for bones, until finally they managed to scoop out a pair of big ones and tip them over the lip of the cauldron and onto the floor.

Poison was about to sit up when something heavy landed on her back and she shrieked.

"It's all right, it's all right," Bram said hastily. "It's just the cat."

Andersen had appeared as if from nowhere and obviously thought Poison would make a convenient cushion for jumping down from the skeletal balcony rail. Now he hopped daintily off her and allowed her to get up. Poison scowled at him. He returned her violet gaze amiably.

"Actually, you're just who I wanted to see," she told the cat. "Can you do us a favour? Go find the dogs and lead them here. We have some bones for them."

The cat blinked at her. She felt faintly ridiculous for talking to him as if he were a person. Then he turned and sloped away, heading down the stairs.

"See?" Bram said.

"I'll believe it when he comes back with the dogs," Poison said. "We should get out of sight."

The cat did come back. By that time, Poison and Bram were hidden behind the remaining pots that stood on the shelf above the stove, safely out of the dogs' reach. Andersen came yowling into the room, and behind him came the two enormous dogs, scrambling and barking as they chased after the elusive morsel. The cat scampered around the cauldron and disappeared from sight, and the dogs raced after him . . . emerging moments later with no sign of the cat. Puzzled, they nosed around the edge of the cauldron, investigating the shadows thrown by the fire. Andersen had outwitted them and was already sitting on the overhead balcony, washing his paw with his tongue. The dogs looked about for a short while before noticing the bones lying on the floor.

"That's it: nice, juicy bones," Poison murmured.

The broth that the bones had steeped in had left an odd stench that would have been overpowering to a dog's sensitive nose, but Peppercorn had said that the Bone Witch's hounds had no sense of smell. Poison watched, holding her breath as they examined their finds. And then one of them pinned his catch down with his paws and began to gnaw. The other followed suit, and soon the two of them were chewing and cracking bones and lapping at the marrow within. The cat observed from above with an expression of haughty disgust.

It did not take long for Poison's concoction to take effect.

She had no idea what she had put in the cauldron, but whatever it was, she had given them a huge overdose. The dogs began twitching and spasming almost in unison: first their legs began to tremble and they began to trip whenever they tried to move; then their muscle control deserted them completely and they fell on their sides, wheezing while their legs flailed spastically about and their heads jerked back and forth. Their tongues lolled, and bloody foam bubbled through their teeth. Finally, they collapsed and lay still, their breath rasping in and out until it ceased entirely.

Bram and Poison looked on, dumbfounded and not a little sickened.

"I just wanted them to die," Poison said. "They didn't have to make such a drama about it."

Bram frowned. "At least it worked. Now what?"

She brushed her hair back from her face. "Now we take care of the Bone Witch."

ᗡᗷᗡ

Night fell.

The mist was still as thick as ever, but a bright and massive moon shone through it, bigger and closer than Poison had ever seen. The house sank into darkness, but the moon cast hard, cold light through the windows and spread rhomboid patches of blue across the shadow. Where it penetrated the cauldron room, it mixed with the firelight and glittered in the wet wash of blood.

Somewhere upstairs, a door creaked. The Bone Witch was awake.

Poison and Bram stood in the corridor that ran from the balcony of the cauldron room past the door to Peppercorn's bedroom. Hearing the noise, they glanced at each other. Poison did not know whether to laugh or feel sick.

"You're certain this will work?" Bram asked for the tenth time.

"I told you, she's blind and deaf," Poison said. "But she'll feel the vibrations if we make a lot of noise. And when she gets here, she only needs to smell us."

Bram swallowed and nodded, cinching the skin of the dog tighter around his shoulders. Both of them wore the dogs' hides like hooded cloaks, bloody shrouds that clung stickily to their hair and arms and cheeks. Both of them were plastered in smeared gore. Relieving the dead creatures of their skins had been an unpleasant task, and Bram was not greatly skilled at it. They had used a knife they found by the stove, though it was the size of a sabre and hard to handle. Peppercorn had appeared on the balcony while they were working below, having found Andersen at last; when she saw what they were doing, she gave a little squeak and fainted. Poison dragged her into the corner of the balcony and left her there. Better to have her out of the way; there was no knowing how she might react if she knew of their plan.

They could hear the Bone Witch creaking about above them now, and her voice drifted down in a sinister singsong.

"*Are you ready, my dear? Ready for Maeb's pot? Tender, juicy bones.*"

"We can still escape," Bram reminded her. "It'll only be a short while till midnight. We can get out through the coal chute."

"No," Poison replied. "We should face her on our terms, not hers. If she catches us hiding, we'll all be for the pot."

Bram listened uncertainly to the witch's cooing.

"Besides," Poison added, "it's time somebody did something about her."

Bram didn't reply to that.

"Come on," she said, and together they readied themselves in front of the door at the end of the corridor. Poison went first; she threw herself shoulder-first against the closed door and bounced off it. Bram did the same, while Poison stamped her boots, and then they both launched themselves at the door again, making it rattle in its frame. It was an odd scene, neither of them speaking, simply clattering about and making as much din as possible.

"Oh! Did my poor dears get shut downstairs? Mother's coming, my pets. Don't fret."

They backed off from the door as Maeb approached. Bram was scared out of his wits, his whiskers quivering, but Poison felt strangely unafraid now. She was tired of cringing from that rancid old hag. This time around, it would be different.

The door was pulled open, and there was the Bone Witch, eleven feet high and twisted as an ancient root. Bram almost fell over in his haste to stumble away, but Poison stood her ground. Maeb paused as soon as she opened the door and took a sniff of the air with her enormous nose.

"I smell blood!" she screeched. "And not man blood, either!"

Poison took that as her cue to flee. Bram had already made a less than heroic retreat and was several dozen feet away down the corridor.

"Come back, my pets!" Maeb cried. "Are you hurt? Has somebody hurt you?" She came lunging after them, sniffing the air as she went. "Come back!"

Poison ran. Having the witch follow her was all part of the plan, but it was no less dangerous for that. Bram was already through the doorway and at the balcony, ushering her frantically. But Maeb had slowed to a halt. Poison looked back over her shoulder, feeling a crawling dread come upon her.

"*You're not my dogs,*" Maeb hissed. "*I can feel your footsteps. You smell like them, but you're not them. Two legs! Two legs!*" She sniffed the air and howled suddenly, "*What have you done with my dogs?*"

Suddenly, she thundered forward with a screech, her wrinkled face in an awful rictus of hate. Her speed took Poison by surprise, and she barely got out of the way of the enormous creature's grasping hands. As it was, she felt the bloodied dog-hide plucked from her back. Maeb screamed in horror as she dangled the skin of her pet in her hand, then flung it aside and came through the doorway, stamping onto the balcony, a monstrous fury upon her.

"*I'll grind your bones to powder and bake them in my bread!*" she cried. "*I'll snap you up and crunch you down!*"

But as she raced into the room, she stepped onto the fresh slick of blood that had been splashed across the balcony. Her feet slid once and her arms flailed — but she was going too fast to stop herself. With a shriek, she crashed into the balcony rail, which cracked under her weight with a splintering of bone and pitched her head-first into the cauldron. Boiling broth geysered over the side with a great sizzling hiss, and the fire was extinguished in a wash of searing water. Silence fell.

Poison and Bram, who had been pressed against the wall next to the doorjamb, ventured to the edge of the balcony and peered over. All they could see of Maeb was the grimy soles of her shoes, poking out of the poisonous brown broth and resting against the lip of the cauldron. They were quite still.

"Hmm," said Bram.

Poison laughed explosively, giddy with relief. "Will you take off that dog skin? You look ridiculous."

Bram raised an eyebrow at her. She looked like she had bathed in blood. He shucked off the skin and threw it into the cauldron after the Bone Witch.

"What about her?" Bram said, tipping his head at Peppercorn, who was still out cold in the corner. Andersen was just curling up on her lap, taking advantage of her inactivity.

"What *about* her?" Poison replied. "She's not our concern. Let her do what she wants."

Bram harrumphed and stroked his moustache, reddening what whiteness remained there. "That's not good enough, Poison," he said. "Can't just leave her here."

"Why not?" Poison challenged.

"It wouldn't be right," he replied simply.

Poison sighed. She had no dislike for Peppercorn, but she had the impression that the girl would be nothing but a hindrance and a liability to them. Still, one look at Bram told her that he would not be swayed on this. It piqued her unaccountably. She had felt somehow *special* when Bram had ventured into the house to save her; now that Bram's kindness extended to Peppercorn as well, the feeling was spoiled a little.

"All right then." She shrugged. She walked over to Peppercorn. Andersen reluctantly gave up his warm spot and circled around behind her, peering past her ankles at his unconscious owner. Poison gave her a shake.

"Wake up, Peppercorn," she said. "Time to go."

Peppercorn made a soft moan and opened her eyes. She took one look at the blood-drenched apparition before her, screamed, and fainted again.

Poison threw up her hands in exasperation. "If you want her, you'd better carry her," she said to Bram.

But Bram was looking out of the window, for the moonlight had suddenly brightened. "The mist is clearing," he said. "Midnight is coming. We should go."

She gave Bram a long, penetrating stare. "Are you sure about this, Bram? Maybe, if you stay here, the house will go back to where it originally started."

"Maybe it will," Bram said. "And maybe it won't. It's phaerie magick. I don't much want to take the risk."

Poison began to argue, but Bram raised one hide-gloved hand.

"I'm here now," he said. "Can't pretend I'm happy about it, but I made my choice. I knew where I'd end up when I came in after you. Now let's not talk about it anymore."

And so it was that when the moon was at its zenith, Poison and Bram walked out of the front door of the house of the Bone Witch, with Peppercorn slung over Bram's broad shoulder and Andersen darting around between their feet. They pushed open the bone gate and stepped beyond. From that moment they were in the Realm of Phaerie.

THE FISHER SAGE

༄ I T WAS just like the stories.

Poison could not resist a smile at seeing how perfectly her imagination had matched Fleet's tales to the land that surrounded her. Of course, he had never pretended to have set foot outside the Realm of Man — Poison would not have believed *that* for an instant, back in the days before she left Gull — but he professed to know people who had. And then there were his books, which he used to read to Poison until she began to borrow them and read them herself. Between one and the other, Poison had built up a picture in her mind of what this wondrous, fabulous, *dangerous* realm would look like. And it looked like this.

The vista was breathtaking. They stood on a small hill, but that hill sat on top of a bigger hill, so that they were high up above the surrounding countryside. The sky was an odd shade of burnished amber with hues of purple, and the sun seemed closer than Poison had ever remembered it, and unbearably bright to look upon. To the west, a river of purest turquoise wound its way through the grassy folds of the land, glittering in the morning light. North and east was a great forest, its trees a riot of reds, greens, and yellows, as if all the seasons had come at once. In amongst these were swaths of blue and indigo, the leaves of trees that Poison had never seen before. Beyond the forest, mountains ridged the horizon, made ghostly by distance. South, the hills were broken by moraines and valleys into which the river plunged in spectacular waterfalls.

Bram glanced back at the crooked old house, a tiny blot on a hill many miles behind them. They had walked all night to get away from it, as if half-expecting the Bone Witch to come screeching out after them, and yet strangely none of them was tired. He shifted Peppercorn's weight on his shoulder and harrumphed, then raised a bushy eyebrow at Poison.

"Any idea where we're going? It'd be a fine thing to get to the Realm of Phaerie and then end up wandering aimlessly till we starve."

Poison shrugged, then looked at Andersen. "Have you got any ideas, cat?"

Andersen narrowed his eyes and blinked sagely, then set off at a trot down the hillside, towards the forest.

"I swear that thing's not natural," Bram murmured again.

Poison shrugged. "Better get used to it. *Natural* doesn't really apply here."

They followed the cat down the hill. It did not seem particularly hurried, detouring now and then to sniff at an exotic flower or pounce on some unseen insect. Poison found herself luxuriating in the hot day, mesmerized by the beauty of the phaerie countryside. Everything seemed somehow sharper and brighter here, her senses tuned more finely than they were at home. She felt the rustle of the grass. She could see individual leaves stirring in the forest from a great way away, as if the clear air allowed her better focus over longer distance.

She was tempted to remark that this place didn't seem so bad, but she knew well enough that the moment she did so, something horrible would happen to them. How was it that life, like a story, had such a sense of comic timing?

They reached the edge of the forest, and there they found a small stream. They laid Peppercorn down and cleaned themselves of the blood of Maeb's dogs. Andersen groomed himself nearby. When they were done, they woke Peppercorn, who had been in a deep swoon so long that she had fallen asleep. Poison half-expected her to faint again when she saw that they were outside the house, but she had no more left in her, it seemed. As they dried in the sun, they carefully explained to her what had happened, leaving out the gory details and giving her only the facts. Maeb was gone, and she wouldn't be coming after them. Peppercorn was free (whether she wanted to be or not). They were in the Realm of Phaerie. They were on their way to visit the Phaerie Lord.

Peppercorn digested all this with something akin to shock on her face.

"You can still go back there, if you want," Poison said, thinking that she should at least offer the option so that she didn't feel like a kidnapper.

Peppercorn shook her head, her blonde curls jiggling with the movement. That was all the response she gave. Poison made a face at Bram, indicating that she didn't quite know what to make of that; when they were dry enough to go on into the forest, Peppercorn came with them without a word.

The forest was as beautiful on the inside as it had seemed from the hilltop. It seemed miraculously free from the mulch of dead vegetable matter that carpeted the floor of forests in the Realm of Man; in fact, not a leaf seemed out of place, nor was there a twig that did not seem artfully positioned to enhance the beauty of the tree from which it sprouted. There was no blight here, none of the entropy that was part of the cycle of life in the Black Marshes. It was like a painting, like a vision: perfect.

Poison didn't trust the forest one inch.

"It's wonderful!" Peppercorn gushed, clasping her hands over her breastbone in awe.

"Aye, and likely as not those flowers would kill you if you sniffed them," Bram said, echoing Poison's thoughts.

"Oh, don't be silly," Peppercorn said, scowling at the older man's grumpiness.

"He's right," Poison said, recalling what she had learned from Fleet. "Illusion is part of the phaerie way. Don't be lulled. This Realm is dangerous to us."

Peppercorn turned up her nose primly at this advice, but Poison noted that she glanced around nervously thereafter.

The day wore on into afternoon and evening, and all day they saw not a single living thing other than themselves. Though the forest resounded with birdcalls and the cries of all manner of strange animals, they did not even see so much as an insect. They stopped to rest in a glade, eating food cold from Poison's and Bram's packs, and though the branches above them stirred with the movement of birds and the branches nearby rustled, they never laid eyes on what was causing the disturbance. It was profoundly unsettling.

Bram was beginning to voice doubts that the cat knew where he was going, but he seemed very definite in the path he was taking, and Peppercorn assured them that Andersen knew his way about.

"It was when the house was in the Realm of Phaerie that he turned up," she said. "I remember, because it was a bright day. It's always bright here during the day; brighter than the other Realm, anyway. I was looking out of the windows when he appeared. He must have wandered in from outside. Anyway, he saw I was lonely, so he stayed to be my friend. Isn't he sweet?"

She gathered up the cat — which mewled in surprise — and

rubbed her cheek against him while lapsing into baby talk and gurgling. Andersen made a show of protest to maintain his dignity and then went limp and began to purr. Poison's expression was one of disbelief at Peppercorn's nauseating display.

"You mean he's a phaerie cat?" Bram asked, before Poison could make some sarcastic remark.

"I don't know," she said, letting Andersen go. "But this is where he came from when he found me. I think he's been all over. He doesn't tell me that much."

And so they walked, following Andersen's lead, never quite certain where the cat was taking them or if he was taking them anywhere at all. Since they had no idea where they were, one direction was as good as another.

Night had begun to cover the Realm when they came across the stranger.

They found him at the end of a narrow trail, arched with tree branches and edged with roots that seemed carefully arranged to look natural and yet did not have a scrap of soil or a spot of blight on them. The trail ran into a clearing, dominated by a small lake that flamed copper-red in the sunset. At one end of the lake was a small house that seemed to have grown out of the bank, a moulded blister of wattle and daub with a thatched roof of yellowed reeds like a lid. From the front of the house, a wooden jetty extended out across the water. At the end of the jetty, a bizarre figure sat with a rod, fishing.

They observed him from a distance, as he had not seemed to notice them. He was a scrawny thing, with moist greenish skin like that of a frog. Two massive, bulbous eyes were set to either side of a nose that was little more than two slits in his face. His mouth was small and disappeared into his neck in the absence of a chin. Long, knobbed fingers curled around the fishing rod. His thin legs hung over the lip of the jetty. Little else could be seen of him, for the rest of his body was engulfed in a great cloak of something like bearskin but bristling with quills like that of a porcupine. His head seemed tiny in proportion to the size of the cloak.

"He seems sad," Peppercorn commented sympathetically, and indeed, as they watched he gave a heavy sigh and continued to gaze morosely into the waters of the lake.

"He's a phaerie," Bram rumbled. "You can't trust him."

Poison wondered when they had all decided the stranger was male, since physically there was no way to tell in a creature so outlandish.

"Well, it's nearly night, and Andersen brought us here so I suppose he must know what he's doing," Poison said. Andersen mewed in agreement, brushing round her legs happily. "Shall we go and introduce ourselves?"

"Just be careful, all of you," Bram warned, his brows beetling together in a frown beneath his hat rim.

The stranger spotted them as they approached, but he made no move to acknowledge them. Instead, he turned back to his fishing and sighed again. They warily joined him on the jetty. Poison could see huge, rainbow-coloured fish swimming lazily in the water beneath, but none of them seemed remotely interested in the lure that bobbed in the water.

Bram coughed.

"Our heroes have arrived, then," the stranger said, his voice a soft, bubbly murmur.

"Excuse me?" Poison queried.

The odd creature put down his rod in a little wooden cradle that rested next to him and got up from the edge of the jetty. He looked them over with his vast, yellowish eyes.

"Hmm," he said gloomily. "You don't seem a bad bunch." He jostled past them and began to shuffle back towards his house. "At least you're not the typical muscle-bound warrior, beautiful sorceress, and amusing thief sidekick. By the waters, did *that* become stale fast."

Poison and Bram looked at each other in bewilderment. Then, as the stranger showed no sign of slowing, Poison caught up with him.

"Umm . . . hello? My name is Poison."

He stopped and looked her up and down again. "Good name," he said with feeling. "I'd have thought you were a Melisande or an Arial."

"Ugh," Poison replied. "Why would you think that?"

"That's what your type are usually called. You're not a princess, are you?"

"I wouldn't want to be," Poison replied. "Everyone wants to be a princess; it's boring."

"Ah! So what do you want to be?"

"I want to be at the Phaerie Lord's palace, so I can ask him for my sister back."

"So you think," came the reply. "But I'll wager that's just the start."

"The start of what?" Poison asked in exasperation.

"You've only just set out! Do you think the Phaerie Lord will just *give* you your sister back? No, there have to be tests, trials, a struggle, setbacks, twists, revelations. You have to *earn* your sister. You haven't met half the cast yet! Mark me, you've still a long way to go."

Poison was utterly unable to fathom what this curious creature was talking about, so after a moment of vague confusion she shook her head and said, "Do you know how to get to the Phaerie Lord's palace or not?"

"Of course." He sighed wearily. "Come inside and I'll tell you." With that, he plodded into his house of dried mud and sticks, and the others followed.

Inside it was dark and cramped, with benches, a fireplace,

a table, and little else in the way of furniture. A shallow pit filled with straw served as a bed. The roof was so low that Bram had to duck to fit inside, and Peppercorn bashed her elbow and squawked noisily as she came in. The stranger went to where the fire was already made, and with a flint and tinder he chipped sparks onto it until the blaze caught. It swelled up eagerly; whatever he had on it was evidently highly flammable. When the flames were strong enough for his satisfaction, he took a black pot and set it to boil.

"My name's Myrrk," he said. "Isn't that uncannily appropriate for one as dismally gloomy as me? Funny how names can be so descriptive. You want tea? I'd offer you food, but I haven't caught anything today. In fact, I never catch anything any day. There's a whole lake out there full of nice plump fish, and I've never caught any of them, not in a hundred years."

"A hundred years!" Peppercorn exclaimed.

"What do you eat, then?" Poison asked.

"Fish, when I can get it."

"But you said you haven't caught any in a hundred years."

Myrrk blinked. "Yes."

"So you haven't eaten in a hundred years?"

Myrrk shrugged. "I suppose."

"Then how are you still alive?" Poison asked bluntly.

"Good question," Myrrk replied. "I suppose *he* didn't think hard enough when he put me here."

"Who?"

"The Hierophant. Aren't I tragic? Always fishing, every day, never catching a thing. I even *look* sad, don't I? But I suppose he didn't bother to work out the details like what I *do* eat if I can't get fish. Shoddy work, if you ask me."

"Aren't you hungry?" Peppercorn asked, her face a picture of concern.

"I just told you I hadn't eaten in a hundred years," Myrrk groaned. "Wouldn't *you* be hungry?"

"I'd be dead," Peppercorn replied cheerily.

"Did you want tea or not?" Myrrk prompted.

"Yes, please!" she piped.

The others agreed to tea as well, if only to placate their host, who was obviously eccentric if not totally insane. Poison did not even trouble herself to ask about the Hierophant; she could not imagine what good it would do to encourage Myrrk's delusions, and she didn't want to get sidetracked from her real task, which was finding Azalea. Yet Poison found an odd logic in his words, a pattern which she could not quite grasp that made her think he might be talking a kind of sense — just not the kind of sense that any of them recognized.

"About the palace . . ." Bram said. Myrrk bustled past him to dig out some cups, and they had to shrink back to avoid his enormous cloak of quills.

"Yes, yes, the palace. Of course, you can reach the palace from anywhere in the Realm, if you have a mind to. Have you ever heard of firewort?" Here he turned back, brandishing a large clump of green weeds.

Poison replied that she had. It thrived around the marshes where she had grown up. But she hadn't thought anything of it.

"Then you must be new to the Realm, if you don't know what it does. Firewort burns in a particular way. You make a fire when the sun goes down, throw on the firewort, and leave it burning. It's what they call a shortcut. So you can keep things moving, see?"

Poison did not really know what he was talking about, but she was all for shortcuts. Patience was never one of her virtues.

"You do wish to go to the palace, don't you?" Myrrk asked,

craning his moist neck around and gazing mournfully at them. "You can't change your mind once the signal is sent."

"We want to go," said Poison unhesitatingly. Peppercorn gave a cheep of alarm, but she did not protest beyond that. Myrrk tossed the firewort onto the growing blaze, disturbing Andersen, who had somehow managed to arrange himself in prime position for the greatest heat source in the room. The fire guttered and then took up again, but Poison noted that the black smoke was shot through with swirls of crimson now, and the fire seemed to glow red from within like molten rock.

"He is coming," Myrrk said.

"*Who* is coming?" Bram asked.

"The Coachman," Myrrk replied.

"We're getting a coach?" Peppercorn asked excitedly, seeming to miss the deliberate capital letter that Myrrk had insinuated into the word.

"Right to the Phaerie Lord's palace," Myrrk agreed. Poison did not much like his tone.

Myrrk brewed them some tea, and in exchange they shared with him some of the food in their packs. The tea was bitter and green, with bits of herb and twig floating in it, but it had a curiously addictive edge that Poison found pleasant. She noted that Bram was not drinking his; he radiated mistrust for the pitiful-looking creature that attended them.

Myrrk sat himself down on a bench. The tiny house was becoming cosily warm now, and the fire threw a homely glow that kept out the gathering night. Poison felt herself relax a little. Myrrk did seem like a sad fellow, but dangerous? She doubted it. Of course, in the Realm of Phaerie, anything was possible.

"I have a question, Myrrk," she said. "Two, in fact. You don't seem like you're happy here. You never catch any fish and you don't eat. Yet you've been here for a hundred years. So my questions are these: how did you get here? And why don't you leave?"

Myrrk blinked and raised his head as if it were a great weight. "You know, nobody has ever asked me that. Why don't I leave? Not once in a hundred years."

"Well?" Poison asked. "Why don't you?"

"I tried, once," he said. "I wouldn't recommend it."

"So what happened?" Poison prompted. He was reminding her of Lamprey all of a sudden, who evaded her questions with vague answers when she asked him about the purpose of his riddles. She wasn't going to let Myrrk get away without giving her some satisfaction.

Myrrk gave her a penetrating gaze for a long time. "Maybe you'll find out, one day. Yes, you're one of those. Like me. A questioner. Shall I answer your first question before your second? How I got here? I don't know. One day I was simply here; that's all I remember. And so I started asking questions. But nobody listened; everyone just wanted to be on their way, as quick as possible, and never to think about what they were doing." He took a loud slurp of tea. "But fishing all day gives you time to think, and I thought. I listened to the stories people told me, people who were passing through, and I worked it out."

"You worked out *what*?" Poison asked.

"How I got here," Myrrk replied.

"And how was that?"

"You'd better ask the Hierophant."

"Why can't you just *tell* me?" Poison urged.

"It doesn't work that way," Myrrk sighed, looking genuinely aggrieved. "There's laws to follow, a way of doing things. You can't find out for a good while yet. It's just too early."

Poison gritted her teeth in frustration. "So what about my second question?"

"Ah yes," Myrrk said. "Well, as I told you, there's a way of doing things. Everyone has their own way to tread, their own little part to play. And if you stop doing what you're supposed to, it starts messing up everyone else's part. Everything's a chain, see? I'm supposed to stay here. I'm supposed to be the one with the answers. Whenever people are lost, they find me and I set them right. I give them a shortcut, just like I did with you." He seemed to deflate a little, his yellow gaze falling to the floor, where Andersen was watching him slyly through one half-open eye while pretending to be asleep. "I wasn't supposed to go wandering. When I did, people started getting lost. Things started breaking down."

"Because you didn't do what you were supposed to?" Peppercorn asked, wide-eyed.

"Because I worked out the way things are," Myrrk muttered. "I had a story myself, once, but I didn't like it and I tried to change it." He groaned. "I'd advise against that."

Poison's next question was forestalled by a sudden wind that whipped up outside, a loud gust that rattled the kettle and the plates. It tailed off in a clatter of hooves, the sound of horses coming to a halt outside.

"You'd better go," Myrrk said, pointing one knobbed finger at the door. "The Coachman won't stay long."

Peppercorn scooped up the cat and they went outside. There at the lakeside stood their coach. Peppercorn's eyes lit up at the sight. Not for the first time, Poison had to remind herself not to be taken in by the beauty of the Phaerie Realm, for what stood before them was elegant enough to make her easily forget.

The coach was all in white and grey, with ivory crossbeams and spokes of gold and hubcaps filigreed in silver. Four lithe horses drew it, snow-maned as clouds, clad in great plates of lacquered white armour. Golden chainmail hung from their backs. They tossed their heads and clacked their teeth as the humans stared at them. Yet beautiful as they were, there was a terrible coldness about them, and their eyes seemed to regard the humans with a baleful arrogance.

The Coachman himself sat hunched in his seat, concealed by an enormous white cloak and cowl, so that only his hands could be seen holding the reins. He was fully seven feet tall and would have dwarfed Bram if he had been standing. He looked down from the driver's bench and glared at them, and they saw a face of porcelain, features perfect, cheekbones high and smooth, and skin pale and unblemished. Yet while the face was handsome, it was as chilling as the horses, for the green eyes of the Coachman regarded them as if they were insects, and his lip curled in a sneer of disgust.

The door to the coach swung open of its own accord.

Peppercorn glanced reluctantly at Bram and Poison, hugging Andersen close to her chest. Poison looked back at Myrrk, who regarded her with a pitying gaze.

"Go and see the Hierophant. He has the answers."

Poison made no reply. They got into the carriage and shut the door.

DEALS AND DESTINATIONS

THE palace of the Phaerie Lord stood at the hub of a dozen rivers and streams, as beautiful and elegant as a jewel. It was a sliver of jade, rising from the lakeland in a multitude of delicate spires and minarets that gradually dwindled as they rose until there was only one left, the most central and mightiest of the towers, which reached high above the others and tapered to a needle at its apex.

The too-large phaerie sun was rising as Poison and her companions approached, and from their vantage point high in the amber sky the scene below seemed wondrous. The morning light shimmered across the pale green surface of the palace and shone gold on the network of rivers and lakes that covered the grassy land all around.

"You have to see this, Peppercorn!" Poison urged, but Peppercorn would not budge. She had curled up with her face against the back of the carriage and her hands over her eyes. She had been in the same position since that first shriek of surprise, when the coach suddenly lifted off the ground and flew, the hooves of the horses beating the sky as if it were solid earth.

Peppercorn evidently had no head for heights, and she cringed from the windows in terror while Andersen licked her face in an attempt to coax her out.

The palace loomed closer as they raced towards it. The journey had taken less than an hour, yet somehow night had passed and it was morning, and the passengers felt as rested as if they had had a long sleep, though none of them had even dozed. When Poison remarked on this to Bram, he replied by reminding her what he had said on the night she left him to break into the Bone Witch's house: "Time is not the same here," he murmured. "We might have already been gone a thousand years from home, and when we get back there won't be a thing we recognize."

Poison thought about that. "I won't miss much. Except Fleet, I suppose. And maybe Father, but he's probably happier without me."

"Is that so? That's a terrible thing to say," Bram observed.

"It's not terrible if it's true," Poison argued. "He and Snapdragon — my stepmother — they only wanted me out of the way after they got together. No matter how much they pretended they didn't." She intercepted his sceptical look. "This is not just a fit of adolescent pique, Bram. I know what I'm talking about. I was just a nuisance to them. Poison."

"Ah, that's why you chose that name," Bram said, his moustache curving as a wry smile creased his face. "Might have known."

"Is there anything you'll miss?" she asked, looking out of the window again. They were almost on top of the palace now.

"That depends what's changed," Bram said. "I'll have words to say to the Phaerie Lord if they've stopped making those sausage pies in the Butcher's Market at Shieldtown by the time I get back."

Poison laughed and hit him across the chest. "You're an idiot!" she said happily.

"Hmm, well," said Bram, grinning; he left it at that.

೦∽౨∿౨

The coach came to a halt inside one of the lower side-towers of the palace, having soared in through a vast, arched portal. As the hooves of the horses clattered onto a solid floor, Peppercorn dared to peep out through her fingers, and when the coach had stopped completely she shuddered in relief. The door opened, once more of its own accord, and Bram helped Peppercorn out, with Andersen hopping down last. When they had all disembarked, the door closed. The Coachman glared at them icily, then turned the coach and snapped the reins. His horses took a few steps at a gallop and then soared through the portal and out into the cloudless amber sky beyond.

They were left in a broad, circular room, its walls and floor of lime-veined marble, with nothing in it except a vast disc of bronze that was set into the floor in the centre, on which the coach had landed. There was a small, arched door in one wall, made of some kind of moulded metal, its surface alive with serpents. As the echoes of the coach's departure faded, Poison, Bram, and Peppercorn looked at one another.

"Now what?" Bram asked.

The door burst open and in came a chaos of noise and chatter, a dense mass of frantic movement. At the centre of the crowd was a thin, pinch-faced man in a brown suit, striding quickly across the room towards them while writing in a large, leather-bound ledger with a quill pen. He was orbited by a gaggle of pale imps: tiny, slender, daemonic creatures with bat-like wings and chirruping voices. They bombarded him with reports, observations, and comments on all manner of things, while he replied to them with orders and instructions and questions. He crossed the room with efficient swiftness and halted in front of the newcomers, then with one dismissive swipe of his hand the imps dispersed like a flock of startled birds, flying through the doorway or the great arched portal until they were all gone.

The man adjusted his round, iron-rimmed glasses on the knife-like bridge of his nose and peered over them at Bram.

"State your names," he snapped.

"Bram of Oilskin, Poison of Gull, Peppercorn of . . ." Bram trailed off.

"Peppercorn of *where?*"

"Lately of the employ of Maeb, the Bone Witch," Poison said formally.

"Ah. And how is dear Maeb?" said the man, raising an eyebrow.

"Dead," Poison replied. Peppercorn, who had guessed as much, merely looked miserable.

"Excellent." The man grinned, showing sharp, cat-like teeth. He scratched a note in his ledger. "That frees up some very desirable real estate." He snapped the book shut. "My name is Scriddle, secretary to Aelthar, Lord of Phaerie. You are aware, I suppose, that due to a frankly tiresome law handed down by Amrae, Hierophant of old, every intelligent being born of the Realm of Man has the right to a single audience with the Lord or Lady of any foreign Realm, in which said being's safety is guaranteed by the honour of said Lord or Lady, at least until the conclusion of the audience, after which all legal obligation has been discharged and, not to put too fine a point on it, all bets are off?"

"No," Poison said with a shrug.

"You are now," Scriddle replied. "Who's this?" He pointed with the feather of his quill to the fourth member of their party.

"This is Andersen," Peppercorn said, picking him up and cradling him.

"How delightful," Scriddle observed, deadpan. He turned on his heel and walked towards the door. "Follow me! The Lord Aelthar will see you immediately."

೧⌒೧

The Great Hall of Aelthar's palace was awe-inspiring indeed, but by the time they had reached it, the newcomers had become so inured to wonder that it barely affected them. Walking through the corridors of the palace had afforded them sights such as none of them had ever seen, feats of majesty that left any of humankind's creations far behind, and which only nature's best could possibly surpass. They had crossed crystal bridges that spanned dizzying drops, with waterfalls plunging past them like sparkling pillars; they had passed a circular window that refracted the sunlight into one enormous rainbow beam and spread it across the floor before them; they had seen rooms decorated with tapestries of such beauty that even Bram's earthy heart was stirred at the sight; and walked beneath the gaze of murals so intricate that they defied understanding.

And then there were the phaeries themselves: elves, naiads, pixies, undines, wisps, nymphs, and dozens more that Poison could not name. They shimmered with cold, unearthly elegance as they passed by, barely deigning to even glance at the verminous humans in their midst. Poison felt suddenly and acutely filthy, like a swamp-lurker that had staggered into a princess's ball. The Realm of Phaerie was glutted with perfection and beauty, and these humans who came sweating and stinking into their land of harmony were an insult to them. It soured her amazement.

I want to be gone as much as you want me gone, she told them silently. *But you took my sister, and I want her back.*

The Great Hall was predictably enormous, built in a cool blue kind of smooth, moist-looking stone. Though it was not so large in length or breadth, its height was startling, for it was built inside a narrow, hollow tower, and it had no ceiling except where the tower tapered to a point hundreds of feet above. Delicately carved ribs soared up towards the apex of the room. Tall, thin windows spread light across the floor, where sat the Phaerie Lord on his great chair atop a dais.

The Phaerie Lord was seven feet in height, and he lounged in his seat with the lazy air of deadliness possessed by a jungle cat. His hair was a shocking flame-red against his pale skin, tousled and ruffled into a style of studied disarray. The morning sun sent blades of gold across his polished silver armour, which seemed on him to be as light as air, and which never clashed as he moved. His face had all the beauty of the phaerie folk, but his eyes were hard and cruel and arrogant. By his side, in an ornamental stand, was a sword of exquisite craftsmanship, a weapon of such perfect design that even someone who had never seen a sword before would know it as the greatest of its kind, the pinnacle of achievement in its field.

Around the Great Hall stood an assortment of phaerie folk, ethereal in their beauty, malevolent in their gaze, watching as Poison and her companions were led into the presence of the Phaerie Lord. Scriddle walked before them, straight-backed, his oiled hair shining and his narrow, sharp face set in an unctuous smile.

"My Lord Aelthar," Scriddle cried, bowing. "Four come from the Realm of Man, claiming an audience with you, under the terms of Amrae's Law."

Poison felt the chill in the room deepen. All eyes were on them now.

"Is that so?" Aelthar purred. His gaze fell to Poison, who returned it sullenly. The sight of him had brought back all the anger she had initially felt at having her sister snatched from her, and she nursed it as a defence against the fear that threatened to overwhelm her. She was in the heart of phaerie territory, as far from help as she might possibly be; she was in no place to make demands, nor had she any way to prevent Aelthar from doing whatever he wanted with them. For the first time she began to question whether what she had done was wise. Maybe Azalea was already dead and gone. Maybe all this was for nothing. Or maybe she had just walked into the jaws of death, and she would never leave this room alive. Phaeries were notoriously capricious, and they might as easily cut her head off now as give Azalea back.

No, not now. Not during the audience. That law prevents it. But afterwards . . .

It was too late, anyway. She had taken the chance, and so had Bram and Peppercorn, who was stroking Andersen nervously and chewing her lip.

The Phaerie Lord let the silence become agonizing before he waved one hand at them. "Well, we must endure these little trials," he said, his voice like molten darkness. "Speak."

Poison's throat was dry. She tried to compose a careful and respectful sentence in her head, but nothing worked. Instead, she opened her mouth and spoke bluntly, the only way she really knew how.

"Your Scarecrow stole my baby sister from me," she said. "I have come to ask for her back."

Aelthar gaped in genuine disbelief for a moment, then burst out laughing. The entire hall joined in with the uproar, surrounding them with cruel mirth. Poison felt her face redden in embarrassment and anger. The Phaerie Lord was roaring with glee, tears running from his eyes. Peppercorn shrank away from the noise, and Bram laid a gloved hand on Poison's shoulder.

"Don't get angry," he whispered.

But Poison *was* angry. She felt it come boiling up inside her, taking her over, and she pushed off Bram's hand and took a step forward to the foot of the dais.

"What is funny to you?" she screamed, and silence fell so fast that the echoes of her demand were left reverberating around the hall like lost phantoms. As if they had never been laughing at all, the phaeries — and their Lord — had reverted to their icy serenity again, and now glared at her impertinence.

"Forgive us," said Aelthar, suddenly becoming indulgent. "But you are such an amusing species."

"You can laugh yourselves insane at us for all I care," Poison said truculently. "But I ask that you give me my sister back, in exchange for the changeling that you left in her place. I've heard many great things about the Lord of Phaerie, but I had never thought I would find him a thief!"

The air seemed to darken, and Aelthar sat up in his chair, his features knitting in anger. "Be careful what you say, little worm. It is no theft to take what already belongs to me."

"No human belongs to you!" Poison challenged. "We may be scattered, divided. We may be leaderless, and your creatures may have overrun our lands. But we're not your vassals. I am Poison of Gull, as my sister is Azalea of Gull, and not one of the folk of Gull has ever sworn allegiance to your kind!"

"Do you think twice to crush a swamp-spider beneath your boot, Poison of Gull? Do you care whether the eyefish you spear and eat has sworn allegiance to you or not? You *own* them; you hold power of life or death over them, as I do over you and your kind. Humans are merely animals to us, albeit possessed of an extreme sense of self-importance. I take or destroy as I choose."

"Your argument is flawed, Lord Aelthar," Poison replied, determined not to be overcome. "I crush a swamp-spider because if I don't, that swamp-spider might bite and kill me or one of mine. I kill an eyefish because I have to eat. Humans can't harm you, by your own admission, and you don't need us. My crimes are committed in the name of survival. Yours have no such justification."

The Great Hall had been following this debate with some interest and was expecting another retort from Aelthar; but instead, he gave a strange smile and slouched back in his chair, arching an eyebrow.

"You have spirit. I'm almost impressed," he said.

He motioned to Scriddle, who hurried up the dais and stood at his side. Aelthar whispered in his ear, Scriddle whispered back, and the two of them looked at Poison. Eventually, Scriddle nodded and retreated.

"Your sister . . ." Aelthar said, curling his lip idly. "Azalea, I believe? Charmingly imaginative names you humans bear."

Poison took a breath to make a snappy comment, then stopped herself, remembering what had happened when she had gotten too cocky with Lamprey.

"We should talk," Aelthar said. "In private."

He waved his hand, and both he and Poison winked out of sight.

❧❧❧

Poison looked around for a moment in surprise, but she was too quick to let the disorientation overwhelm her. One moment she had been standing in the hall of the Phaerie Lord, and the next she was here, atop the highest tower of the palace. At its very tip was a round balcony; no stairs or ladder led to it, and it was quite unreachable by any means except flight or by magick. She was magnificently high up, balanced on the point of a needle, and the clouds seemed close enough to touch. It was as if she could see the whole land from here: the lakelands giving way to forests and mountains, the sparkling line of the coast, and beyond, the masts of phaerie ships as they sailed out across the Realm.

A cold wind whipped her hair across her face, and she brushed it away and squinted at the Phaerie Lord. At seven feet tall, he dwarfed her in comparison. The magnificent sword that had rested by his throne now hung from his belt.

"Why are we here?" she asked.

"I have a proposition for you," he said, his eyes like slivers of gemstone. "And it would not do to have my people know that I stooped to bargaining with a human."

"I'm listening," Poison replied, sloughing off the insult. If it got her Azalea back, she could endure all the insults he had.

"I'm not certain how much you know, so I'll be brief. The Realm of Phaerie is not the only Realm besides your own. There are many Realms, and each has its own Lord or Lady. Within our domains, we are all-powerful, but outside them, we are vulnerable to the master or mistress of that Realm. The exception, of course, is your own weak land, which has no leader worth speaking of."

"What has this to do with Azalea?" Poison asked.

"You will complete a task for me," he said. "And when it is done, I will restore your sister to you."

Myrrk's words came back to Poison suddenly, with all the weight of a prophecy: *Do you think the Phaerie Lord will just give you your sister back? No, there have to be tests, trials, a struggle, setbacks, twists, revelations.*

"Why me?" she asked, automatically choosing to question rather than accept what he had offered. "Why deal with humans, if you despise us so much?"

A spasm of annoyance crossed the Phaerie Lord's face. "Your species' lack of magick has a useful side effect. You can slip into and out of the Realms unnoticed. If I sent my phaeries, they would be caught in a moment and it would be plain who had sent them. This task is . . . *secret.*" He hissed the word as a threat, leaving her in no doubt as to what might happen if she betrayed the trust he was placing in her.

Poison crossed her arms. "Then what must I do?"

Aelthar paced back and forth across the tower top. "The good Lady Asinastra possesses a very special dagger, a dagger with a blade that splits into two prongs, like fangs. It is unique, and very valuable. I want it. You must get it for me."

"And where is it?"

"In her castle. In her chambers." He held out a fist and opened it; inside was a small glass orb, the size of an apple, and so black that it seemed made of darkness, eating the light all around. "As soon as you have the dagger, break this."

Poison took the orb. It was cold as frost. She slipped it into her pocket.

"What does it do?"

Aelthar smiled nastily. "You'll see. Don't you trust me, human?"

"I'm not stupid. Tell me what it does."

Aelthar shrugged. "No," he said simply. "Use it when you have the dagger, and not before. If you don't like the terms of our deal, you can always refuse."

Poison glared at him hatefully. He knew full well that she had no choice. He was just antagonizing her for the sake of it.

"So how do I get there?"

"I will send you."

"And how do I get into the Lady's castle once I'm in her Realm?"

"That," said Aelthar with a toss of his flaming hair, "is your problem."

Poison thought for a moment, but her heart had already decided.

"I have your word of honour as a Lord that my sister will be given back to me after I return?"

"I swear it," he replied, with a smirk.

"Then I accept."

"I thought you would."

⌒⌒⌒

The wind moaned in the mountains, and Bram held his hat on as he looked at the passing-place. Behind them, the Coachman waited, his face obscured by his white cowl. The horses champed and stamped. Peppercorn hugged herself and shivered.

"In there?" she asked.

Poison nodded gravely. "In there."

They were assembled on a ledge high up on a mountainside, a rough jut of black stone amidst an endless landscape of rock and snow. It was impossible to see anything else of the Realm of Phaerie from here, only an eternal procession of peaks, capped with white. It was freezing at this altitude, and the wind cut to the bone.

Before them was a narrow gash in the rock, barely ten feet high and only wide enough for Bram to just squeeze into, if he had a mind to. His expression showed that he did not. It was curtained thick with spiderwebs, and spindly black shapes with fat bodies moved with a hunter's grace along the surface of the sticky veils.

"Aelthar said the Coachman would take us anywhere we wanted to go," Poison reminded them. "None of you has to come."

Peppercorn glanced down at Andersen, who was sitting with his tail curled around his legs, looking as miserable as it was possible for a cat to look. He mewed piteously, obviously unhappy at the cold.

"This is like an adventure, isn't it?" she said tremulously.

"That's exactly what it is," Poison said, though the adventurers in the stories she read had always seemed a lot more certain of themselves than she was, and they had usually obtained at least one magickal item by now to use at an opportune moment. Then she thought of the orb in her backpack. Still, what earthly use was *that*? Just like the phaeries in Fleet's stories, to give her something and not tell her what it did.

Peppercorn chewed her lip, her pretty features uncertain. She was like a doll that had suddenly found it had been discarded by the child who used to play with it; having never had to choose her own way before, she seemed vaguely lost.

"What about you, Bram?" Poison said. "You can go back home, if you want."

Bram scratched the back of his neck. "Hmm. The thing about that is, you'll still be going on into that place, with or without me."

Poison tilted her head. "True enough."

Bram sighed. "Well, until you stop throwing yourself into these things like a fool, I suppose I'm stuck with you. All the sovereigns in the world wouldn't mean much if I turned my back on you when you needed me."

"Don't flatter yourself!" Poison laughed. "I don't *need* you."

Bram gave her a knowledgeable look from beneath his bushy brows.

"What's that look for? Don't come over all wise with me, Bram. I can do just as well without you, you know."

"Of course you can," Bram said.

"You didn't mean that!" Poison accused, frustrated.

"Are we going?" Peppercorn said quietly.

Poison and Bram stopped arguing and looked at her. "Sorry?"

"Are we going?" Peppercorn repeated. "Andersen's getting cold."

"You're coming, then?"

"I always wanted to go on an adventure," she replied simply.

Poison couldn't argue with that. "You're not scared of spiders, are you? Either of you?"

Bram grunted a negative. Peppercorn shook her head. "I don't like rats very much though," she added.

"That's all right," Poison replied. "I imagine the spiders will have eaten all the rats."

And with that, she swept aside the first veil of cobwebs, and they stepped into the passing-place.

SPIDERS

IT **WAS** dark in the Realm of Spiders. The sky was a mottled velvet colour, wisps of purple cloud drifting across the cold points of starlight, far away. No moon lit this realm, and yet it was as bright as the brightest night in the Realm of Man, for everything glistened here.

Poison, Bram, Peppercorn, and Andersen stood on a high, rocky ledge overlooking the palace of the Lady Asinastra. Behind them was the narrow mouth of the passing-place, where they had forged their way through a thousand webs to arrive at the other side of the defile. Strands of spider silk hung from them in tatters, stirring in the faint breeze. Poison's skin crawled with the memory, and she could not convince herself that she did not still have some of the foul things in her hair; she counted herself lucky at least that nothing poisonous had bitten them. Bram, who had gone first, had showed her the numerous tiny puncture marks on his thick gloves and remarked that he would probably be dead if they had reached bare skin. He seemed surprisingly unconcerned about the whole affair.

The palace of the Lady of Spiders stood inside a great

mountain bowl, with peaks rising high all around it. It was set in the midst of a thick green forest, boughs frosted with spiderwebs that must have been massive to be visible from this distance. The palace itself consisted of a dozen towers of varying height, placed in no particular pattern or order, connected by bridges at seemingly random elevations. It was made of what appeared to be black stone, with purple parapets, but much of its shape was disguised by the immense strings of webbing that reached between the towers and spread out all the way to the rock walls that surrounded it, so that the palace was the centre of a web that encompassed the entire mountain bowl. Huge veils of white, sticky fibre hung between the strands, gently filling with air like sails in the breeze and stirring the web around them.

Nothing moved, except for the vast shifting of the web.

"Should we think about getting down?" Peppercorn suggested, peering over the lip of the ledge to the tops of the trees, hundreds of feet below.

"I think we can climb," Bram added. The rock face was thick with ledges to rest on, and it was folded enough so that handholds would be no problem. "We can put the cat in my backpack."

Andersen gave him an offended look, then began licking his paw daintily.

"Not yet," Poison said. "There's no hurry. Let's have something to eat, watch, and wait."

"I'm all for that," Bram said, shucking off his pack and sitting down.

"I don't like the look of that forest," Poison murmured absently, gazing into the web-laden depths of the trees. "We'd never see them coming."

They ate cold meat, bread, and dried fruit on the ledge, considering themselves relatively safe for the time being. They could always dart back into the crack in the rock if anything threatened, and they could see an enemy approaching long before it got to them. Poison was thinking. The route through the forest was both too obvious and too dangerous. If there were spiders big enough to spin webs like that, then they would stand less than no chance in the close, dark confinement of the trees. There had to be another way.

"Look!" said Peppercorn suddenly, pointing. The others looked up to see a beautiful moth-like creature come swooping over the edge of the mountain bowl. Its wingspan was enormous, but its wings were gossamer-thin and almost transparent, patterned in delicate colours. Its body was slender and frail and six-legged, and leaf-like antennae waved above its segmented eyes as it tested the air.

"It's pretty!" Peppercorn smiled.

"Don't get too attached," Poison said.

A moment later, Peppercorn saw what she meant. The moth was swooping directly into the web, apparently unable to detect the obstacle with whatever method of navigation it used. Peppercorn sucked in a breath as it glided towards a ropy strand as thick as a man. At the last moment, it seemed to notice something in its path and banked aside, but it was not fast enough; the trailing edge of a wing caught on the sticky fibre, and the rest of its body was pulled back by the snag, slapping into the web where it was caught.

The spider was on it in a matter of seconds. Peppercorn gasped as the vast, bulbous monster darted out of a cave in the wall of the mountain bowl and raced along a thread towards the hub of the palace, then back out again along the spoke where the moth was struggling. It bundled itself around the hapless victim, which shuddered as it was bitten. The moth's thrashing grew more desperate, and then weakened and ceased. They watched for a time as the spider cocooned its prey, then saw the creature tuck its prize under its abdomen and scuttle back to its cave for a feast.

Bram seemed to have lost his appetite. "They're so cursedly *quick*," he muttered.

But Poison seemed less put out than he was. The drama had given her an idea. "They *are* quick, which is why we won't go through the forest," she said. "They'd catch us in a moment."

"So how are we going to get into the palace?" Peppercorn asked plaintively.

"We're going to climb along the web," Poison replied.

༄

Of all the places Bram might have imagined himself ending up in his middle age, he had never seen himself spread-eagled across a cliff face in the Realm of Spiders with nothing but air between him and a messy death in the trees below. He mumbled and muttered oaths and blew his white moustache, but still he clambered on, working the toe of his boot into a crack, sliding his gloved fingers into a fold in the rock, until finally he put his foot down safe on a ledge, and there before him was the strand of spiderweb.

By happy chance, one of the massive tendrils of white silk was anchored to the wall not far from where Poison and the others had entered the Realm. Poison had outlined her plan to them in detail, but it relied on several factors about which they were not yet certain. One was how sticky the web was; the other was how strong. And there was a third factor, too. Who was more patient, the spider or the flies that sought to evade her?

Bram heartily disapproved of the whole affair, but he had volunteered to go even so.

"I'm the strongest climber," he said. "And besides, the sooner I prove to you that this won't work, the better."

The ledge was wide enough for Bram to relax a little, and was close enough to the strand so he could reach it without stretching too much. He caught his breath, then looked over at where Poison and Peppercorn had been following his progress.

"Touch the web!" Poison called. "Gently! You don't want to bring the spider!"

Bram swore under his breath. She had to mention that, didn't she? If he *did* attract the spider, there wasn't anywhere he could go. Still, if he remembered rightly some tale an old minstrel had once told him about mandolin strings, they didn't vibrate so well if they were plucked at the ends; it was only by striking them in the middle that they made a noise. He hoped the same principle applied to spiderwebs.

Gingerly, he reached out a hand and laid it on the webbing. At worst, he reasoned, he'd lose a glove. The web was thick and flexible, but he could feel the immense strength in its construction. The glue on its surface oozed between his fingers. He let his hand rest there for a moment, then tried to pull it away. The glue resisted, but it gave up with a little effort. Bram harrumphed to himself. The glue was weak, all right. It was probably designed to catch those winged moth-things, which — large as they were — were terribly frail and probably possessed little physical strength. He glanced down the web, but there was no sign of the spider.

"I think we can climb on it, anyway," he called. "But it'll be slow going."

Poison flashed a grin of triumph. "Now use your knife!" she cried back.

Bram gave her an irritated glance and did as she said, slicing a little way into the web. It took some sawing to get the blade in, but once he had he found he could pull it away as if he were peeling a string of celery.

"How is it?" Poison asked.

"I think it might work," Bram said grudgingly. "We'll see if it stretches."

He tied the narrow string of webbing round his waist and climbed back to the ledge where Poison and Peppercorn waited. Every few feet he had to stop and tug the webbing to unpeel it a little farther from the main body of the web, and each time he held his breath in case the movement would bring the spider. But it never came, and eventually Bram reached his companions and sat down for a rest while Poison excitedly untied the webbing from him.

"No wild idea goes unrewarded," she declared, weighing the sticky silk in her hands.

"Only in stories, Poison," Bram reminded her. "Haven't you learned to tell the difference yet?"

"*Is* there a difference?" she asked. "Here, come here. We'll all need to pull on this. And be ready to run."

"Run *where?*" Peppercorn bleated.

"Back into the crevice," Poison replied as Bram wearily took hold of the rope. Peppercorn did so, too. They looked as if they were about to engage in a bizarre tug-of-war.

"Now!" Poison cried, and with that the three of them pulled the rope as hard as they could. The strand tore a little farther down the length of the web, but it held easily. "Release!" Poison called. "Now pull again!"

They pulled, relaxed, pulled, and each time the shaking of the great strand of webbing that they were attached to increased. At first it was a tremble, then a noticeable swing, and then —

Peppercorn shrieked as the spider burst from its cave, scuttling to the centre of the web before racing outward again, seeming to grow in size with terrifying speed as it hurtled towards them. But they had already dropped their silk and fled into the narrow slash of the crevice, huddled in the darkness there. The creature reached the end of the strand and stopped. Close up, it was truly grotesque. Eight eyes shone a dull red above enormous mandibles, and its bloated abdomen was furred in spiny black bristles. Its legs were spindly in proportion, but they were still as thick as Bram's arm. Poison did not doubt that if the spider caught them, it could kill them in a flash.

But it had not caught them. It had not even seen them. Instead, it waited, puzzled, processing the anomaly in its arachnid brain. Something had been struggling here; yet now the hunter had arrived, the prey was gone. It was not completely outside the spider's experience — after all, every so often a moth managed to pull free of the web, usually at the expense of a leg or a chunk of wing — but it was rare enough to be unsettling. Though it sat motionless for a long while, Poison felt it stewing in suspicion. Then, finally, it backed up the thread, scuttled away, and retreated to its cave.

When it was gone, Poison emerged again. "Come on," she said. "That was only the beginning." She picked up the loose string of silk that Bram had sheared off the main thread, and the others joined her.

"Where's Andersen?" Poison asked, keen that the cat would not give them away next time the spider appeared.

"Over there," said Bram, thumbing towards the shadows of the crevice. Andersen looked up with a faintly guilty expression, with four spider legs protruding from his mouth, still waving weakly.

"Stay there," Poison told him. Andersen didn't need telling.

They heaved again. This time the spider bolted out of its cave on the very first tug, and they dropped the string and hurriedly squeezed themselves back into the crevice just in time. The spider once more found itself without prey. As before, it sat motionless over the spot where the disturbance had come from, as if waiting for the phantom moth to reveal itself. Eventually, it gave up and retreated once more.

It took them a dozen more times before the spider eventually quit. It was Peppercorn that first noticed it was slowing down, proceeding more cautiously on the fifth or sixth time, as if it suspected a trick was being played on it and it did not want to seem foolish. Once, it waited until they had stopped tugging and had decided that it was not going to come, then flashed out at lightning speed. They barely scrambled to safety in time. But after that, the spider had had enough. Whatever was causing the disturbance on that strand of the web, it was not food, and hence the spider was not interested. They tested it six more times after it had stopped emerging altogether, just to be certain. It was impossible to be too careful. Once they were out on the thread, they had nowhere to go; if the spider came out for them, they would be dead.

"I think it's safe," Poison said, though she was unable to keep a trace of doubt from her voice.

But Peppercorn was shaking her head, trembling. Her nerves had been shot to pieces by dicing with the spider. "I'm not going!" she said. "I'm not going!"

Poison laid a hand on her arm with uncharacteristic gentleness. There was something about Peppercorn that she could not place, something that made her feel protective rather than short-tempered. The girl was timid beyond belief and painfully naive, and yet instead of annoyance — which would be her usual reaction — Poison felt a sort of sympathy for her. Despite the fact that Peppercorn had done nothing to earn her favour, besides sheltering her from Maeb that first time, she liked the girl. She just couldn't understand why.

"You don't have to go," Poison said. "You came this far. That's enough." She turned her violet gaze on to Bram. "Nor you." Bram took a breath to protest, but Poison cut him off. "I know what you're going to say, but this is too dangerous to risk. Where's the sense in us both getting eaten? Besides, you're too heavy. On my own, I might be able to get by without attracting that thing's attention. You'd set alarm bells ringing all over the web."

She had expected Bram to argue, but instead he let out a long sigh. He must have been genuinely afraid to allow himself to be persuaded so easily.

"You do what you have to, Poison," he rumbled.

"If I get in trouble, I have the orb from the Phaerie Lord," she reminded him.

"And what will *that* do?" Bram asked. "You can't trust a phaerie! He'd as soon see you dead as come back with that dagger. The orb could kill you as fast as that spider would! The phaeries are tricksters, Poison! And you're placing your life in their hands."

"Well, I wish I had a choice," Poison said. "I'll be careful. I'm not suicidal, Bram."

Bram raised an eyebrow and looked towards the sinister edifice of Asinastra's palace. "That's open for debate," he muttered.

❧❧❧

If she thought it had been bad in the house of the Bone Witch, this was worse. Poison had never experienced fear like she did when she first clambered on top of the great thread of webbing that ran from the wall of the mountain bowl to the palace of the Lady of Spiders. The raw helplessness overwhelmed her. She would have to crawl the whole length of the thread, hundreds of feet up, and if at any moment during that time the spider decided to emerge, she would meet a horrible and grisly death. Could she really go through with this? she wondered. Was it worth dying to try and save her sister's life?

Yet she found that it was not so much the thought of her baby sister that kept her going but something else — a sense of something started that she had not finished. She had to keep going forward, because that was the only way left. On that day when she had chosen to leave Gull behind, she had set herself in motion, and nothing could stop her now, not even herself. It was a heady feeling, giddy and reckless, and she clung to it as she clung to the webbing, as a lifeline to stop her from falling into despair.

The thread was as thick as Bram was broad, stout as a young tree. Had it been on the ground, Poison could have walked along it with no problem. But it was hanging in a black-and-purple abyss, and death waited on either side. So she crawled, clinging to it with her knees and elbows. She had tied up her long black hair and slid it down the back of her collar, to prevent it sticking to the webbing, but it seemed the least of her worries now. The glue sucked at her coarse dress, making every move an effort; each time she jerked an arm or leg free from the adhesive she felt sure that the spider would come.

She concentrated on nothing but the webbing. She dared not look up at the spider's cave, nor down at the trees below, nor back at the ledge where Bram and Peppercorn watched her in agonized silence. Every moment passing seemed like the slow draw of a blade. She touched the orb in her pocket, making certain that it was tucked away safe. There was nothing to smash it on up here. Would it break if she squeezed it? And if so, what would it do then?

Questions, questions, but they were all useless now. For she was far from help, halfway across the gulf, and the palace loomed larger than ever, its web-strewn towers daggering towards the dark sky. She had never felt so alone.

On and on she went, stopping every few feet after a particularly violent jerk made the web tremble, keeping her eyes fixed on the sticky white silk because she dared not look up to see if the spider was coming. The glue gave her a deceptive sense of security, but she knew that if she fell, it would not hold her to the web.

"Poison!"

She heard her name, Peppercorn's voice, and by her tone she knew it was not going to be good news. She looked back, and saw Peppercorn pointing.

There was another moth, sailing lazily on the night air over the palace.

Poison wiped sweat from her lips with the back of one glue-gummed hand. She gauged how far she had to go. Too far. She was perhaps three-quarters of the way to the palace, but that had taken her a long time. The towers rose up tall on either side of her now, close enough so that she could see broken windows and crumbling brickwork. Ahead, other strands of webbing reached out to join with the one she was following. Would it be possible to make it to one of the outlying towers?

No. She dared not move. For now she looked over to the spider cave in the mountainside, and she saw what she had most feared to see. The creature was crouched in the entrance, its eight eyes of dull red fixed on the moth as it soared closer.

Closer to Poison.

She tried to will herself small and invisible, but the moth appeared to have spotted her and was trying to make out what manner of thing she was. Poison had no idea what kind of diet these moths subsisted on, but she suspected that she looked like a particularly fat grub, and that meant trouble if the things were carnivorous. Yet if that thing came too close and got caught in the web, the spider would be on it — and her — in a moment.

Poison wanted to scream at it, to frighten it away, but it might attract the spider. She could only hold still, and hope.

The moth fluttered nearer, so that she could feel the wind of its gossamer wings on her skin. Its six legs flexed in a ripple; its segmented eyes bobbed inquisitively in their sockets. Though it did not appear to have any kind of toothed mouth, Poison was not in the least reassured. It was still big enough to pick her up.

Then she remembered how feeble the things were, how they were not strong enough to fight their way out of the weak glue of the webbing.

An idea occurred to her. She pulled a hand free and reached over her shoulder into her pack, and from there drew out the first thing she could find — an apple. The moth dove down in front of her, its antennae bobbing. She flung the apple at it.

The effect was startling. The apple punched through the moth's wing like it was a paper screen, and the moth squealed. It launched itself away with a great beat of its wings, and Poison had to cling onto the web to prevent herself from falling. But the moth's injury seemed to have ruined its ability to fly; it spiralled away crazily, swooping in great arcs and unable to gain any height, until it crashed into the web some distance from Poison. The spider lunged out of its hole, eager not to let this one get away. Poison had to bite back a whimper as she saw the vast, bulbous thing come scuttling out, moving with the horrible gait of its kind. It was upon the moth in moments, biting it again and again with venomous fangs. The moth, after a brief struggle, accepted its fate silently. It did not take long for it to go limp.

But the spider did not cocoon it as it had the other one. Instead, it adopted that awful posture that it had done when Poison and her companions had tricked it, as if it were listening, or thinking deeply. Splayed across the dead husk of the moth, its legs resting on several individual strands, it remained motionless.

It knows I'm here, she thought, feeling panic rise. *Knows, or at least suspects.*

Could it see her? She doubted that the spider's vision was very good, as it had never noticed them hiding in the crevice earlier. But did it *feel* her? Ah, that was another matter. There was something amiss in the web, and the spider sensed it.

Slowly, the spider rotated, and she felt a sick dread as it came to rest once more, facing her.

The mandibles worked uncertainly, chewing on air. Its eight eyes glared blankly in Poison's direction.

She held herself as still as she could. Something was attracting it. But what?

The answer came to her with cruel certainty. Her heartbeat. If she could have halted the thumping in her breast, she would have done so at that moment. For the spider was close now, and it felt the dull rhythm through the web. She was betrayed by the beating of her own heart.

Yet it was an unfamiliar sound, and faint, and there were none of the struggles that usually accompanied prey. Still unsure of the evidence of its own senses, the spider came forward a little way. Poison had to fight to suppress a noise. It was only a few yards from her now, close enough for her to see the hairs on its bloated abdomen and the edges of its mandibles. She fumbled for the orb in her pocket, but the fear kept her from using it. Aelthar had said only to break it when she had the dagger. Did she dare to go against his instructions when she had no idea what it did?

"Hoi!" came the distant cry. Bram. "Hoi! Over here!"

And with that, Bram and Peppercorn began pulling at the web-string that attached them to the great strand that Poison had climbed along. The spider reared up, darting forward. Poison almost screamed as it flashed towards her with lightning speed . . . and then was gone, scuttling away. It had passed over her as she lay trembling.

She tore herself up from the web, knowing that this would be her one and only chance before the spider returned. To her left and right were two of the crumbling towers of the palace. She began to crawl as fast as she could towards the nearest, caring nothing for stealth anymore, heading for a narrow, broken window that lay just above a strand of webbing. She spared a glance towards the spider, who had reached the end of the web strand to discover that it had been duped yet again, and that there was nothing there. But as she floundered along the sticky web, hanging above the abyss, she saw it turn. It sensed her properly this time, struggling like prey.

"Poison! It's coming!" Peppercorn yelled.

With a burst of terror, she pulled herself upright, freeing herself from the glue. The only thing she feared more at this moment than the terrible fall was the jaws of the spider, and so she stood up and *ran* along the web. The strand sucked at her feet, but it was wide enough so that she did not fall.

She felt the thrumming of the strand beneath her feet, heard Peppercorn scream, *sensed* the great black bulk of the spider coming up behind her, fast, faster.

She jumped towards the window, throwing herself into its glass-toothed maw, and a split-second later there was a crash as the spider collided with the wall of the tower, unable to check its momentum in its eagerness to catch this elusive prey. Poison felt a sickening moment of vertigo, for she did not know whether the other side of the window held an endless drop or a bone-breaking set of stairs; and then she hit the floor with a force that knocked the wind out of her, stars sparkled in front of her eyes, and she blacked out.

THE LADY OF COBWEBS

WHEN she awoke, the spider was gone.

Poison raised her head from the cold stone floor, pulling out strands of her long black hair that had somehow gotten into her mouth. Her first reaction was puzzlement; then, as memory reassembled itself, relief. Whatever this room had once been, it was now dark, cobwebbed, and empty. Remnants of broken furniture had become convenient anchors for the ubiquitous arachnids of this Realm, though thankfully they appeared to be of the usual size instead of the monster that had very nearly claimed her life a short while ago.

She winced as she raised herself. How long *had* she been out, anyway? Her ribs blazed with pain and felt brittle, as if they would snap inwards at the slightest touch. There was a thin trail of dried blood on the floor, which she traced to a scabbed-over scratch on her thigh, where a jagged bit of glass from the broken window had scored her. She counted herself lucky that she had not been more badly hurt. A quick check also revealed that the orb in her pocket had managed to escape intact, which was a small miracle in itself.

She dusted herself down, checking her arms and legs for

any further injuries. She tutted at the rip that had been made in her dress. Hard-wearing and unglamorous though it was, like all marsh-clothing, it still pained her to see it damaged.

Well, she thought stoically to herself, *the sooner I get this over with, the sooner I can leave this place.*

She rolled her shoulders to work out the kinks, and then set off to explore.

It did not take her long to establish that the palace of Asinastra was a ruin, and a deserted ruin at that. For long hours she wandered through the corridors and passageways, finding only crumbling walls, faded tapestries, ancient furniture, and cobwebs, cobwebs everywhere. At first she proceeded warily, creeping silently about and peering into every room before daring to enter. As her confidence grew she became more blasé and gave up trying to sneak past things that clearly weren't there. Eventually, she began to despair of seeing anyone at all, and it was hard to resist the temptation to call out in the hope of attracting someone.

But then always there were the spiders: big ones, tiny ones, deadly ones, and harmless ones, spiders that hid and spiders that spat. Poison was used to spiders, and even the venomous ones did not concern her much. She had been brought up in the Black Marshes, where virtually everything that moved was poisonous. You just had to know how to avoid them, or deal with them if they got in your way.

So many spiders. Now where are all the flies? she wondered.

It was strange. Since leaving Gull, there were just too many things that did not seem to add up. Lamprey's riddles, uncannily like something out of a phaerie tale. Myrrk, with his cryptic nonsense and the fact that he claimed not to have eaten for a hundred years. Of course, Myrrk could well have been insane, and Lamprey, too, but both of them seemed to *know* things. Both of them had obliquely cautioned her against having ideas above her station; both claimed to be examples of what happened if a person overstepped her mark. Yet both seemed reluctant, even uneasy, when faced with a straight question.

And now, here, in this place with a million spiders but no flies, she found herself wondering what they could possibly be feeding on, and she was reminded of Myrrk's words about the Hierophant and how he had not bothered to work out the details of Myrrk's diet. Who was the Hierophant and why did Myrrk believe he had such control that he dictated what the strange fisherman ate? Was the spider-and-fly puzzle the same thing, or was she missing the point? And how did any of this apply to her?

It was too much for the moment. She could barely manage to deal with what was in front of her, with the overwhelming *newness* of the world she had stepped out into a few short weeks ago. Or had it even been that long? Time did not mean what it used to mean. The fact that her father and Snapdragon might have already died of old age in the hours she had spent in the Realm of Phaerie was just one of many things that threatened to unbalance her sanity if she thought too hard about them.

No. She dared not dwell on what might be happening at home. What if the message that she had given to the surly girl on her way to Gull had never gotten through? All she had done was entrust a few words to a stranger. What if her father never knew the reason why his eldest daughter disappeared, never to return, leaving them burdened with a changeling for the rest of their days?

Azalea. She had only to focus on Azalea. That was her goal, her purpose: to get back her sister.

She rested for a time and ate an apple from her pack,

vaguely regretting the one she had thrown at the moth. The only sound in the vast emptiness of the palace was the noise of her munching, and the occasional echoing squeak or tap as she moved slightly. She might have been alone in the world. She was certainly lost in it.

Eventually, she got back up and began to walk again. She still did not feel sleepy, even though the last time she had actually slept properly was days ago. More evidence of the skewed time frame that existed outside the Realm of Man. She considered how long she might be wandering these night-soaked halls before she came across anything, or if there was anything to come across. Was Aelthar's dagger even here? And where was the Lady Asinastra?

It was hours later that she found something. What it was, however, she was by no means certain.

She had taken to breaking up bits of furniture, picking up rocks and suchlike, and placing them in the centre of each room when she departed, pointing in the direction she was leaving. She could not shake the suspicion that she was going in circles. Apparently, she was mistaken, however, for she did not once come across any of the little markers she had left for herself, which only depressed her more as it meant the scale of the place was enormous. Up winding stairs she went, into rooms, along corridors, until finally she saw the dead woman.

At least, she looked dead. Poison could not tell, and she did not trust the evidence of her senses. Certainly, she had been cobwebbed where she sat on a grandiose wooden seat, indicating that she had not moved for a very long time. She was slumped forward, her hands on the armrests and her legs apart. She wore a white dress, tattered and faded by the ages, and her long, filthy black hair showed just enough of her face so that it was possible to see she had a veil concealing her from forehead to chin. But perhaps most disturbing of all was the great bulge in her lower belly. Whether still alive or dead, she was heavily pregnant.

The room was scattered with old and mouldering treasures. Indeed, it seemed as if the entire palace had been scoured of anything interesting just to have it brought here. Whereas Poison had seen nothing more remarkable than a table since she had started exploring the palace, here she found a wealth of glory, left to rot. Ancient suits of armour cluttered the corners; magnificent swords had gone to rust; paintings in gold frames had faded and were spotted with fungus; piles of coins had gone green with the uncountable years. And every-where cobwebs — though, oddly enough, no spiders. Poison had become so used to seeing out of the corner of her eye the swift, jerky movements of the palace's eight-legged inhabitants that the absence of them was unsettling.

Then her eye fell on something that made her heart leap. A dagger, with a blade that split into two prongs, like the fangs of a snake. It was dull but not rusted, poking out of the hollow of a horned helmet, webbed in place by a thick curtain of silk. There was no question in her mind: that was Aelthar's dagger.

She glanced at the corpse once again, but her gaze was drawn back by the dagger. She crossed the dark room silently, still mistrusting the dead woman, afraid to make the slightest sound in case it might wake her. Morbid curiosity urged her to touch the woman's withered hand, to set her mind at rest that she was really harmless — and yet, the child in her still shied from it, expecting at any moment that the corpse might come to her feet and lumber into attack.

Forget her, Poison told herself. *Get the dagger.*

She crouched down next to the tumbled suit of armour, its pieces connected by sinews of thick white web. The dagger's blade protruded from the helmet towards her. Unable to resist one more nervous glance at the motionless figure on the chair, she steadied the helmet and reached a hand into the sticky mass of silk that filled it, shuddering in repulsion. At any moment, she expected to feel the swarm of spider feet racing up her arm towards her face, clambering in her hair, angry at the disturbance of their web. But nothing so terrible happened. She groped for the hilt of the dagger, found it, and pulled it silently out. For a few long seconds, she looked at it, weighing it in her hand. Then she sighed, stood up, and turned around.

The corpse was gone.

She felt an icy jolt inside her, an instinctive reaction to the absence of something that should not have been able to move. The cobwebs were torn away, leaving a great, ragged hole where the withered woman used to be. Panic took her, the deep-rooted fear of the dead that humankind possessed on a subconscious level. She looked about desperately, but there was no sign of the woman anywhere in the room. Stumbling a step in retreat, she tripped on a flagstone and fell backwards onto her pack. The fall was not painful, cushioned as it was by the food and clothes within; but then she opened her eyes and screamed.

The woman was on the ceiling. Her emaciated fingers and toes clutched the stone and held up there as easily as if she was crawling along the floor. She had craned her neck around at an impossible angle, and her matted hair hung down across her dirty veil. But the veil had slipped, and Poison could see her eyes now: black, blank pearls, like the eyes of the changeling Poison had left back in Gull. She felt the terrible weight of that gaze, and it froze her in place.

The woman dropped, suddenly releasing herself and plummeting down towards Poison. Poison's instincts cried out, telling her to throw herself aside or at least put her hands up in front of her face. But nothing moved. Her muscles seemed empty of life. The woman landed lightly on her fingertips and toes, foursquare over the prone body of Poison, her face inches from Poison's own, her swollen belly pressing into Poison's. The marsh girl trembled in terror, but she could not tear herself away from those black, empty eyes, could not break the contact that paralysed her.

<thiiiief>

The voice was an awful, drawn-out rasp, lisping and strange, as if it were being made by a mouth that was not adapted to human language. Her breath stank of decay and something more acrid. Her hair hung over her face and onto Poison's, trailing dusty strands of cobweb across her skin. Poison realized with a terrible certainty that this was the Lady Asinastra, and that she was now helpless against her.

<husband told me> <about her?> <about she> <the lady knew you'd come> <I?> <I, the lady of cobwebs>

Poison barely heard what the creature was saying, for her attention was fixed on the dark abyss of her gaze, the eyes that seemed to reach into her and rob her of her will to move. She was only barely aware of the insane rhythm of the spider-woman's sentences, the question-and-answer that Asinastra seemed to be conducting with herself.

<husband doesn't dare come in> <he knows what the lady will do> <yes, he knows> <when the heir is born> <won't he be fine?> <a fine heir to the realm>

Husband? Poison was still not following her, but how did a husband figure in any of this?

<husband guards the palace> muttered Asinastra, as if she had heard Poison's thoughts. *<husband gave me child>*

Poison tried to shake her head in denial as the realization set in, but her muscles would only twitch. She couldn't mean the thing outside? She couldn't mean the *spider*?

Asinastra took Poison's hand and laid it on her belly. Poison attempted to resist, but there was no strength in her while Asinastra's gaze was locked with hers. For a moment, she felt nothing; then something repulsive shifted beneath the dress, beneath the skin, something large and curled and many-legged. Poison felt tears of fear and horror spring to her eyes. Asinastra let her hand drop away.

<child>

Poison could not have spoken even if she had been able.

<she wants the dagger> said the Lady, and Poison realized that the dagger was still clutched in her hand, though it was useless to her now. *<our dagger?> <my dagger> <what does she want it for?> <she doesn't know> <maybe she does> <do you know?>*

The silence that followed her mumbling dialogue with herself made Poison realize that the last question had been directed at her, but she could not answer.

<who sent her?> <who sent you?>

Again, Poison tried to force a word out, but this time Asinastra seemed to realize what the problem was. Her eyes tightened fractionally, and Poison felt her throat unclench a little.

<speak>

Poison dragged in a breath.

<speak!>

"I want an audience," she croaked. "Under Amrae's Law."

Asinastra shrieked in anger, springing backwards off Poison as if she had been stung. Poison felt the weakness fall away from her as she was released from the Lady's paralysing glare, and she slowly levered herself upright and got to her feet while Asinastra prowled and hissed around the room.

<she wants an audience> <under the law?> <the law!>

"And you cannot harm me," Poison reminded her, recalling the words of Scriddle. "On your honour as a Lady."

<oh, she thinks she's so clever> <horribly clever> <but she's not so clever yet> <we can wait> <I can wait> <when the audience is done> <the lady will have her then>

But Poison did not intend to be there by the time the audience was done. She still held the dagger in one hand, and with the other she reached into her pocket and drew out the orb: the cold, black orb given to her by Aelthar.

Bram's voice came back to her with the force of a prophecy: *The orb could kill you as fast as that spider would! The phaeries are tricksters, Poison! And you're placing your life in their hands.*

<what have you got there?> Asinastra rasped, peering through the tangle of her hair. <what has she got?>

No choice. Poison raised it above her head. Then, in a capricious act of spite, she decided that she owed Aelthar an ill for what he had put her through this far. Marshalling her courage, she said, "Lady Asinastra, I am the Phaerie Lord's thief."

<aelthar!> <aelthar!> the Lady howled. <thief!> <thie —>

But Poison heard no more, for she had already flung the orb down onto the hard stone floor of the chamber, and as it smashed, its blackness flooded out and Poison was engulfed, with the echoing shrieks of the Lady of Cobwebs fading after her.

THE TROUBLE WITH PHAERIES

~~~~~~~~

WHEN Poison next opened her eyes, she was staring at the inside of a beautifully ornate waiting room.

She blinked. It took a few instants for surprise to set in, then a few more for her to reassert herself. She recognized the finery by now. They were in the Phaerie Lord's palace.

Andersen mewed at her feet.

"Oh, you're all right!" Peppercorn cried, throwing her arms around Poison.

Poison hugged her automatically in return, still a little bewildered. The orb had brought them back — and what was more, it had brought them back together. Bram was there, too, clearly unhappy at having his world turned inside out and fiddling with his moustache while he tried to get over the shock of being magicked into another Realm.

Poison felt a flood of relief wash over her; until this moment, she had dreaded a trick from Aelthar. But it appeared that, against all odds, he had not let her down. Though he had tormented her with uncertainty by refusing to tell her what the orb did — something which Poison would not soon forget — the orb had saved her. No wonder he had forbidden her to use it until after she had the dagger. He didn't care anything about her. He simply wanted to be sure that she got out with his prize.

The door of the waiting room burst open and Scriddle hurried in, attended by his usual gaggle of imps who were wittering reports and requests at him in a seemingly incomprehensible frenzy. As before, he fired commands at each of them in turn, and then waved them away when he reached the humans. He grinned a sharp-toothed grin, slicked his hair back afresh, and then held out his hand.

"I believe you have something for the Lord Aelthar?" he said to Poison.

She looked down at the dagger in her grip. "Where is he?" she asked.

Scriddle's grin became strained at the edges. "Preparing for an extremely important conference," he replied.

"Well, tell him I want my sister back before he gets this," she said.

"Human, you don't seem to understand," Scriddle said through gritted teeth. "I have three Lords just arrived in the palace, representing three Realms, each with their own retinue, their own likes and dislikes, and their own personal needs, and the person responsible for coordinating everything to everybody's taste is me. That makes me *very busy!*"

"In that case, I'd hate to hurry you," Poison replied, asserting herself admirably. "Do tell Aelthar that we'll wait until he's ready, and then we can talk about trading this dagger for my sister."

Scriddle tutted. "Ridiculous girl. You humans really do have bloated egos. This is the Phaerie Realm, the land of my master. You have no leverage to bargain with."

He held up his hand, and in it was the forked dagger.

Poison's hand closed on empty air, and she looked down in puzzlement to see that the dagger had disappeared from her grip.

Scriddle turned on his heel and stalked out. "You will wait here until my Lord decides how to deal with you," he said over his shoulder. And with that he shut the door and a key turned in the lock.

"Well," said Peppercorn in the silence that followed. "That was rude."

"'Deal with' us?" Bram quoted. "I don't much like the sound of that. Doesn't sound like someone interested in a fair swap."

"No," said Poison. "No, it doesn't." She looked around the room. "In fact, I'm beginning to think it would be better if we weren't here when Scriddle gets back."

"Are you sure?" asked Peppercorn. "What if he really does mean to give you your sister?"

"He'd better, after what I've been through," said Poison. "But I'd feel better if we weren't locked in here. I think we should go and find *him*. I'm not going to let him think we can be pushed around. He owes me."

Bram's and Peppercorn's misgivings were plain in the glance they exchanged behind Poison's back, but both knew her better than to talk her out of it.

Poison tried the door, more out of lack of any other inspiration than in the hope it would actually open. After that, she looked around the room. Despite the opulence of their surroundings, it was surprisingly secure. The only other way out was an arched window that looked out over the Realm, where Peppercorn was already peering out. Poison knew what Peppercorn would say before she said it.

"It's a long way down," she commented. Poison sagged. "But there's a ledge."

"A ledge?" Poison asked, hurrying over to look. Her hopes

were soon dashed, however. What Peppercorn had called a ledge was little more than a few inches wide, an ornamental frill that ran around the tower and out of sight. Poison looked out over the achingly beautiful lakeland and tried to think.

"Won't there be other windows farther round the building?" Peppercorn suggested.

Poison sighed patiently. Peppercorn had an uncanny talent for missing the point. "Probably," she said. "But what does it matter if we can't get to them?"

"*We* can't," Peppercorn said. "But Andersen can."

All eyes turned to the cat. Having not been listening to the conversation, he suddenly found everybody looking at him expectantly. Feeling hunted, he backed off a few paces towards the corner, uncomfortable at the sudden attention.

"Can you?" Poison asked. "Climb along this ledge?" She had become quite used to talking to Andersen as if he were another person, rather than an animal.

Andersen reassembled his dignity and made a great show of idly licking his paw and drawing it across his furry skull, cleaning himself. Poison gave Peppercorn a look; Peppercorn shrugged as if to say: *That's just how he is.* Eventually, when Andersen had determined that they had waited long enough, he slid up to the window and jumped up onto the sill. He looked out at the ledge, then back at Poison. It was hard to imagine how a cat could express disbelief, but nevertheless that was the impression Poison got, as strongly as if Andersen had opened his mouth and said: *You expect me to climb along that?*

"Well, if you can't do it, we'll have to find some other way," Poison said.

Andersen looked affronted. Reverse psychology appeared to be particularly effective on a creature as proud as a cat. He daintily put one paw down onto the ledge, then after a moment he followed with the rest of his body in a graceful cross between a hop and a lunge. Poison could have sworn she saw him shake his head — *I can't believe I'm doing this* — before he set off along the ledge at what seemed a recklessly fast trot. Peppercorn chewed her lip anxiously until he was out of sight.

"Oh, I hope he'll be all right," she said.

Poison tried to think of something genuine and comforting to say, but being nice was not her strong point. She and Peppercorn were complete opposites; where Peppercorn was helpless and sweet and painfully naive, Poison was hard-edged and suspicious and capable. Yet she felt an almost sisterly protectiveness towards the blonde girl. It pained her to think how she had almost left her behind in Maeb's house. Poison felt responsible for her now, having been the one who dragged her from the darkness of the Bone Witch's domain out into the light. Peppercorn needed looking after, and Poison found that it was an oddly pleasing role.

But it was not only that. Poison envied Peppercorn's sunny disposition, her innocence. Poison had grown up in the deadly gloom of the Black Marshes, but Peppercorn must have had an equally unpleasant childhood; yet they could not have turned out more different. Poison wished sometimes that she could be like Peppercorn and not be weighed down by the cares of the world. But it was a fancy, and she knew it. Cynicism was a one-way path, and once taken the way back was lost forever.

They waited. Time passed. Poison, unable to be patient when imprisoned like this, applied herself to searching for alternative ways to escape in case Andersen should fail in getting them out. It was only after he had gone that she began to doubt that Andersen *could* do anything, even if he was free. Who could help them? And what could a cat do?

She was still racking her brains when she heard a scratching on the other side of the door.

"Andersen!" Peppercorn cried, racing over. The others

crowded round. A moment later, the scratching stopped, and something rattled.

"What was that?" Peppercorn asked.

"The key," Bram said. "It's still in the other side of the lock."

The key rattled again as Andersen batted it.

"There's no way he's going to be able to turn it," Poison said. "We have to knock it through."

Andersen mewed in agreement.

It took them only a few moments to find something long and thin enough to jab into the lock — a candle spike from a candelabra — and with a little effort they worked the key out. It fell with a clatter on the other side. Moments later, they heard it being scraped along the floor, and it was slid under the door to them. Peppercorn clapped in delight as Poison picked it up, unlocked the door, and opened it. Andersen was grooming himself smugly on the other side. Peppercorn scooped him up and ruffled his fur, tickling him and cooing over him until Poison felt almost embarrassed for her.

"That cat's not natural," Bram murmured once again.

"You can't argue with the results, though," Poison replied.

They looked down the empty corridor, made of the same beautiful jade stone as most of the Phaerie Lord's palace.

"Now where?" Bram said.

Poison looked at the cat. "I don't suppose you might be able to find Aelthar for us?" she ventured. She had learned not to discount any possibility where their odd companion was concerned.

Andersen sprang down from Peppercorn's arms, shook himself, and mewed at them.

"Sounds like a yes," Peppercorn said.

"Oh, good," Bram said sarcastically.

⤳⟲⟳⤵

If she had thought Andersen was strange enough before, the next half hour made Poison realize that she had fallen far short of the mark. The cat's powers of navigation were nothing short of phenomenal. He led them unerringly through a maze of corridors, up and down stairs, taking them along routes that were rarely used and hardly trafficked. They passed a few phaerie folk along the way — at least to begin with — but their presence was treated with disdain and they were ignored, which suited Poison fine.

Eventually, they came to a small, innocuous door, recessed in an alcove in a deserted corridor. Andersen obviously intended them to go inside, so they did — and found themselves in a narrow squeezeway, only wide enough for them to pass through in single file. There was no light but that which filtered through a few distant grilles, rectangles of sun glowing in the blackness.

"What is this place?" Bram asked.

Poison shut the door behind her, plunging them into deeper dark. "At a best guess, I'd say we were between the walls."

"Between the walls," Bram repeated flatly, prompting for elaboration.

"A place as big as this needs airways between the rooms," Poison explained. "For ventilation. Even phaeries need to breathe. Most of them, anyway."

"How do you *know* all that?" Bram asked, faintly irritated at seeming ignorant.

"Remember I told you about that story, with the prince and the tigers? Later on, he used the ventilation system of the palace to find his way to the princess, by following the scent of her perfume. Then he stole her out from beneath the nose of the Vizier."

"That's so romantic!" Peppercorn cheeped.

"I'll tell you the whole tale one day," Poison promised, and was surprised to find that she meant it.

"I think I should hear it as well," Bram put in dryly. "Seems more like a survival manual than a story."

Poison didn't reply to that one; it was a little too close to the bone. How could she articulate that strange sense that she had, that ever since Gull she had felt as if pieces of the stories she had read were coming to life around her?

"Are you sure you know where you're going?" she asked Andersen. Andersen gave an offended meow in response.

"He wandered into Maeb's house from the Phaerie Realm, remember?" Peppercorn said. "He knows his way around."

"You mean he's been here before?" Poison asked. "In the palace?"

Peppercorn shrugged. "Why not? He seems to have a good idea of where he's going, hmm? He could have lived here for years. He never told me."

"Is that right?" Poison asked Andersen — but the cat kept his secrets.

Andersen was not done with them yet, however. The squeezeways ran for what seemed like miles and went through many twists and turns. Soon they were hot and sweaty and covered in scrapes from the walls. The ornately wrought grilles alternated in height as they passed by them, affording glimpses of the palace's rooms. They passed a kitchen swarming with needle-toothed pixies arguing over the preparation of food and swearing like sailors at each other. They saw a room plush with jewels and such a profusion of gold edging that it dazzled the eye. They peered out over a vast library, its aisles stretching away beneath them. But always Andersen hurried them on, hissing at them impatiently when they lagged.

It was because they were hurrying so that Poison did not at first notice they had left Peppercorn behind. But then with a shiver of fright, she tugged on Bram's shoulder to stop him. Andersen scuttled back to see what the problem was.

"Wait here," Poison whispered, conscious that their voices could be heard through the grilles by the phaeries in the rooms all around them. "I'll go back."

She found Peppercorn just around the next corner, her fingers clenched in the fine ironwork of a grille, standing on tiptoes to gaze through it. Poison came up alongside her.

"What are you *doing?*" she whispered.

"Look," Peppercorn cooed dreamily. "She's so beautiful. A princess. Just like that story."

Poison rolled her eyes and then nudged her aside so she could humour the younger girl. Her scepticism evaporated, however, when she laid eyes on the lady in question.

She was like a vision, something half-dreamt that had found its way to reality. Tall and slight, her face was a perfect oval; her hair falling down her back in streams of white and gold, stirring slowly as she moved, seeming to curl and sway with a life all its own. She wore a dress in tones that matched her hair, clinging to her slender figure, a fabric as light as air and which shimmered like the mist at the foot of a waterfall. Her skin was pale as milk and inhumanly perfect, and her features were alien, resembling those of a woman and yet not, seeming smoother somehow, as if she were moulded rather than born. Her eyes were pools of endless blue, with no pupils to mar their colour, like the sky on a spring morning.

Poison could hardly breathe. The phaerie woman was mesmerizing. She was standing alone in a room, waiting for something or someone, and yet even the slightest of movements that she made seemed to wrench at the heart. She sighed, and the sound was like the wind stirring fallen leaves in autumn, or birds taking flight. Poison could not help wondering who she was, why she was here, what she was waiting for ... but with an effort of will she tore herself away from such thoughts. They had no time for idle fancy. Steeling herself against the temptation to gaze on the lady again, she grabbed Peppercorn by the wrist and pulled her away. Peppercorn made a small noise of complaint, but she did not resist. They rejoined the others, both of them feeling as if they had left a small part of themselves behind, that by sacrificing that beauty they had betrayed themselves.

"Are you done gawking?" Bram said, bringing them back to earth.

They went on through the squeezeways for what seemed like an age, and when finally Andersen stopped and they caught up with him, they were exhausted. He was sitting next to a grille that was just like dozens of other grilles they had passed, a barely visible silhouette in the gloom. Poison crouched down next to the cat and peered through.

The room beyond was an elegantly furnished chamber, hung with tapestries of war and immaculate in its finery. It was empty.

Poison frowned. "Andersen, why did you ..." she began, and then trailed off as she heard the sound of approaching footsteps. She cast one last, suspicious glance at the cat and then returned her attention to the room beyond the grille.

She could have predicted who would walk in then, even before she saw him. Andersen did know where he was going; he must have wandered these squeezeways long ago, back in the shadowy depths of his past.

It was Aelthar who entered, and with him was Scriddle, his obsequious and prickly secretary. These were the Phaerie Lord's chambers.

"Shut the door, Scriddle," Aelthar said. The tone of his voice betrayed his mood. He was angry, and short on patience.

Scriddle did as he was told.

"We must make plans," Aelthar snapped suddenly, pacing the room. "This cannot go on."

"I agree," Scriddle replied, his sharp head bobbing. "Something must be done."

"Humans!" Aelthar spat. Poison felt a thrill of fright.

"They are indeed a most annoyingly pestilent breed, Lord," Scriddle agreed. "May I ask if your private conferences with the other Lords bore any fruit?"

"Ha!" Aelthar cried bitterly. "When have any of us been able to agree on anything? Grugaroth is still bitter about Myghognimar; he can barely suffer to be in the same room as me. The Umbilicus is so overcautious that it never acts at all. Only the Gomm has the will and the strength to be an ally to me in this matter, but it is like trying to chain a bull. He understands nothing of subtlety."

Poison felt Peppercorn burrowing in alongside her, trying to get to see what was going on. She shifted over a little to make way.

"What's happening?" Peppercorn whispered. Poison hushed her.

"My Lord should not be too downhearted," Scriddle said, raising an eyebrow above his round glasses. "There is still the issue of our visit to the Hierophant. Every Lord and Lady of the Realms will be there. And many are frightened by what the Hierophant is up to, Lord. They won't stand for it."

"Of course they're frightened! Who knows who will come out on top when the barrel is shaken?" Aelthar suddenly crossed the room to stand before the grille where Poison and Peppercorn watched. Peppercorn was about to make a noise of alarm when Bram's glove clamped over her mouth.

"How ridiculous it seems," the Phaerie Lord mused. "Humans

are the lowest rung on the ladder of the Realms, and yet a single one of them can inspire such panic. What is it about them, Scriddle? How is it that only *they* can become Hierophants?"

Scriddle paused for a time before answering. "Perhaps they have something that the other races do not?" he suggested.

"And what might that be?" Aelthar laughed, tossing his flame-red hair. "A complete inability to cooperate? A tendency to embark on long and pointless acts of genocide upon their own kind? I swear to you, even the animals of their Realm count higher in my estimation than humans do. Their gift of intelligence they have squandered by selfishness and barbarity. One day, the day they lose their precious guardian, I will march my forces into their lands and wipe them from existence, and I will be counted a hero by all for doing so." He stamped to the other side of the room, exclaiming "Vermin!" as he went.

"My Lord," Scriddle said, adjusting his glasses with an embarrassed cough, "may I remind you that I myself am half human?"

"And a shame it is," Aelthar said. "Were you pure phaerie, I would have you as my right-hand man instead of merely a secretary. You have everything I ask for in a subject, Scriddle, but not the blood."

"I am honoured to have risen this far in your employ, my Lord," Scriddle replied humbly. "I ask for no more."

"Well," Aelthar said, taking a few breaths to calm himself after his tirade against humanity. "We must prepare a retinue. Assemble them in the library. We leave immediately for the Hierophant's castle."

"Lord?" Scriddle queried, his ledger appearing in his hand and falling open. "There is one matter yet to attend to."

"What matter is that? Oh, the humans?"

"Indeed."

"Need I even tell you?"

"I would be loath to second-guess my master and choose incorrectly," Scriddle said smoothly.

"Kill them, Scriddle. Kill them, of course."

Poison felt her blood run cold.

"I suspected as much," Scriddle replied, snapping his ledger shut. And with that, the two of them left the room.

Peppercorn and Poison stood up in the narrow squeezeway and looked at each other.

"Kill us?" Peppercorn squeaked.

"That's the trouble with phaeries," Bram muttered. "You can't trust them as far as you can spit."

"They'll find out we're gone!" Peppercorn said, her voice rising as she began to panic. "They'll come looking for us!"

"Don't worry, Peppercorn," Poison said, her violet eyes shining in the hot darkness. "We won't be here."

There was iron in her voice. The Phaerie Lord's words had shaken her — not because she feared for their safety, but because she knew now that he had intended to betray them. He had never meant to give Azalea back and honour his side of the bargain. Poison's entire plan up until now had relied on Aelthar returning her sister of his own volition. Now she saw that it had been a false hope. For an instant, she teetered on the brink of despair. But then a new resolution took the field and dragged her back. If the Phaerie Lord would not give her Azalea, Poison would *take* her. By whatever means necessary. And while she herself was too weak to threaten a being as mighty as Aelthar, she had learned by now that there were other beings that he *did* fear.

"We won't be here?" Bram echoed. "Where will we be?"

"You heard him say that they're heading for the Hierophant's castle," said Poison. "I've been meaning to have a word with him anyway. And by the sounds of it, we'll be safer there than anywhere. At least he's human."

"You want us to stow away in the Phaerie Lord's retinue?" Bram asked.

"You *are* sharp," Poison said. "That's exactly what I want."

Bram ruminated for a moment. "I wish I had some better ideas," he grumbled.

"After what we've been through so far, you're worried about a little bit of sneaking around?" Poison grinned, slapping him encouragingly on the shoulder. "How hard can it be?"

Andersen mewed sarcastically at her feet.

STORYTELLING

⌇⌇⌇

THE Hierophant's castle stood on the rocky heights of a mountain, glowering darkly in the storm-lashed night. Rain swept across the surrounding peaks, and the blanket of black cloud was periodically underlit by a silent flicker of lightning, before thunder would barrel across the landscape and into the distance.

The castle was the only sign of life in this bleak Realm; it crouched massive and alone, sprawling over the mountaintop, a shiver of turrets and crenellations, parapets and spires and towers, all carved from the stone of the mountains. It had been built on uneven ground, and so it was uneven in shape, following the contours of the cruel, bare rock and giving it a lopsided appearance, with its western wing set lower than the main body of the castle. In the darkness, it was a shadow of deepest black against the sky, and dozens of lights burned inside its silhouette, a scattering of man-made stars in the storm.

⌇⌇⌇

If Poison had a plan in mind for secreting herself and her companions among the Phaerie Lord's retinue, it turned out to be unnecessary. Still thinking along human lines, she had envisioned a train of carriages such as the coach that had brought them here; but the ways between the Realms were not bound by the laws of distance.

Remembering Aelthar's words, they had backtracked along the squeezeways until they came to the vast library that they had seen through a grille earlier. With a little muscle and some wriggling on Bram's part, they had dislodged it and slipped through, clambering down a bookcase to one of the balconies that ringed the aisles. There, they had found a place to hide until Aelthar arrived shortly afterwards.

Poison's heart sank. His retinue consisted only of ten phaeries, four of which were guards and the rest an assortment of naiads, undines, and dryads. Scriddle was there, practically twitching with nervousness and irritation; he had no doubt discovered that the humans had slipped his clutches by now. Poison wondered whether he had told Aelthar or not.

Still, the small satisfaction of the discomfort she had caused Scriddle did nothing to ameliorate the disappointment she felt. There was no way they could hide among Aelthar's retinue. The best they could hope for was to follow them and see where they led.

As they watched, Aelthar approached a great book that lay closed on a stand at the end of an aisle beneath them. It was enormous, bound in faded red leather with its pages yellowed. Aelthar opened it without ceremony, found a page somewhere in the middle, and began to read from it. Poison craned to hear, but the words were in a language that she did not know. It was only when Andersen hissed softly that she began to notice that something was happening.

The cat had its hackles up and was pressed low to the floor, burrowing under Peppercorn as if he feared the roof falling on his head. Peppercorn herself was cringing, and loose hairs were beginning to lift away from her blonde curls, drawn up by static. The air seemed to tighten around them, and Poison found that she had to labour to draw breath into her lungs. Bram was frowning darkly beneath the broad brim of his hat, and his moustache was trembling. There was a sensation of building energy, registered on senses that they did not even know they had; everything seemed to *flex* at once; and then it was done, and normality was restored. Poison exhaled a low sigh of relief.

"What happened then?" Bram muttered. "Some kind of phaerie magick?"

"Perhaps," Poison said, but she was watching Aelthar as he closed the book and then stalked out of the library, his retinue assembling to follow.

"Come on," said Bram. "We'd better get after them."

They hurried down to the ground level of the vast library, by which time the phaeries had departed through a huge set of double doors. Their footsteps tapped in the echoing stillness, muffled by the weight of knowledge contained in the books that surrounded them. When they reached the doors, Poison opened one of them a crack and peered through. She looked back at the others with a puzzled expression. Then she pushed it open and they left the library, finding themselves in an entirely unexpected place.

It was a T-junction in a corridor. That in itself was not remarkable, but what was strange was that the palace itself appeared different. Gone was the elegant jade and carven finery that had characterized the Phaerie Lord's palace; instead, the walls were made of vast blocks of black stone, lending the scene a much grimmer air. Even the atmosphere was different: colder and more moist. There was a faint and constant susurration. Bram inclined his head, listening hard to try and determine what it was he was hearing, before a roll of angry thunder passed overhead and he realized that it was rain.

Poison put together the strange feeling of dislocation they had felt in the library, the sudden change of decor, and the drastically different weather and came up with a conclusion as surprising as it was gratifying.

"We're here," she said.

"Where?" Peppercorn asked, trying to coax Andersen out of the corner where he had fled at the sound of thunder.

"The Hierophant's castle," Poison announced.

"Indeed you are," said a voice. "And I've been waiting for you for some time now."

They turned to see who had spoken, but Poison knew who it was even before she saw the rangy old fellow. Though he was wearing a fine robe now, when she had never seen him in anything other than the battered marsh-clothes he used to wear, she would have known that voice with her eyes shut, for she had spent so long listening to it recount tales of mystery and wonder, in that hut back in Gull.

"*Fleet?*" she cried in disbelief.

"Poison." He grinned as she flew into his arms and hugged him hard. "Steady there! You'll snap an old man's ribs!"

∽∾∽

The fire crackled in the hearth; Andersen lay asleep on the rug, his flank rising and falling gently.

Poison, Bram, and Peppercorn sat in armchairs around the small, cosy room. The chairs were a little threadbare and well used, but all the more comfortable for it. Bram was on the verge of dozing, tired out by the heat and the delicious meal they had just eaten. Now they sat and sipped mugs of chocolate coffee — potentially the best thing Poison and Peppercorn had ever tasted, for neither had grown up within reach of good food.

Fleet sat nearby, watching them amiably and puffing on a gaudily decorated hookah. This room was not unlike the one back in Gull, where he and Poison had sat for hours and talked about this and that; there was the fire, the chairs, the wall slotted with great volumes of lore, and a clutter of scrolls and notebooks scattered about. Fleet was evidently a man who knew his own mind when it came to his surroundings.

Poison sighed contentedly. It was the first time since she had left home that she had felt truly safe. She had been so unwilling to spoil the joy of the moment that she had so far held herself back from asking the dozens of questions she had for her old friend. Instead, she told him of her journey, for now *she* had a story for *him*, and this one was undisputably true, and just as exciting as any phaerie tale. The storm raged outside, but within the massive stone walls of the Hierophant's castle, they were immune to its fury.

"Answers," Fleet creaked at length, his wrinkled face a landscape in the firelight. "I expect you'll be wanting answers."

Bram stirred lethargically. He was not concerned either way. Poison turned her attention reluctantly to Fleet; whatever answers he had might disturb the rare tranquillity that she had found. Peppercorn was rapt with ecstasy at the taste of the chocolate coffee and had little time to spare for anything else.

"What's happening at home?" Poison asked. "Start with that."

"I don't know anything more than you about that," Fleet replied apologetically. "I left several days after you did. Your father and stepmother were . . . coping. With the changeling. Some of the village mothers were helping them."

"And what about the girl? The girl with the message?"

"What girl?" Fleet asked, and Poison explained about the girl she had met in Shieldtown whom she had charged with delivering her apologies to her father.

"If she ever turned up, it must have been after I was gone," Fleet explained.

Poison felt an unwelcome sadness settle on her. The very

fact that Fleet was being so sparse with information indicated that the situation was not good. How could it be otherwise? She passed over it, deciding that she would rather not know.

"I didn't know about Lamprey, Poison," Fleet said. "I'm sorry. If I'd have realized how dangerous he was . . ."

"Why didn't you just take me?" Poison asked wearily, interrupting him. "It seems you have no trouble getting out of the Realm of Man, since you're here. You could have brought me to the Phaerie Lord. Why . . . why put me through all that?"

"I couldn't interfere," he said emphatically. "I couldn't. Not like that. You had to make your own way. All I could do was point you in the right direction."

"That makes sense," Poison said sarcastically. Lamprey, Myrrk, and now Fleet? She was sick of evasive and circular reasoning. "Just tell me what and who you are, Fleet."

Fleet did so, his voice slipping into that easy rhythm of tale-spinning that had lulled Poison through her childhood. "There are many of us; I do not know how many. We recognize each other from time to time, but part of our purpose is to be anonymous. Those who know of us — and there aren't many — call us the Antiquarians. It's as suitable a name as any, I suppose."

He stretched his spine with a grunt and a loud crack, then settled back deeper into his chair and drew on the hookah pipe. The mood of his audience was relaxed, so he paced his delivery to match.

"We are the biographers of the Realms," he continued. "Collectors of lives. We do not only gather stories, we attend them, witness them, and, where necessary, help them along. The Antiquarians are not bound by race or loyalty; the calling can strike anyone, human or phaerie, troll or dwarrow, or any of a hundred other species. We soak up the tales, histories, myths, and legends of our people, and we watch as new ones are created. All of these we record, and we store them here, in the Hierophant's castle." He paused for dramatic effect, taking a drag on his hookah and blowing out a thin stream of aromatic smoke. Then, with an expansive gesture, he added, "Within these walls lies the tale of creation, from the time that the Realms began until this very instant. Everything of importance that has been said or thought or done in all of history lies in our libraries."

Poison's eyes widened. "That's impossible," she breathed.

"The Hierophant decides what's possible," Fleet advised her.

"Show me," Poison said.

∾᠊ᢔᢕᢕ᠊∾

The library of the Hierophant's castle simply defied belief.

Poison had never seen so many books, but more overwhelming even than that was the impression of how many more she could *not* see. For the Great Library was a labyrinth of corridors and aisles so dense and compact that it was impossible to guess how far it stretched. The corridor in which she stood had six balconies, stretching up into the sombre dimness of the upper levels, and each balcony represented a different level of the library, not counting the one they stood on. The seven levels, so Fleet informed them, were built to different floorplans, so that they intercut each other crazily; sometimes the ceiling would plunge so that it was only a little higher than a man's head, other times it would soar away, with bridges leaping across chasms of books high above. The corridors curved and twisted like living things, and Poison felt as if she was inside a twining snake with shelving for ribs.

"How big is it?" she asked, amazed.

"Size doesn't really apply here," Fleet said. "The Great Library is not constrained by walls, or even the barriers between the Realms. It reaches into any place where books are kept. You can get to any library in any Realm through these aisles, if you know how to look."

Poison found herself wishing that Bram or Peppercorn had chosen to come with her and see this, but they had been content to sleep in their chairs, exhausted, and so she had gone without them.

"Can I see one?" Poison asked. "How do you find your way around?"

Fleet laughed. "One question at a time. Finding your way around the library is part of the apprenticeship we all go through as Antiquarians. Let's just say it's not easy, so don't lose me, Poison. Now, you want to see a book? Let me get one for you."

She followed him into the shadowy corridors of the Great Library. Lanterns burned in sconces at intervals, but the place was too vast for them to overwhelm the darkness that lurked all around. Poison raised a quizzical eyebrow at the lanterns, but Fleet intercepted her thought.

"Don't worry. There are more magicks on this place than you can count. You could no more burn a book with that lantern flame than you could tear one with your hands."

Poison looked Fleet over as he walked. He was still the same old Fleet, with his floppy grey-white hair and large, solid nose and kindly eyes. Putting him in a scholarly robe had not changed him much. Except now he had told her he was an Antiquarian, some kind of collector of lives, and that meant he was something other than the Fleet she had known back home.

"Why didn't you tell me, Fleet?" she asked as they walked.

"Are you angry?" he replied.

"No," Poison said. She didn't feel particularly betrayed by his deceit. "No, I'd just like to know."

"I couldn't," he told her.

"That's what I thought," she said. "Because you were watching me?"

"Very quick, Poison," he said approvingly. "I was watching you. Among others. I did travel a lot, you know. But of all the folk I kept an eye on, I was watching you the closest."

Poison nodded, digesting this. "What made you choose me?"

"I have an instinct for that sort of thing," he said. "All who are called to the Antiquarians have it, to a lesser or greater extent. Time teaches you to spot the seeds of adventure in a person's heart, even when they are young."

"But if Aelthar had not sent the Scarecrow to steal Azalea —"

"You would still have gone eventually, Poison," Fleet interrupted. "Aelthar's intervention was just the trigger you needed. If it had not been that, it would have been something else. Although, perhaps not." He shrugged. "The nature of our work is inherently random. Often those who have the potential to be great choose not to fulfill it. Circumstance or fate decide otherwise. That is why we spread our nets, we choose our targets, we watch and wait. Heroes and villains are made on the turn of a sovereign, Poison. Sometimes we miss that moment, and we must work to retrieve it by deciphering stories, tales, and legends to filter out the facts. But sooner or later, all knowledge comes to us."

"Is there a book for me in here?" Poison asked.

"Of course," Fleet replied.

"Can I see it?"

Fleet smiled indulgently. "Not until it is done, Poison."

"Are you writing it?"

"No," Fleet said. "No, our purpose is merely to observe. Through us, the books write themselves."

Poison frowned. "I don't understand."

"See, then," Fleet said. He hauled down a massive tome with studded iron bindings. Taking it to a recess, he laid it down and turned up the lantern that hung overhead. There was a bench there on which he and Poison sat while they looked at the book that was laid on the table before them.

"Alambar Burl," Poison read aloud. It was embossed on the cover in fading gold. Fleet hefted the book open to a page in the middle. The writing was in perfect script, written in ink without a blemish or smudge.

Fleet leaned over it and read.

"But though men and women fell to the left and right of him, Alambar would not retreat from the battlements, and it seemed as though he was charmed. The phaerie arrows cut the air all around, but none found their mark in his breast. With his sword raised high, he called to rally, and the people of Jemar heard his cry and took heart, and they swarmed to the battlements with new strength. Then were the phaeries dismayed, for the defenders did cut them back, and the earth at the base of Jemar's walls was darkened with phaerie blood."

Poison had already read on several paragraphs by the time Fleet had finished. "So who was Alambar Burl?" she asked.

"He was a hero of the latter days of the Many-Sided War," Fleet explained. "After our people had split themselves apart and fought to exhaustion, the phaeries came. It was a different Phaerie Lord back then, but they have not changed much in the intervening years. The struggle was a terrible one, but the phaeries eventually drove us from the plains and into the high and low places, the mountains and mines and swamps. Alambar was a great fighter and a legend of those times."

"How did he die?" Poison asked, turning the pages in great

sheaves until she reached the last one. She skimmed the final paragraphs.

> *At that, Alambar took Sisella's hand, looked into her eyes, and spoke gravely. "I swear to you, we will not be long skulking in the shadows. Adversity will make us stronger. We will unite, and united we cannot fail; by the strength in our blood we will take back our Realm."*
>
> *Then Sisella knew that her husband spoke true, and together they walked back into the mountain settlement, where the skeletons of the first buildings stood against the setting sun.*

Poison looked confused. "I thought these were biographies. How can you finish a biography if they're not dead?"

"You always did have a morbid streak, Poison." Fleet grinned. "A biography doesn't have to end with someone dying; that's an obituary. No, Alambar lived till a ripe old age, and Sisella with him. His death is recorded elsewhere. You see, this is his *story*. Though he lived on after it was finished, this tale was done. It began with a boy enlisting to fight in the Many-Sided War and saw him become a man and a hero, but it ended with the defeat of the human armies by the phaerie and their retreat. Before this tale, and after it, there is little of interest in his life. We are storytellers, Poison, working for the Hierophant, who is the master storyteller. Storytellers do not include details unless they are necessary. We leave the boring work to the historians."

"I think I see," Poison replied. "Then a person has only one tale?"

"No, some have two or three separate ones or more," Fleet said. "Some people have many tales. Sometimes they are linked into one big tale, sometimes they are utterly distinct. Most people do not have one at all. Though the Antiquarians are many, we cannot cover every life. So we take only those lives that are most important to the world. What we see and learn, the books know. It is part of the Hierophant's magick. And they then write themselves."

"So my tale has begun?" Poison asked, brushing her black hair behind her ear.

"Yes."

"So why can't I see it?"

"Because all the pages are blank."

Poison made a noise of incomprehension.

"You can't tell half a tale, Poison. You can't write half a book. Whatever you choose to do next will completely change the aspect of what has gone before. If you decided to suddenly kill your friends as they slept —"

"Why would I do that?" Poison interjected.

"Bear with me," Fleet said patiently. "If you *did*, then the tale would take on a whole new light. Instead of being the journey of Poison from Gull to save her sister, it would be the terrible story of how a young girl became a cold-blooded killer. The way it would be written would be different. Do you see? Or you might die right now, and it would turn out that it wasn't *your* tale all along, it was Bram's or Peppercorn's, and you were just one of the sideline characters. The whole story has to be known before it can be recorded; otherwise it might suddenly change. That's the beauty, Poison. You never know what's going to happen next. When the tale is ended, then the writing will be visible to your eyes; until then, it is unwritten."

Poison pinched the bridge of her nose. This was too much to understand. "When did my tale begin, then?" she asked.

"When you left Gull, I should think," Fleet replied. "Well, probably a little before. The story of how you got your name is quite an interesting one. And we needed to know about your family so we could learn about Azalea, and how she was taken."

"This is wrong," Poison said, feeling bewildered and weary.

"This is my *life*, Fleet. This is my sister being stolen, and . . . and the tears I've cried over her . . . and the times I've been scared to death and nearly eaten alive . . . and all of that is just a *story?*"

"Everything's a story," Fleet replied. "I told you that before. It just depends on your point of view."

AN AUDIENCE WITH MELCHERON

ᕤᕙᕤ

"**W**E demand to see the Hierophant!" Aelthar's voice rang out across the hall.

"The Hierophant will see none of you until his work is done," boomed the gargoyle.

Poison's knuckles gripped the stone parapet of the balcony as she looked over the scene being played out below her. The sight of the flame-haired Phaerie Lord and his secretary filled her with rage and disgust, for in them she saw the creatures who had stolen her baby sister, and who had later double-crossed her so as not to give the child back. What purpose had they for taking her in the first place? Poison did not even know that much. Where was Azalea? What had she been suffering since she had been taken into the Realm of Phaerie by the Scarecrow? Was she even still alive?

Poison bit down on that thought. She would not be discouraged. There would be ways. She was far from beaten yet.

The hall was one of many in the Hierophant's castle, a vast, high-ceilinged chamber of black stone with mighty pillars supporting a broad balcony upon which Poison stood with Fleet and a few other observers. On the floor of the hall, where fine rugs were laid and where time-dimmed pennants hung against the walls, were those Lords and Ladies of the Realms who had chosen to attend. Poison studied them closely.

Foremost was Aelthar and his retinue. He was arguing with an enormous, stone-skinned gargoyle that crouched on a broad set of steps, guarding the double doors at the top. Poison took a moment to adjust her perspective. Aelthar was about seven feet, so the gargoyle was easily ten — fifteen when it flexed the bat wings that grew from its shoulders. Its fanged face was set in a snarl, and its eyes glowed like coals.

"He cannot deny us!" Aelthar cried, losing control in his fury. "The masters and mistresses of the Realms are all here assembled. We insist upon an audience."

"You may insist," the gargoyle rumbled, "but the Lord Melcheron will not see you. He is writing, and will not be disturbed."

"We know he's *writing*!" Aelthar snapped. "That's why we're here! Now let us pass!"

"In the Realm of the Hierophant, as in your Realms, his word is law. You may not pass."

Poison let her eyes range over the others assembled in the room. She had already enquired of Fleet their names, though she had forgotten some. One she remembered particularly well was Grugaroth, the Ur-Lord, the Troll King.

He was the only one in the room that was an equal in size to the gargoyle, even stooped as he was. He had short, thick legs, massive forearms, and an enormous lower jaw from which two tusks protruded, one of them broken. Fleet had informed Poison that he had broken it in a cataclysmic three-day battle with his predecessor, Mgwar, from whom he took the mantle of power. His skin was thick and brown and leathery, plated with natural armour and tufted with thick clumps of hair. He was dressed in besmirched brown and scarlet, and carried an improbably huge hammer across his back. Bloodshot eyes burned red in his soot-smeared face. He was a mountainous creature, dark and dirty from the deep mines and belching fire pits from which he came. But most important to Poison, he was an enemy of Aelthar.

"Fleet?" she asked.

"Hmm?"

"Who or what is Myghognimar?"

She remembered the name for its sheer unpronounce-ability; Aelthar had mentioned it when they had eavesdropped on his conversation with Scriddle.

"It's the sword that Aelthar carries," Fleet replied. "It was forged by a legendary dwarrow master in the mines of Grugaroth's kingdom: the finest blade in creation, so they say. Many centuries ago, the phaeries and the ur-people made war on each other, and Aelthar — who was a great general at the time — was responsible for defeating and slaying Grugaroth's half brother Nuiglan at the Battle of Karss Forge. He took Myghognimar as the spoils of his victory. The phaeries were eventually driven out, but Grugaroth never forgot. He hates Aelthar, and every sight of that blade reminds him of the vengeance he owes the Phaerie Lord."

Poison watched the Troll King with interest. After a time, she glanced over the other Lords and Ladies of the room. They came in all sizes and aspects, a dozen or so, each with their ret-inues eyeing each other warily. There was the Daemon Lord, his skin a sulphurous black. There was the manifestation of Eternity, a sparkling, blank-faced humanoid who, it was said, was responsible for regulating the natural laws of the worlds — to make sure up was up, down was down, time flowed, and so forth. She spotted the Umbilicus, the mouthpiece of the Spirit Lord, who could not take on physical form but who spoke through this corpselike entity, hanging in mid-air as if suspended on invisible meat hooks, surrounded by an unearthly green glow. The Gomm, whom Aelthar had referred to when they were eavesdropping, was not present. But there was one other that she was looking for, one she hoped would not be here. . . .

She felt a tickling on the back of her hand, where it gripped the balcony. Looking down, she saw with a thrill of horror that a large beige spider was crawling across her knuckles, unhurriedly walking over her skin. With a spasmodic twitch of disgust, she sent it flying from her hand and over the balcony.

"What is it, Poison?" Fleet asked, having noted her violent movement.

"A spider," she said, looking around. Just a little too much of a coincidence that a spider should appear at the very same moment she was thinking about . . .

Ah. There she was.

Asinastra was at the end of the balcony, her face and her dreadful gaze covered by a moth-eaten white veil, hunched amid the straggle of her own filthy hair. Even though Poison could not see those black, paralysing eyes, she knew that Asinastra was looking malevolently at her.

Poison felt herself go cold inside, but she refused to show it. She met Asinastra's veiled stare levelly. The Spider Lady had not forgotten who had stolen her dagger.

"She can't hurt you," said Fleet at her shoulder. "Not here. The Hierophant's protection extends to everyone within his Realm."

Poison did not break the stare. "I hope you're right," she replied quietly.

As she watched, Asinastra slipped away, disappearing through a doorway. She felt a palpable relief that the creature had left, but it was soured by a terrible foreboding. Asinastra was here, and she would be coming to visit Poison sooner or later. Only the Hierophant's protection provided any shield for her; it seemed a thin shield indeed, the width of a word.

"Why are they all here?" she asked Fleet suddenly, indicating the Lords and Ladies below.

Fleet stirred and cleared his throat. "The Hierophant has begun to write," he said. "Sometimes a Hierophant takes personal charge of writing a tale. That tale is invariably important in some way — more important than most."

"But they're scared of him. Why?"

"The Hierophant's stories are not just stories," Fleet replied. "They change things. You see, the Antiquarians are recorders; what we know goes into the books in the Great Library, which write themselves. We can only observe. But the Hierophant is a *creator*. What is written in the Hierophant's handwriting becomes truth, becomes law. You already know of Amrae's Law. When he wrote that down, all Lords and Ladies were bound by it. Not just by choice, but *bound*. They *cannot* refuse a human their single audience; they *cannot* harm you while it is in progress. It is impossible for them to break that edict. Amrae wrote that law to give humans a fairer footing in the other Realms, so that their voices could at least be heard. The whole of the Realms waits now to see what new laws might come from the tale that the Hierophant is writing. And they tremble in fear."

"What will he do?" Poison asked.

"Who can say?" Fleet answered with a shrug. "What would you do?"

"I'd write a great leader for humanity," she said, without hesitation. "Like Alambar Burl, but better. One who would unite us and lead us in driving the phaerie out of our Realm, so that no more babies would be taken, no more lives lost to the cruel places that we are forced to live in. I'd create him or her, and give this leader to our people, so that we can claim back what is ours."

"An admirable notion," said Fleet approvingly. "Something like that is exactly what Aelthar fears. But there is no way of knowing. The tale cannot be read until it is finished; like the books in the Great Library, it will not be visible until the last line is written. Only the Hierophant knows what it is that he is creating."

At that moment, Aelthar turned away from the gargoyle in a fury, and he chanced to look up to the balcony. His eyes met with Poison's and his brow clouded like thunder. She felt a terrible chill in her heart as she met that gaze, but she forced herself to return it with sullen violet intensity. Scriddle followed his master's eyes to Poison, and then blanched as Aelthar turned his stare upon his secretary. Poison guessed that Scriddle had not told the Phaerie Lord that the humans had escaped him. Aelthar stalked away, with Scriddle and the other phaeries following him. Grugaroth sneered as Aelthar passed by, and the dwarrows, ogres, and trolls that surrounded the Troll King growled at the phaeries, who ignored them disdainfully.

Poison found that she was sweating. It had been unwise to come here; better that Aelthar did not know where she was, since he wanted her dead. Between him and Asinastra, she had some powerful enemies here.

"Don't be afraid, Poison," Fleet reminded her, guessing her thoughts. "All guests are under the protection of the Hierophant while in this castle. None dare harm you here."

"I know. You said before," Poison replied, unconvinced. She watched as the Lords and Ladies dispersed slowly from the hall, their faces — those that had any — disappointed and angry.

"Come on," said Fleet suddenly. "Would you like to meet the Hierophant?"

Poison blinked in surprise. "But I thought . . ."

"He won't see any of *them*," Fleet said, with a twinkle. "But I'm sure he won't mind a little intrusion on our part."

Poison was glad of any excuse to leave. "Why not, then?"

~~~

They entered the Hierophant's chamber quietly. Fleet put a finger to his lips to hush her as they slipped through a small side door, and she crept into the room behind him. There had been a guardian outside — much like the gargoyle that defended the more ostentatious double doors that Aelthar had been trying to gain access to — but this one had ignored them completely.

"They are trained to allow through certain people," Fleet explained in a whisper. "I am one of them — and since you are with me, then so are you."

The chamber was large and predictably lined with books. A plush four-poster bed rested in one corner. One wall was taken up by an enormous round window, with a patterned frame of concentric circles, against which the rain lashed. Every so often, lightning flickered and thunder boomed, but Poison was so used to the storm by now that she barely noticed. It had not abated one bit since she had arrived here.

The Hierophant was sitting at a vast and ornate writing desk, his quill wagging as he wrote in a massive leather-bound volume. He seemed unbelievably old, thin and wrinkled with a long white beard that trailed down over his lap. His bald head was marked with liver spots, nicks, and bumps. A thick robe of green velvet was draped across his shoulders, burying his shrunken frame in its folds.

For a long while, Poison watched him. The only sound apart from the storm was the scratching of the quill nib. The Hierophant was staring hard through his round-lensed glasses at the paper, and writing with furious vigour. Eventually, he stopped with a sigh and glanced up at them. Though they had not made a sound, he had known they were there all along.

"Ah, Poison!" he said in a thin, dry voice. "How good to look upon you with my own eyes. My name is Melcheron, the Hierophant."

Poison glanced uncertainly at Fleet. "It's my honour to meet you," she replied. "I didn't know I was expected."

"Everyone's expected," the old man said, tapping the side of his forehead with one wrinkled finger. "I knew you'd come. I brought you here."

"How did you bring me here?" Poison said, unable to keep the scepticism out of her voice.

Melcheron did not answer her question; instead, he beckoned her. "Come closer. Let me see you. Fleet, could you give us a moment alone?"

Fleet bowed. "I'll be outside," he said, and departed.

Poison approached the Hierophant with some measure of wariness. She did not like his faintly disconcerting manner, nor the impression she got that he knew more than he was saying. As she got close, she glanced at the book he was writing in. As Fleet had said, there appeared to be nothing there; but the inkpot on the desk was filled with something that looked like particularly viscous water, which she assumed he had been writing with.

He squinted at her with eyes that seemed to have yellowed with age, like parchment.

"Yes, yes, I see I was right. You know, don't you?"

"Know what?" Poison said automatically, before cursing herself for saying the most obvious thing.

As she had guessed, the Hierophant's answer was evasive. "You know, even if you won't admit it to yourself. You're trying to second-guess me, aren't you? Ha! Good! Good!"

"Do you remember Myrrk?" Poison asked him suddenly.

He cackled with glee. "Good! Good! Change the subject; go on the offensive! Oh, you'll be a gem, my little Poison." He took off his glasses and wiped a tear from his eye with one bony knuckle. "Myrrk, you say? Yes, I remember him. A sad sort."

"He remembers you," Poison said. "He says you didn't bother to work out all the details, like what he eats since he can't get fish. Do you know what that means?"

"Assuredly!" Melcheron said. "I do it all the time! I can't account for every single thing in the world, Poison! I'd go mad!"

Poison's expression indicated that she thought he was halfway there already.

"Still," he continued, growing suddenly sombre, "Myrrk's not the only one who complained about it. It's been happening more and more, you know. People are *noticing*. Do you think I'm slipping, Poison? My memory's not what it used to be. Do you think they see the holes?"

"What holes?" Poison asked, feeling a growing frustration inside her.

"The holes!" Melcheron said. "The plot holes!"

Poison could take no more.

"*Tell me what you mean!*" she cried, losing her temper. "Everyone I have met since I set foot outside my hometown has been incapable of giving me a straight answer! What does it mean? Why do I keep coming across parts of the world that seem taken straight out of a phaerie tale? Why did Myrrk seem to think that you were responsible for him not having anything to eat? *Who are you?*"

Melcheron did not seem in the least shocked by her tirade.

"You already know, Poison," Melcheron said slowly. "You don't need me to explain it."

Poison felt something sink into a cold, dark abyss inside her.

She *did* know. She had had a growing suspicion since the start, a nameless idea that fed on every experience, every sight, every sound. But it was an idea too terrible to contemplate, too awful even to dare think.

"You know," he croaked. "Though you will not admit it to yourself."

"I need to know for *sure*," she said. "I need to hear you say it."

"Wouldn't you rather live with the uncertainty? In time, you can forget. You can persuade yourself that you were only being foolish. You can be like the others, the ones who never question, like Aelthar and Peppercorn and Bram, even like Fleet. He doesn't know. None of them know but you, and me, and a few others like Myrrk. And look what became of him."

The words were a temptation that was almost greater than Poison could bear. She wanted to shut her eyes and clap her hands to her ears and run away from this. She wanted the bliss of ignorance. But that was not her way, and never would be.

"*Say it*," she hissed.

Melcheron sighed and bowed his head gravely.

"All of it: the Realms, the Lords and Ladies, your parents, even you, Poison. All of it is fantasy. All a creation. You, Bram, Fleet, Peppercorn, Aelthar — you dance to my tune, whether you will it or not. My words shape your destiny. I am the author of you, of everything you have been and are. You are merely my character, albeit an important one. But a character nonetheless, a fiction. *My* fiction."

He raised his head and looked her in the eye.

"All you know is a story, Poison. And I am the storyteller."

The void in the pit of her stomach yawned dizzyingly, threatening to swallow her. She felt the strength flee her limbs, and she had to hold onto the edge of the Hierophant's desk to stop herself from falling.

"I . . . I don't understand," she stammered.

"I am telling a tale, Poison, and you are part of it," he repeated patiently. "Hard to grasp, I know. Myrrk had the same trouble. He was part of another tale I wrote, a long time ago. A minor cog, a plot device to speed along the heroes, but he really became quite impossible once he learned what the role was. I shouldn't have made him quite so bright. . . ."

"You're lying," Poison breathed. "You can't . . . you don't control the world."

The Hierophant cackled gleefully. "Of course I don't. But I control *your* world, Poison. The Realms were created many aeons ago, in a time lost to history, by the original Hierophant. Since then, there have been uncountable successors, each one telling his stories, each adding stitches to the tapestry. But a character will take on a life of its own, as any storyteller knows. The tale that Myrrk was part of finished a century ago, yet he lives on somewhere. You see, the world around you is merely an accretion of stories, built over endless time; it evolves of its own accord. But now and then it becomes necessary to manipulate that world." He tapped a forefinger to the side of his wrinkled head. "And that, as they say, is where I come in."

"This is idiot philosophy," Poison protested desperately. "You insane old man!"

"You know it in your heart, Poison. You've felt it. You never existed before I brought you into being. The Black Marshes never existed, nor your family, nor the wraith-catchers. They were all my latest additions to the world. I created you for the purpose of my tale. Of course, Aelthar has been around for a long time; I didn't need to make *him* up. But he is as powerless to resist the force of my tale as anyone else, and just as ignorant."

"Why are you doing this?" Poison whispered, her shoulders sagging.

"Doing what?" the Hierophant asked innocently.

"Why are you telling me this? Why torture me so?"

The Hierophant studied her with rheumy eyes. "Because you asked me," he said. "It's in your nature. I wrote you that way."

MALAISE

SHE could not even cry anymore. There didn't seem any point.

Poison lay in Fleet's bed, curled up in a fetal position with the blankets wrapped tight around her. She had been there for days now. Where Fleet slept, or even *if* he slept, she did not know or care.

At first, there were tears, constant and unending. She felt as if her heart had been ripped out with a hook, and the hole that was left kept filling with sorrow and hurt and raw *betrayal*, so much that she had to weep it out or she would drown. Fleet was as bewildered as he was distressed by her condition. She would not speak to him about it. He would not understand. He was just a fantasy, like she was.

He doesn't want to know. Nobody wants to know. I wish I didn't know.

But what was learned could not be unlearned.

Fleet had put her to bed. She remembered Bram and Peppercorn swarming around her; it must have been quite a shock to see their indomitable friend reduced to such a state. She could not muster the effort to answer their questions.

What did they care? They were falsehoods, just like she was. They were not real. *Nothing* was real.

And with that thought, Poison simply gave up.

It was easy. Those few words from the Hierophant had sucked all of the fight out of her, and now the most natural thing in the world was to go limp and stop struggling. The possibility that he was lying did not even enter her head. She knew, on an instinctive level, that he had been telling the truth. She knew the truth even *before* he had told her. Her subconscious had pieced the puzzle together long ago.

None of it was real. None of it. She was living in a phaerie tale, and she was just a puppet of the story, like they all were. All the choices she had made, all the effort and heartache she had suffered, all were just an illusion of free will. None of it had been *her*. She had simply been following the story.

Had anything she had *ever* done truly been her choice, or had she merely been given the appearance of independence?

It was too much for her. The ground had been pulled out from beneath her feet, and her entire world had toppled into the abyss that was left. Everything had become worthless. Nothing had a point. What use was anything if she was dancing to someone else's tune? How could she ever make another decision without questioning whether she was simply doing the will of the author, that she only *thought* she was choosing for herself?

Truly, why bother?

So she stayed in bed. Most of the time, Andersen slept in the hollow of her stomach. Bram and Peppercorn and Fleet sat by her in shifts, talking to her all the time, asking her what was wrong, what had happened to her, why was she like this? She never replied. Bram seemed to have convinced himself that

Poison had discovered Azalea was dead, and that the grief had broken her heart. Poison felt like laughing. Azalea's death would be nothing compared to this. Why should she even care about Azalea now? She was just a fiction, like Poison was, acting out her little play.

But she *did* care. That was the crux of the pain. Even though she knew what she knew, her life — such as it was — continued on. She still felt the trails of the tears against her cheeks. She still felt the warm heat of Andersen napping on top of the blankets. She still felt the loss of Azalea, and she still felt that giving up on her sister would be a terrible betrayal. No matter how much her head told her that she was living in a fantasy, she could not convince her soul or her senses. Yet, painful though it was, it was not enough to give her the strength to move.

Days passed, though they could have been hours, or weeks, for who knew how time twisted in foreign Realms? Fleet read to her from the old books that she used to read as a child, not realizing the irony of telling her phaerie stories when they were living in one. Did the characters in his books also possess a life like hers? Did they also believe they were alive? And what about the Hierophant, the author of *her* world? Was he merely a creation of someone else, unaware? Wouldn't that be a fine joke! Like two mirrors placed opposite each other, endlessly reflecting, worlds within worlds with no beginning or end.

Just to think about it bent her mind like a sapling on the verge of snapping.

Fleet gave her tidbits of information now and then, hoping to spur her interest in the goings-on in the castle. Some of the Lords and Ladies were drifting away now, either angry or resigned, having realized that they would not get to see the Hierophant after all. Grugaroth had departed with his retinue of ur-people. Aelthar, however, was unbowed, and he had resorted to terrible threats now in his demands for an audience.

Poison barely listened. She had not eaten since she took to bed and had barely drunk a thing. She was pale, her sweat smelled unhealthy, and her long black hair had gone limp and straggled across her face. She began to mutter in her sleep. Her friends — how hollow the word seemed now! — tried to convince her to eat something, anything; but the desire to eat had gone, and even the hunger was only a dull, distant ache inside her.

So wrapped up was she in misery that she did not notice what was happening around her until it was too pronounced to miss.

It was while Fleet was reading to her that she spoke the first conscious words she had said since she had gone to bed.

"Fleet," she croaked. He looked up instantly, his eyes shining with hope. "Fleet, you're sick."

He *was* sick. She saw it now. His cheeks were sunken; his flesh was wasting off his bones. She could see the sockets of his eyes. It was as if *he* were the one starving, not her. And yet . . . it was more than simple lack of food. There was something else about his condition, something beyond illness or physical need, but she was too dazed by hunger to understand it.

"We're all sick, Poison," Fleet said.

"Peppercorn and Bram, too?" She felt a faint stab of concern. "Andersen?"

"*Everyone*," Fleet replied. "The servants, the Antiquarians, even the Lords and Ladies. Even Aelthar has succumbed."

"What is it?" she whispered. "What's happening?"

"I don't know," Fleet said. "It's like the castle is full of ghosts. Everyone's listless, everyone's . . . tired. The doctors can't find a cause. They talk of plague and disease, but it's none of those things. . . . It's in the walls, too. . . . Even the castle itself seems weaker now, paler . . . less solid than it once was." He sighed. "It's like it's all just fading away."

"But . . ." Poison began. "How . . . ?"

"I don't know . . . I don't know . . ." he whispered. He seemed so weak then, an impostor, not the tough, wiry Fleet she had always known. He raised his head and fixed her with a weary eye. "Poison, I've heard you talking when you sleep. It doesn't make sense. . . . I . . . I can't understand it . . . but you have to stop whatever you're doing."

"Me?" Poison was shocked enough to be indignant. "I'm not doing anything. Literally." She surprised herself that she still had the ability to make a joke, however feeble.

"You're . . . you talk about stories, Poison. What did the Hierophant say to you? What did he do?"

But Poison was remembering the words that Myrrk had spoken to her, back in his hut by the lake. How the world had gone wrong because he gave up his role and tried to make a different life for himself. *I had a story myself, once, but I didn't like it and I tried to change it. I'd advise against that.* He had refused to tell her what he meant, saying that it was not the right time; now, in a moment of sudden clarity, she knew.

"It's me," she said through parched lips. "It's me. I *am* doing this."

"What are you doing, Poison? Why?" Fleet's tone of hurt was like a lead block on her soul.

"I stopped cooperating," she replied.

"With who?" Fleet asked.

She levered herself up a little on her pillows. "You can't see it, Fleet. You can't see it because you don't want to. But this is a phaerie tale; that's all it is. Conjured by the Hierophant. I won't be a part of his game, like some chess piece for him to move. If I can't decide for myself, I won't play at all. If I can't have free will" — she dropped her gaze — "I'd rather die."

She could see Fleet glazing over as she spoke, but he was struggling to comprehend. She had presented him with an entirely impossible concept, one that was beyond his ability to grasp.

"I don't understand," he said. "I don't. I don't know how this is linked with this . . . malaise that has fallen on all of us, but I know it's to do with you, Poison. What is so terrible that you have lost all will to live? Don't you see that you're taking us all with you?"

Poison would have shed a tear then, if she had any left. "You're fictions, all of you. Just like me."

"How can you think that?" Fleet cried, suddenly spurred to animation. "We feel, we love, we cry, we bleed, we sacrifice. . . . If that is not life, then what is? What's your definition, Poison? How can you think that the Hierophant is controlling you somehow? Don't you make your own choices? Didn't you choose to come on this quest?"

"Did I? I don't know," she said, sinking back to the pillows. "If ever I needed proof that my choices are illusions, you have just given it to me. Look what happens when I refuse to do as he wants. The story is fading around me. Why can't I choose to give up?"

To that, Fleet had no answer. Poison turned over in bed, facing away from him, and eventually she heard him leave.

❦

They came to her often, now that she had begun to speak again. They saw it as a good sign, but it really wasn't. She merely wanted to tell them she was sorry for what was happening. Though they did not understand as Fleet had not, they pleaded with her to eat, to regain her strength. They were dying, fading, becoming nothing as the story unravelled around her. But how could she ever pull herself back from the pit into which she had sunk? How could she live on in the knowledge that she was reading off someone else's script? She endured Peppercorn's tears and Bram's silence, not knowing which was worse. But she would not flex. She would fade, and they with her, and so it would go. It was the one choice she had made for herself, and if she could only thwart the Hierophant by her death, then that was what it would have to take. It was his fault for making her such a contrary character. The harder she was pushed, the harder she pushed back.

❦

She lapsed in and out of consciousness, weakness periodically swallowing her and spitting her out. Day and night meant nothing to her. Time had fractured into brief windows of lucidity. She was starving and dehydrated. Sometimes she woke with moist lips, where one of her caregivers had dribbled honey or milk into her mouth as she slept, relying on the swallowing reflex to ensure she took it down. But it was not enough to stop the decline. She was dying, and she knew it . . . but at least it was her decision.

One night, she woke in near-darkness, to see Bram sitting by her bedside. A single lantern burned on a table nearby, casting its glow across one side of his face. His eyes were shadowed by the brim of his omnipresent hat.

"Bram . . ." she croaked, somehow managing a smile.

He was silent for a long while, and though she could not see his expression, she sensed that it was grave.

"Bram, what is it?"

"I've been thinking," he said. "And you're going to listen to what I have to say."

He tilted his head up and the lantern light fell across his face, and Poison gasped. She could almost see his skull through his skin. His moustache was thinning and limp. His bull neck had withered and hung loose with flesh. His eyes were spidercracked with blood.

"Oh, Bram . . ." she moaned. The sight of him was like a spear through her chest.

"Save your sympathy," he replied, and his voice was harsh and brittle. "I've heard your apologies before. I'm not interested."

Poison was taken aback by this sudden change in his manner, and too weak to form a retort.

"You're a selfish girl," he growled. "Look at what you're doing. Take a good look at me. Have you seen Peppercorn? Fleet? Even that cursed cat? Have you seen what your principles are doing to us? You're killing us, you spoiled little brat, all because you won't stand up for yourself."

Poison quailed at the raw anger in his voice. She had not known Bram to be capable of such. For such a kind soul to be so turned . . .

"You're fictions . . ." she protested weakly.

"Yes, yes, I've heard that, too," he snarled. "Fictions. Ridiculous! I'm as alive as you, and you're as alive as the Hierophant. We're all *alive*, Poison. By any definition you have, we're alive. Even if you think we've been given life by someone else. We all have dreams and ambitions, we all have plans and wishes, and you're taking them all away from us." He stood up, making a gesture of disgust with one gloved hand. "Didn't you ever believe in a god, Poison?"

"When I was young . . ." she croaked.

"Then how is this different?"

"Because then I believed . . . I had control of my own destiny. . . ."

"But don't you see?" Bram cried. "You've proved your point! You *do* have control over your own destiny. You're choosing to die, choosing to kill us all with you. Nobody has stopped you; nobody *can* stop you except yourself. It doesn't matter what the consequences of your choice are, but you made it yourself."

Poison was frankly surprised that Bram had thought that up himself. "That's not . . . good enough," she said, wiping the lank strands of her hair away from her face. "If the only way to make the world right . . . is to do what he wants me to do . . . then it's no choice at all."

"You don't have the right to kill us all!" he cried.

"How do you know . . . you're even alive?" she countered.

"How does anyone? How does anyone know anything? There's never any true answers, Poison. Everything is uncertain. That's *life*. We can only deal with the world as we are presented with it. Don't you appreciate that? All I want from life is to get back home, to buy that house in the mountains, and to never have to think about phaeries and Hierophants ever again! You're robbing me of that dream, Poison! What gives you the right to decide whether all of us deserve to live?"

"Because . . ." she whispered. "Because you're all dying. Because you're all dying because I'm dying. What gives you the right to make *me* live? How can you make me responsible for the whole world?"

"You *are* responsible for the whole world!" Bram said, suddenly triumphant. "And do you know what that means?"

Poison frowned. "I don't . . ."

"It means this is *your story*, you fool!" he cried.

Poison was bewildered. She had thought Bram, like Fleet, had been unable to see the strings that manipulated him; and yet here he was, using her own logic to argue with her. It must have been a terrible stretch for a man as down-to-earth as he was to encompass the concepts that Poison was offering. Did he really believe what he was saying, or was he just using the architecture of her delusion to try and outwit her?

"It means you have power over it just like the Hierophant does!" Bram cried. "If I die, if Peppercorn dies . . . well, the world will go on as normal. But because you're dying, the whole tale collapses. Don't you see? You're the heroine! This is your story. Without you, it doesn't work." Bram's eyes were flashing now with manic enthusiasm. "So if this is your tale, then take control of it! Fight back! Do something!"

"Do what?" Poison said weakly. "How can ... how can I fight?"

"I don't know!" Bram said, stamping around the room. "You're the clever one. You've overcome everything that he's thrown at you so far. Fight back, and there's a chance, a chance you can do something about your situation. Are you willing to throw away your life — all our lives! — without being *certain*? Try! And if you fail, you can always give up again."

He was right. He was right. The fact that she could bring the Hierophant's world to the edge of ruin was proof that his tale was about *her*. All about her. So much so, that the entire story collapsed if she was not in it. There was power in that. There was influence. She felt a stirring of something long-forgotten inside her, something she had once known as hope. Perhaps she *could* do something. Perhaps she could turn it around.

Was she really alive? Was Bram? Didn't everyone feel at one time or another that they were the only one who was truly alive, and that everyone else was an actor in a play put on for their benefit? Was there ever any way of telling?

No. Bram was right. She could never be certain until she was dead, and maybe not even then.

Whatever the truth about the manner of life she was living, it wasn't worth dying for.

"Eat," Bram commanded, proffering a bowl of cold soup that had been lying by her bedside since Peppercorn's last attempt at feeding her. "Damn you, eat. Don't be so selfish. Get up and fight and stop feeling sorry for yourself."

Poison's eyes flickered feverishly over the bowl. To cave in now, when she was so close . . . was she sure that Bram's words made sense?

But the faint sliver of possibility that Bram had presented her with was all her natural willpower needed to reassert itself. Nursing the spark of that tiny hope, defiance roared into flame inside her. She would not resist the Hierophant with her death; she would resist him with her *life*. She would not thwart him, she would *beat* him at his own game. There would be a way. Somehow, there would be a way.

She took the bowl from Bram and spooned the cold soup into her mouth. Foul-tasting as it was, it seemed the most delicious nectar to her, for it brought her strength, and with strength she could fight.

Bram sat down with a long sigh of relief, watching her as she ate.

"You had me scared, Poison," he whispered. "You had me scared."

"Do you believe me?" she asked quietly, between mouthfuls. "About the story, the fantasy? About the fiction?"

Bram's moustache quirked in a grin. "Not a word of it," he said. "But I know that if you get better, this wasting sickness goes away. That's all I need to know."

~~~

Poison's recovery was quick, and within days she was out of bed and walking again. With the return of her strength, the malaise that had overtaken the Hierophant's castle seemed to recede like a bad dream. Colour came back to the cheeks of the castle's inhabitants and flesh to their bones. The walls seemed to become denser, until they were once again the indestructible stone they had always been, as mighty as the foundations of the mountains. Storms lashed the castle with renewed fury.

The most remarkable thing, aside from the rapid recovery of all concerned, was the amnesia that seemed to come with it. Nobody remembered the strange fading sickness; like a nightmare destroyed by the sunlight, it existed only in faint tatters of recollection. Whenever Poison mentioned it she was met by puzzlement, even from Bram, and told that she had not quite recovered from her own illness yet. As far as anyone was concerned, Poison had gone down with the flu and they had nursed her back to health; but if she pressed anyone for the specifics, they evaded the question.

She let the matter pass for now. Her thoughts were on other things. She was plotting how to overcome the creator of this place, how to outwit the one who was writing her life for her. She spent days in deep contemplation while in bed, and when she was up she paced the room, her brow furrowed and her eyes even more intense than usual.

She need not have troubled herself, as it happened. It was on the day that Fleet declared her fully fit and well that the Hierophant was murdered.

ASSASSINS

HE lay slumped over the great leather-bound tome that he had been writing in when Poison had seen him last, the quill still held lightly between his dead fingers. In fact, it might seem he had simply fallen asleep at his work, if it were not for the handle of Asinastra's dagger that protruded from between his shoulder blades. Poison could not draw her eyes away from that dagger — the dagger she had stolen from the Lady of Cobwebs, which was now buried up to the hilt in the Hierophant's back.

There was no blood. It was as if the fanged blade had simply drunk it out of him. On the blank pages of the book over which he lay, there was not a stain or a smear.

The storm crashed outside, drumming on the segmented circle of window glass that commanded the room. Poison looked around at the others who were assembled in his chamber. The gargoyles had stopped guarding the doors once it was clear that their master was dead, but four robed Antiquarians stood sentry over the corpse to ensure that nobody touched it. Most of the Lords and Ladies who had stayed while Aelthar demanded an audience were here assembled; the discovery of the body was only minutes old, and they had rushed to see the truth of it for themselves. Poison, Bram, Andersen, and Peppercorn had come in with Fleet, and nobody had challenged them. To Poison's relief, Asinastra was notably absent.

Poison was aware that Aelthar was there, too, glaring at her hatefully from beneath his flame-red fringe. She returned the glare. The dagger that she had brought him had found its way into the Hierophant's back. She had more than an inkling of who was responsible.

But more than that, for there was one thing that troubled her above all else. Having only lately recovered from the crushing weight of knowledge that the Hierophant had placed on her, she found this almost impossible to cope with.

The Hierophant had been murdered. The storyteller had been killed by one of his own characters.

So who was writing her story now?

But any time for contemplation that she might have had was taken from her, for then walked in a vision of ethereal beauty, wearing a dress of silver that shimmered like sunlight on water. She passed into the room with a grace and elegance that captivated the eye of everyone present, and they moved aside to let her through, until she stood at the side of the Hierophant's desk.

"It's her," Peppercorn whispered in awe.

"Who?" Bram asked automatically.

"We saw her," Poison said, her voice raw with suspicion. "At the Phaerie Lord's palace."

The phaerie lady's endless blue eyes looked over the body of the Hierophant, and she let loose a sigh of terrible lament, like the stirring of the wind through the yews of a graveyard.

"Her?" Fleet queried. "Are you sure?"

"It was her," Poison said. She was not an easy creature to forget. "Why, who is she?"

The assembly watched the phaerie lady as a single tear of purest crystal slid down the smooth, pale planes of her face.

"That's Pariasa, Mistress of the Aeriads," Fleet told them. "She's the Hierophant's wife."

"His wife?" Poison asked, turning to Fleet. "The Hierophant had a wife?"

Fleet nodded.

Poison thought for a moment, her face a picture of concentration. Everything seemed to fit. The dagger, the phaerie lady, Aelthar . . .

"We need to go," Poison said. "There may not be much time."

~⌒⌒⌒~

They rushed through the dour stone corridors of the Hierophant's castle, Poison in the lead, Andersen dodging between their feet. Bram huffed and puffed as he brought up the rear. Poison was looking around nervously as they went, shying away from the shadows and regarding every stranger with a wary eye.

"What is it, Poison? Where are we going?" Peppercorn asked, hurrying along behind her.

"We're getting out of here," she said. "We're in danger. All of us."

"Danger?" Bram panted. "Why?"

Poison pulled to a halt so that the older man could catch his breath. Fleet, despite having at least twenty years on Bram, was not even sweating.

"Listen," she said, glancing up and down the corridor. "The only people who know about that dagger are us," she said. "Everybody else — if they knew anything about it at all — would think it came from Asinastra. Don't you see? Whoever did that to the Hierophant wants us dead; we're the only people who can point the finger at anyone other than the Lady of Cobwebs."

"Then who did it?" Bram asked.

"Aelthar!" Poison, Peppercorn, and Fleet replied in unison.

Bram scratched the brim of his hat. "Seems unanimous, then," he replied, a little embarrassed at being the last one to figure it out.

"I'll explain later," Poison said. "Right now we've got to get to safety."

"But wait," Bram said, stalling for time so he could rest a little longer. "Why didn't you just tell everyone in the Hierophant's chamber just then? And I thought we were safe in this castle?"

Peppercorn gave a long-suffering tut. "We were under the Hierophant's protection," she explained. "That's not much good now that he's dead, is it?"

"And I can't accuse Aelthar yet," Poison added. "I need some sort of proof, or at least someone to back me up. There's nothing to stop him from just killing us right now." *Or Asinastra*, she added mentally, remembering their encounter on the balcony earlier.

"Proof . . ." Fleet muttered, then suddenly his eyes lit up. "The library."

"What's in the library?"

"Melcheron's tale! The Hierophant was an Antiquarian like us — the Head Antiquarian, really — so it will all be recorded up until the point of his death. If he saw who it was who killed him . . ."

"It'll be written in the book of his life!" Poison finished. "What he knows, the book knows! Perfect!"

"But I thought we were going somewhere *safe*," Peppercorn mewled.

"Afterwards," Poison promised. "But we have to do this first. If Aelthar thinks of it before we do . . ."

"Well, let's stop all this hanging around then," said Bram, as if it had not been him they were waiting for. "Come on!"

The Great Library was eerily empty.

The companions walked softly through the labyrinth of aisles, dwarfed by the shelves of books that stretched up several storeys above them. Darkness hovered at the edges of the lantern light, and the quiet seemed to suffocate sound. All of the Antiquarians were elsewhere, having heard about their master's death by now, and Poison was beginning to think that perhaps it had not been the best idea to come here. In this endless maze, anything could come upon them and they would have no hope of help.

They followed Fleet around corridors, between shelves, up stairs, and over narrow bridges. Whatever method he used to navigate the library was a mystery to Poison; even Andersen seemed content to trail meekly along behind instead of scouting ahead as he usually did. When finally he halted, it was in a small chamber where two sets of shelves leaned in close and a single lantern-lit desk sat unused against the wall. Poison found herself wondering how the lanterns stayed alight, then decided it was magick, then changed her mind and assumed it was merely some Hierophant's lack of attention to detail. It made her head hurt to think of such things — especially when there could be a perfectly rational explanation for the endlessly burning lanterns — but she could not help herself.

Bram was right, though, she thought as she watched Fleet searching the shelves for the book with Melcheron's name on it. *I would have let myself die, without a struggle, if he had not talked me out of it. But now the Hierophant is dead. Am I controlling my destiny now? Did he ever really have power over me at all?*

There was so much she was unsure of. How was it that the world went on without the Hierophant, the one who had created her — and yet when she was on the verge of death, it began to fall apart? Within this story, she was more important than the man who professed to write it; that much was evident. What if Melcheron had been wrong? What if there was some higher, unseen Hierophant, one who had created Melcheron as Melcheron had created Poison, an overseer of all the Realms to whom Poison was indispensable but Melcheron was not? She felt suddenly, terribly small and alone in the light of such an overwhelming concept.

"It's not here," Fleet said. He checked the shelves again, as if disbelieving his own eyes, then shook his head. "No. Gone."

Poison sagged. "Are you sure?" she asked, scrabbling for a straw to cling to.

"Sure as I can be," said Fleet. "They must have planned the theft in advance. They took the book, knowing it could be used against them."

"How can someone just *take a* book from here?" Poison cried. "I thought this place was guarded by magick."

"The books are indestructible," Fleet said. "They are not immovable. Most people can't take them out of the library but some of us can: Antiquarians, and a few other people Melcheron trusted. Had the Hierophant been alive, he would have known of the theft through his magick."

"So they took the book *after* Melcheron was murdered?" Bram said, catching on. "Someone close to Melcheron?"

"Exactly," said Poison.

"Are you even sure it's Aelthar?" Bram asked, stroking his moustache with a gloved knuckle. "I can't imagine Melcheron trusted him very far. And how did he get past those gargoyles and into Melcheron's room? They didn't let him through before."

"Because it wasn't *just* Aelthar," Poison said. "We should go."

Andersen hissed suddenly and the sound froze them all as efficiently as if someone had said: *Listen!*

They listened. The silence of the library weighed upon them. Poison looked down the long aisles of books, to where they tapered into darkness. Something had jarred in her memory a moment ago, something that had been too faint for her to hear. But the cat had heard it.

Something . . .

Distantly, almost too quiet to hear, came the chime of a small silver bell.

Poison felt her heart lurch and the blood drain from her face. Andersen began to make a strange crooning noise of menace in the back of his throat.

It came again, a clear ring, echoing through the library. Louder this time.

"It's here," Poison breathed, remembering . . .

. . . *reaching through the page . . . the touch of a fingernail on her wrist . . .*

She felt her head go light with terror. "The Scarecrow's here."

"The what?" Peppercorn quailed.

"Aelthar's sent it after us," Poison said, grabbing her hand. "Run!"

They did not need any further prompting. They fled through the aisles, away from the sound, racing out of the small chamber and over a narrow, arched stone bridge that vaulted a chasm of books. They plunged back into the confines of the shelves again on the other side. It was only moments before they came to a starfish-shaped five-way junction. Poison made for a random direction, but Fleet grabbed her arm and pulled her back.

"Don't be so headstrong, Poison. If you get lost in this place, you'll die in here."

"You guide us, then," she snapped.

"Where are we going?" he returned.

"You said this place can get into any library in any Realm." She did not even wait for Fleet to nod. "Take us to Grugaroth."

"The Realm of Trolls? Why?"

The bell sounded again, a pure tone that seemed to ring inside their skulls.

"Just do it!" Poison cried.

Fleet threw up his hands, resigning himself. "That way," he said, pointing.

"*Thank* you," Poison said irritably, and they were off again, Fleet in the lead.

"I don't want to meet trolls!" Peppercorn wailed, her dress tangling around her feet as she ran.

"You want to meet the Scarecrow even less," Poison assured her. Glancing back at Peppercorn's miserable expression, she felt compelled to say something else to take the harsh edges off her comment. "Listen," she said between breaths, as they clattered down a set of steps. "We can't go home. Aelthar will find us. And I can't give up till I've got my sister back. The only safe place is another Lord's Realm."

"But why *him*?"

Poison rolled her eyes heavenward. "Because he hates Aelthar. And so do we. That's one thing we've got in common."

"I don't hate anyone!" Peppercorn protested.

"No," Poison murmured, with something like envy in her tone. "No, you probably don't."

They raced through a dizzying series of corners, then down another set of stairs to what Poison thought of as the ground floor of the library. They were pursued by the chime of the Scarecrow's bell, getting steadily closer and closer, seemingly unobstructed by the shelves and unhindered by Fleet's attempts to shake it off. Poison felt panic rising within her, but she kept it off her face. She was running hand in hand with Peppercorn, and she could almost feel the fear emanating from the blonde girl, passing through their palms. Bram was thumping along behind, having picked up Andersen to prevent him from tripping them — he had a potentially fatal habit of winding between their legs.

They came out from the narrow alleys of books into a wider, shelved corridor. Fleet pulled to a halt suddenly, looking one way and then the other. The endless volumes stretched away in either direction, disappearing into the gloom. A lantern sat on a table nearby, casting strange shadows sideways across their features.

"What have you stopped for?" Poison demanded.

"I'm thinking, curse you!" Fleet snapped back, surprising her. He was obviously on edge. Like Bram, the fact that he almost never got angry made it all the more effective when he did. "Do you think it's easy to remember my way through a place this size?"

"I thought you were an Antiquarian!" Poison cried. "I thought this was your *calling!*"

"Shut up, Poison," Bram growled. "You're not helping."

Poison was shocked into silence. She subsided, still furious. Fleet glared at her for a moment and then returned to his attempts at remembering the next stage of her route. Poison became suddenly, acutely aware that the bell had gone silent.

A moment later she saw the sparkling flakes come drifting down like snow to settle on them. It took an instant for alarm to register, and then she looked up.

The Scarecrow was above them, standing on a bridge that spanned the corridor, its eyes two yellow slits in the shadow of its hat. It was scattering the flakes into the air, a cloud of the stuff that fell lazily towards them.

"Poison, I feel sleepy . . ." Peppercorn said from behind her. Poison felt Peppercorn's grip slacken in hers.

"*Get it off you!*" she shrieked, beating at her clothes and hair. She could feel the lethargy settling on her already, the tiredness seeping into her bones. She made an attempt to wipe the flakes from Peppercorn, but she could not spare more than a few pats, and it was too late anyway. Peppercorn slipped to the floor with a sigh and fell asleep amidst the thin dusting that had coated the floor. The others had seen the danger now and were copying Poison — but they were already well coated in the stuff, and it was a losing battle. Bram had dropped Andersen, who barely managed to land on his feet before slumping down, asleep; Fleet had sunk to his knees. Bram was battering at himself, great drifts of flakes sloughing off the brim of his hat; he was fighting to keep his eyes open. And still the flakes kept falling.

Poison felt the warm wash of sleep caressing her. She saw Fleet gently lay himself down and sink into oblivion, and thought how wonderful it would be to surrender herself to that. Her hands felt heavy now, pawing halfheartedly at her clothes to rid herself of the stuff. Already she was half-asleep, drowsing, unable to fight the magick of the phaerie substance. She heard a groan and a thump behind her as Bram succumbed, and then there was only her. Her and the Scarecrow.

She did not know how it had gotten from the bridge to the ground floor. Whether it had jumped or flown or moved by some altogether more mystical means, she had not noticed. She was drifting in and out of consciousness, swaying on her feet, and the thing was coming closer now, as if in a nightmare. Thin, wrinkled hands poked from the sleeves of its long, ragged coat; its slit eyes glowed beneath the huge brim of its hat, wider even than Bram's. In one hand, it held the tiny bell, twitching it now and again. The chime was hypnotic, lulling

Poison towards the folds of sleep. She swayed on her feet now, unable to even muster the strength to wipe away the flakes that had settled on her. If she slept, she died ... and yet even knowing that, she could not stop the tide of unconsciousness.

The Scarecrow rang its bell again.

She stumbled towards the nearby table, coming down hard on it with both hands, propping herself against it as the muscles of her legs betrayed her. The lantern was a soothing glow, inviting her to sleep in its soporific light.

"No ..." she said through gritted teeth, and she summoned up a picture of Azalea in her crib, Azalea who had been taken by this creature. She thought of the changeling, the black-eyed monster that had been left in her place. *This* thing had begun it all. It was because of this phaerie abomination that she had suffered everything since. She squeezed all the hate and anger she could feel out of that. She wanted *revenge* before it all ended, and that desire gave her a last surge of strength, drawing what tiny reserves she had for one final, desperate ploy.

With a weak cry, she turned around, snatching up the lantern and flinging it at the Scarecrow. It smashed into her enemy full in the chest, spraying its contents all over and igniting. The Scarecrow shrieked as it was engulfed in flame, licking tongues of fire spreading greedily along its coat. It flailed helplessly, staggering this way and that, crashing into bookshelves — which, protected still by magick, did not catch fire — and screaming as the flames grew thicker and fiercer. The air filled with the ugly stench of charring. Poison swayed, the last of her energy gone, and slumped to the floor. She fell towards oblivion with the agonized wails of the Scarecrow in her ears, her eyes trying vainly to focus on the column of fire where the evil phaerie had collapsed into a smouldering pile of rags.

And then, as if a heavy blanket had been lifted from her

shoulders, the tiredness fell away. She felt vigour seep back into her, pouring strength into her muscles and sharpening her thoughts. She pulled herself up, got unsteadily to her feet. The flakes had lost their power now that the phaerie was no more. A fierce grin of disbelief spread across her face. She had beaten it. She had killed the thing that had stolen her sister.

The others were stirring now, awakening from their unnatural sleep. Poison dragged them up, one by one, and instructed Peppercorn to pick up the cat. She obeyed dazedly.

As her companions gathered themselves, Poison watched the blackened heap of clothes that had been the Scarecrow, admiring the play of flame and smoke across its corpse. A smile flickered on her face.

Revenge had never felt so good.

THE UR-LORD

～⌒∽⌒∽⌒～

THE castle of Grugaroth hung over the mouth of a volcanic furnace, a great maw of bubbling magma that writhed and slid, belching noxious fumes into the air. The enormous magma pit was enclosed within a massive cavern, somewhere deep beneath the dark, hard earth of the Realm of Trolls, roofed in from the sky by millions of tons of stone. The castle was held aloft by a great ring of iron, which in turn was supported by five chains with links that were ten yards thick. The ring girdled the castle at its base, where it joined the solid stone of its foundations; the foundations hung beneath the ring, tapering away to jagged points above the lava. It was as if the monstrous construction had been ripped from the earth where it was built — roots and all — and imprisoned here, clamped in place above a seething, hellish inferno. Which, as history had it, was more or less the truth.

The castle itself was a terrifying sight to behold. It was a black edifice of iron, low and squat like some kind of enormous anvil, all hard edges and spikes. The red light from below gave it a daemonic aspect; square windows glared out over the magma. A portcullis, like a set of gritted metal teeth, stood at the end of a vast bridge that linked the castle to the edge of the furnace. The whole construction hung there in defiance of physics, an impossible thing; yet there it was, and none could deny it.

The walls and floor of the cavern were a latticework of wooden platforms and ladders, pillars and lintels and joists. Tunnels ran deep into the walls, pits gaped in the ground, and all through them swarmed the troll folk. Dirty-faced dwarrows mined for ores, leather-skinned gnomes drew charts, ogres stamped to and fro with boulders. The air reeked of sweat and sulphur. Sparks flew as great iron machines were welded; red-hot metal hissed deafeningly as it was plunged into icy water; the cries of the foremen rose from all about, as did the chants of the workers as they chipped and mined for their master in his castle.

Grugaroth sat on a throne of black iron amid the red shadows of a vast hall. He was slouched in recline, his small eyes lost beneath his heavy brow, drumming his fingers on the armrest of the throne. There he had brooded for hours now, the Troll King, his immense hammer by his side. He had heard of the Hierophant's death, for even he had his spies, though he disapproved of subtlety in general when brute strength would do. Now he cogitated on the matter, processing the implications in his slow, methodical way. He was neither as quick nor as intelligent as some of his peers, but he was canny and shrewd. It had kept him on his throne for a long while now.

The arrival of a gnome, barely as tall as his shin, went unnoticed until the nervous creature's third cough roused him from his reverie. He shifted his attention to the newcomer with a grunt, noting with mild surprise the sullen-looking human girl that had followed him in.

"Your pardon, Majesty," the gnome said. "My name is Babghoh, your humble servant, and one of the keepers of your mighty stone library."

Grugaroth was not interested in this, but he had the patience of a glacier, so he merely waited for the gnome to continue.

"A short while ago, a group of humans arrived in your Realm, Majesty. One of them, this female adolescent named Poison, has invoked Amrae's Law and wishes to speak with you."

Grugaroth made a rumbling noise deep in his chest, which was his way of offering an affirmative.

"Furthermore," said Babghoh, "she asked me to tell you that she has information for you. About the Phaerie Lord Aelthar. She asked me to tell you that she shares an enemy with your Majesty."

Grugaroth slowly raised an eyebrow, his red eyes rolling to fix on Poison.

Let her speak, he boomed.

❦

There was no night or day in the Hierophant's Realm, only an endless storm; therefore, it was hard to keep a common time there. By the human chronometer, however, it was a mere twelve hours after Poison and Grugaroth had talked that the troll folk returned to the Hierophant's castle, led by their King.

Nobody was really surprised. Many of the Lords and Ladies who had departed in exasperation at the Hierophant's refusal to address their concerns about his new masterwork had come back in the last few hours. The Hierophant's death changed things. There would have to be a successor, and who that successor might be was of great interest to them all. For the Hierophant had trained no apprentice, named no heir to his legacy. That meant a new appointment would have to be made. Of human blood. It was, like Amrae's Law, an immutable decree.

Uncertainty was everywhere. Usually, the Hierophant devised some kind of arcane test for his apprentice, a seemingly impossible task that would prove his or her worth to take the mantle of Hierophant, the lawmaker. As time had gone on, the tests given to the apprentices had become more subtle, more convoluted, until sometimes they could scarcely be recognized as tests at all. But never in all of remembered history had a Hierophant died before he had passed on his office. There was no precedent for this. For the first time, the position was up for grabs.

But which human would dare to take it? It was not simply a matter of declaring themselves Hierophant. The Lords would tear them limb from limb. A person did not lightly take on the most powerful office in the Realms.

Further consternation was caused upon the arrival of Grugaroth, as he called for an immediate assembly of all the Lords and Ladies in the largest hall of the castle. And particularly Aelthar.

The summons was heeded by all. At a time like this, even the smallest thing might be too important to miss.

They came together beneath the great stone arches of the hall, the nobles gathering in the space between the gargantuan pillars that propped up the ceiling. Their retinues watched from the cloisters all around, a great crowd surrounding their masters. The Lords and Ladies stood in a circle, a phantasmagoria of strange beings illuminated by a huge ironwork candelabra overhead. The storm lashed the high windows at either side of the hall.

Finally, all were assembled.

"We are here, Grugaroth," said Aelthar, with a mocking sneer in his tone. He was wearing Myghognimar at his belt, knowing how it would inflame the Troll King. "Time to reveal what it is that is so important to you."

Grugaroth made a warning rumble, his brow darkening and his massive lower jaw clenching.

Poison, he snarled. ***Step forward.***

And so she did. Peppercorn squeezed her arm in support, and Bram laid his hand on her shoulder; and then she slid through the ranks of dirty dwarrows, gnomes, and trolls to stand at Grugaroth's side. She seemed minuscule in the presence of the Lords and Ladies, all of whom towered over her, but she was far too defiant to be cowed by their size.

"*This* one again?" Aelthar sighed. "What a thorn you turned out to be."

Grugaroth ignored him. ***Let all here witness***, he bellowed. ***This human girl and her companions are under my protection in this place. They shall not be harmed.***

There was scarcely even an acknowledgement of this by the assembly. They were waiting to see what would happen next. Poison's eyes flicked over the Lords and Ladies: the Umbilicus, floating in the air, a disembodied corpse; the Daemon Lord, all flame and horn and hoof; sparkling Eternity; Gomm, the enormous tree-like golem of wood; ethereal Pariasa, the widow of the Hierophant. There were others that she did not recognize, but once again, no Asinastra. Had the Spider Lady gone to ground, back to her Realm, knowing that she might be blamed for Melcheron's murder? Or was she lurking unseen somewhere nearby, waiting for the chance to even the odds?

Poison felt scarcely better now that she had struck her deal with Grugaroth. His protection, in return for helping him exact revenge on his hated enemy. Simple enough. But how safe was she, really, against these creatures? For once she opened her mouth to speak, Aelthar and any of his allies would seek her death more keenly than ever before.

Why was she even doing this? Why not just disappear? But she knew the answer to that. Unless she tackled Aelthar here, he would never stop hunting her until she was dead. She knew too much. And besides, there was the small matter of Azalea. Unless she got leverage over him somehow, she would never get her sister back. She was already unable to picture Azalea's face without seeing the black eyes of the changeling instead.

"I know who it is that killed the Hierophant," she declared, her voice ringing surprisingly loud. "And I accuse Aelthar, the Lord of Phaerie, and Pariasa, Mistress of the Aeriads."

The hall erupted into pandemonium. The assembled retinues roared in outrage, whether at the gall of this insignificant human in accusing a Lord, or in support of her. Aelthar was a most powerful Lord, perhaps *the* most powerful now, but he was not the most popular. He had many enemies to whom Poison's announcement afforded the prospect of long-awaited retribution.

As to the accused, they did not react with half so much emotion. The Lady Pariasa barely gave a flicker to indicate that she had even heard Poison, only watched her with those fathomless alien eyes. Aelthar was smirking with arrogant contempt. He raised his arm, and silence fell at his command.

"Do explain," he said, his tone as patronizing as he could make it.

Poison held his gaze a moment too long. She was worried, and it showed. He was too self-assured, too cocky in the face of her accusation. Did he have something up his sleeve?

She swallowed, feeling the accumulated weight of all the eyes upon her.

"A short time ago, I visited the palace of Aelthar to reclaim the sister who he had snatched from me," she said, her words vanishing into the stillness that had come across the gathering. "Once there, he offered me an exchange: I was to steal an item for him in return for my sister's safe return. That item was a dagger, a *forked* dagger, belonging to the Lady Asinastra."

"I don't deny it," Aelthar said, folding his arms and tossing the fringe of his hair. A murmur ran round the hall.

"Then you also admit that the dagger found in the Hierophant's back was the dagger you sent me to steal?"

"There's only one of it in all the Realms," Aelthar replied with a shrug. "A blood-drinking knife; one of her most prized possessions, I believe. Extremely valuable."

— *the human implies that the dagger you procured was used by you to kill the Hierophant* —

It took Poison a moment to work out where the soft, broken whisper had come from, and then it was only by following Aelthar's gaze. The Umbilicus, the floating corpse in its aura of ghastly green light, had spoken. Or rather, the spirit that animated it.

"I know what she implies," Aelthar said. "But please, let her finish."

Poison was still perturbed by Aelthar's unshakable confidence. She glanced at the phaerie lady, the second victim of her accusation, but Pariasa was unreadable.

"After I stole the dagger, Aelthar had me and my companions imprisoned. We escaped and overheard him ordering his subordinate to have us killed. We were, after all, the only ones who knew about the dagger. Not even Asinastra was to have known who took it." *Except that I told her*, Poison added silently, with a twist of satisfaction. *That's one more enemy you have, Aelthar. One more for stealing my sister from me.*

"Go on," Aelthar prompted.

"It was that dagger that was used to kill the Hierophant; but it was not Aelthar who killed him. It was Pariasa, the Hierophant's wife. Who else could have gotten past the gargoyles guarding the doors to his chambers? Of course, any of the Antiquarians might have done it, but where is their motive? I saw the Lady Pariasa in the Phaerie Lord's palace only a short while after I returned with the dagger. And she *does* have a reason to want her husband dead."

Poison was watching the proud, haughty face of the Phaerie Lord as she spoke, and was satisfied to see that this last piece of information seemed to shake him a little. He glanced at Pariasa, but she was still watching Poison. Aelthar had not known that Poison and Peppercorn had seen Pariasa in his palace.

"She is Mistress of the Aeriads," Poison continued, drawing strength from Aelthar's momentary weakness, "but the Aeriads are phaeries, and she owes her allegiance to Aelthar. It's no secret that the Hierophant was working on something new, something that all of you here were concerned about. But would you be concerned enough to murder? Would any of you? Or did Aelthar already know what the Hierophant was writing, which he would go to any lengths to stop?"

It had the desired effect. Outrage. Grugaroth hunkered down next to Poison and glared around the room. This time they had to wait for silence.

"I believe that Pariasa knew. I believe that the Hierophant told her what he was doing. Why wouldn't he? Perhaps he did not suspect her of being disloyal. Perhaps he did not know that she would go to her true master, the Lord Aelthar, and tell him what she knew. The Lord Aelthar was, of course, the loudest voice when it came to demanding that the Hierophant reveal his new masterpiece: a show for your benefit. Aelthar already knew, and whatever it was, it was bad for the phaerie folk. Between the two of them, Aelthar and the Hierophant's wife murdered the Hierophant, knowing that his work would never be finished, and thus would never be read or become law. You would eventually trace the dagger back to Asinastra, for if Aelthar had gotten his way, my friends and I would be dead, and you would blame her for the crime."

— she makes a convincing case — whispered the Umbilicus. Its puppet body did not move, merely hung limply in the air.

"Without producing a shred of proof, of course," Aelthar countered.

Proof is for human courts, Grugaroth rumbled.

Aelthar shrugged again. "You're right, of course. Thankfully, we have none of the tediously exacting — and ultimately ineffective — standards that the humans are so fond of. This is not a court. You are not judges. The circumstantial evidence — were it true — is quite enough to convict me in your eyes." He examined his fingernails. "Unfortunately, it's not true. I'll admit I was going to have her killed when she got back from Asinastra — you all know how fond I am of humans." This raised a smattering of laughter from the phaerie contingent. "But not for the reasons she says. Quite simply, she didn't hold up her end of the bargain. She never came back with the dagger."

"That's a lie!" Poison called out.

"Hmm?" Aelthar said with a roguish grin. "And I suppose that nobody but you and your *human* friends saw you with the dagger?"

"Scriddle did," Poison said, already feeling her heart sink.

"Scriddle?" Aelthar called. A moment later his oily secretary was at his side. "Is this true?" he asked theatrically.

"Not at all," Scriddle replied with a grin. "She came back empty-handed."

Aelthar turned to the assembly, spreading his arms. "You see? I'll admit I sent her for the dagger; I'll admit I wanted it for myself. But it was only a whim. I sent her on an impossible errand as a reward for her impertinence in demanding an audience with me. I sent her there fully expecting her to die in the jaws of Asinastra's spiders. Still, just so you do not think me too cruel, I did give her the means to escape if, by some miracle, she did happen to lay hold of the dagger I sought. I am fond of a gamble. Not that I would have given her her sister back anyway. As if I would *lower* myself to bargaining with a human!" More of the crowd laughed this time. "Typically for her chicken-hearted race, she chose to return empty-handed. I doubt that she even tried."

Poison seethed inside. She could feel an angry flush creeping up her neck and colouring her cheeks.

"As to the Lady Pariasa, if she will permit me to speak in her defence, she has most certainly not been meeting with me, neither recently nor any time since the Hierophant married her. My subjects will no doubt be able to account for my whereabouts between the time of the audience I gave to this human girl and this very moment — I have scarcely been alone at all, having met several of you Lords here present at my palace and then travelling directly to this castle."

He appealed to the audience once more: "I admit I wanted the Hierophant dead. I want *all* humans dead, verminous whelps that they are. I despise them. But I did not kill him, nor did the Lady Pariasa. The girl is a natural storyteller; she spins a fine tale. But the truth is that she is bitter. I took her sister, many years ago, and she has borne a grudge against me ever since."

Poison felt her mouth go dry. *Many years ago?*

She heard Bram's voice in her head, the words he had spoken to her as she was about to enter the Bone Witch's house and head for the Realm of Phaerie. *Time is not the same there as here.*

"Then what it comes down to, in the end, is this human girl's word against mine and the Lady's," Aelthar was continuing.

"No," Poison heard herself say, though her mind was barely on her own words anymore. *Many years ago?* "No, there is a witness. The Hierophant himself. The book of Melcheron was stolen from the Great Library, some time after the murder. That means the murderer knew his name would be recorded inside its pages. The books know what the Antiquarians know, and Melcheron was Head Antiquarian; he must have known who was in the room when he died, and so it would have been written in the book and made visible after his murder — for that was the end of his tale. I believe only one person could have taken it, only one person not prevented by the Hierophant's magick. Pariasa, his wife, whom he trusted. That book is indestructible. We find the book, we find the murderer."

A flicker of concern crossed Aelthar's face as the room suddenly simmered with murmuring. The theft of the book was news to the Lords and Ladies.

"Search Aelthar's and Pariasa's rooms," Poison said, "and perhaps we will find the answer."

"I refuse!" Aelthar replied. The room went silent.

Is there something you are hiding? growled the Troll King.

"Not at all," Aelthar replied with a sneer. "But the idea of troll folk pawing through my belongings disgusts me beyond measure."

There was more outrage at this. Poison flinched. The room was far too volatile for insults like that to be thrown around, and there was no protection from the Hierophant anymore. Everyone here was vulnerable while they remained in a Realm with no Lord to rule it.

"Wait!" she said, and her tiny voice had the curious effect of quieting them all. "Wait! I have a solution. Send the Antiquarians. They are neutral, and they will treat your rooms with respect."

Aelthar considered this for a moment. "Not him," he said, a single accusing finger picking out Fleet among the troll folk. "But otherwise, I agree. Search my rooms and those of the

Lady. You will not find Melcheron's tome there. We — *all* of us — will stay here until this matter is resolved."

Agreed, Grugaroth rumbled.

An Antiquarian left the hall to pass on the message, and all they could do was wait.

There was a moment of impasse. Poison turned her attention to the phaerie lady whom she had accused. Her heart would have ached to condemn such a beautiful thing if she were not convinced of the creature's guilt. She looked back at Bram and Fleet and Peppercorn. Peppercorn was wringing her hands, while the others looked grave.

How did I get to here? she thought to herself. *What's the purpose of it all? I just wanted Azalea back. If this is truly a tale, then where is it going? And who's writing it, now that Melcheron is dead? I don't understand any of this.*

"Well," said Aelthar, after a time. He rolled his shoulders inside his gleaming silver armour and flashed a grin about the room. "Since we have nothing to do but wait, and since I am entirely certain of our innocence, I have another matter to bring before the assembly.

"The Hierophant has died and no successor has been named. There is no precedent for this, but there must be a Hierophant. Therefore, I propose that we put forward our own candidates."

— *the Hierophant must be of human blood* — whispered the Umbilicus — *it is law* —

"Indeed," said Aelthar. "And so they shall be. Choose them from the Realm of Man. Search far and wide for the greatest and wisest of men and women. And at a time in the near future, we present them and decide between them at council."

There was much discussion of this, but it seemed a fair resolution of the situation and was agreed upon grudgingly.

"Then, my Lords and Ladies, allow me to be the first to present my own candidate," Aelthar said. "I confess I had made some preparations against just such an eventuality as this. Humans are so terribly short-lived, don't you think? Patience is all that is needed."

The candidate stepped forward, and Poison felt the earth drop away beneath her feet. It all made sense now. In her mind, the connections suddenly clicked into place.

The Hierophant must be of human blood, thought Poison. *But nobody ever said how much of it had to be human.*

"Lords and Ladies, I give you my most loyal secretary, Scriddle," Aelthar was saying, but Poison swayed and felt faint. She could see Aelthar's intention as he turned his piercing gaze upon her, saw the spark of malice in his eye.

He's going to kill us all. He's going to wipe us out. The entire Realm of Man.

Poison was so overcome with terror that she barely heard the return of the Antiquarians, nor the announcement that there was no book of Melcheron to be found in the chambers of the accused.

A PROPOSITION OF THE HEART

❧

"**W**E have to *do* something," Peppercorn sobbed.

"Someone must be told," Bram agreed. "If they knew ..."

"They *do* know!" Poison said, pacing Fleet's room like a caged animal. Andersen was watching them attentively from where he sat upright near the hearth. The never-ending rain battered at the thick window; sheets of water slipped and slid down the pane. Nobody in the room even noticed the thunder or lightning anymore — not even the cat, who had been terrified of the storm at first.

Fleet was sitting in his favourite armchair, his fingers steepled and resting on his lips. "Poison is right," he said. "They do know. Whatever the truth of it, there's no question that Aelthar is behind this somewhere. I knew he hated humanity, but I never guessed how much. . . ."

"So why don't they stop him?" said Peppercorn. She was hugged inside the great circle of Bram's arm, her eyes red; she had taken Poison's revelations rather hard.

"It's not so simple," Fleet replied wearily. "Aelthar is the most powerful Lord; his armies are the mightiest of all. The only reason he did not utterly crush humankind during the Many-Sided War is because the Hierophant intervened. None of the other Lords or Ladies can stand against him."

"But if they *all* did . . ." Poison suggested.

"Why would they?" Fleet replied. "None of them cares a fig for humankind. In their own Realms, a Lord or Lady is virtually all-powerful; but now this Realm has no Lord, and it is open to invasion. This pretence of deciding who will be Hierophant is a sham. By putting Scriddle forward, Aelthar is delivering a message; he is saying: *I claim this Realm. Who will oppose me?* Aelthar can act with impunity, because he knows that the only way he will be beaten is if the other Lords and Ladies unite. And that they will never do. They are too divided. Too many old hatreds fester between them. They will bluster and protest, but they can't stand up to him. He will take this Realm in a bloodless coup."

Poison stared into the fire, and flames flickered in the violet of her irises. "Aelthar will put Scriddle in the Hierophant's place, and then there will be nothing to stand between him and wiping us out entirely. Scriddle might be half-human, but his loyalties and heart are phaerie. The Realm of Man will be ended."

"You knew it was hopeless," Bram grunted at Fleet. "So why did you let her do this? Why did you let her accuse Aelthar?"

Poison gave her friend a sad smile. "I had to try," she said. "You knew that, didn't you, Fleet? I would have done it anyway."

"At least it is out in the open now," Fleet said. "All is not lost yet."

"All is not lost," Poison echoed from where she sat in her chair; then she fixed Bram with a strange look. "You taught me that once, Bram. When I was on the brink of death. You brought me back."

Bram looked shocked, his small eyes going wide in the shadow of his hat. "What? What are you talking about, girl?"

Poison shook her head at her idiocy. Of course, he didn't remember. None of them did. The malaise that had nearly destroyed them all had been wiped from their memories.

"Never mind, Bram," she said. "Let's just say you taught me something important."

"Then what is left, Poison?" Fleet asked. "What can we do?"

"Well, there's still that missing book," Poison said.

"Melcheron's tale?" Fleet asked, sitting up. "Even if we could find it, what good can that do now? We'd have proof, but we won't be able to stop Aelthar."

"Perhaps not," Poison said. "But we might learn what it was he was writing that scared the Phaerie Lord so much. It will surely be mentioned in the book of his life."

"You're right," Fleet said, getting up. "You're right!"

There was a knock at the door of Fleet's room, making Peppercorn jump. Fleet frowned, then levered himself out of his chair and went to open it.

There in the doorway stood Scriddle, besuited as always, his hair freshly slicked and his round glasses freshly polished. He gave a cruel smile, showing his short, sharp teeth.

"Is Poison here?" he asked. "My Lord Aelthar would like a few words with her."

❦

It had taken many assurances before Poison could be persuaded to set foot in Aelthar's chambers, but she finally agreed. Aelthar had insisted on meeting her alone. Poison had replied that she would not come unless she had a retinue — after all, she did not trust the Phaerie Lord's promise that she would be safe. He had broken it once.

Eventually, Grugaroth himself came along, with a dozen

trolls. They were not permitted to enter, but they were allowed to wait outside. If they heard Poison's cry, Grugaroth promised, they would burst in and protect her. Poison was scarcely reassured; by the time she made a noise, she would probably be dead. However, the threat of Grugaroth's retribution ought to be enough to hold Aelthar back from outright murder; a dozen trolls stood a good chance of getting to him before his phaerie guards could prevent them.

The door closed behind her, and she was alone with Aelthar. The room was hung with tapestries to cover the black, grim stone of the walls, and scattered with fine furnishings, not so elegant as the Phaerie Lord's palace, but possessing a grave kind of charm. He sat in his deadly, jungle-cat slouch on a carved settee, a goblet of red wine in his hand. Poison took the settee opposite. They regarded each other over a stained-glass lantern, in which a marshwraith glowed and fizzed fitfully. A marshwraith! Poison could have laughed. It all began with the marshwraiths. . . .

"You truly are a monstrous annoyance to me, Poison," Aelthar said slowly.

"Glad to hear it," she replied.

His lips quivered into a smile, and then as he watched her over the rim of his goblet he sipped his wine. "You know, your little . . . accusation has made things very difficult. This would all have gone smoothly, if not for you. Now there are Lords and Ladies causing me all kinds of troubles. They think I murdered the Hierophant to install my own puppet Hierophant in his place."

"You did," Poison said simply, unrepentant.

"Oh, but it's not true," he replied. "I did take advantage of the situation; indeed I did. And I had planned for it for more years than your kind can count. But I did not plot to kill him." He sipped his wine again. "I suspect, however, that Scriddle did."

Poison scoffed. Despite the fear that being this close to her enemy provoked, she kept up her façade of disdain. It was the best defence she had.

"Believe it or not," Aelthar said, "I think Scriddle got tired of waiting. He could never rise in the ranks of the phaerie because of his polluted blood. So he set his sights on being Hierophant instead. That, really, was why I had him spawned as a half-breed in the first place." The Phaerie Lord looked thoughtful. "He's *very* ambitious. I shall have to keep my eye on him."

"You expect me to swallow that? You knew nothing about the murder?"

"I assure you, dear human, that it was as much a surprise to me as to you. I told you the truth when I said I never received the dagger you stole. I really did set you the task because I thought you would never manage it. Yet you apparently did succeed, and you say you gave the dagger to Scriddle. I suspect he gave it to the Lady Pariasa, and *she* put it in the Hierophant's back. You see, the dagger was really not important to Scriddle's plan. An ordinary one would have done just as well. But when you appeared with a dagger that everybody knew belonged to Asinastra, he saw a perfect way to throw the other Lords and Ladies off the scent. It was merely a fortunate happenstance; he was already plotting the Hierophant's murder before you arrived. Scriddle knew that he was the only real candidate for a replacement in my eyes. He knew I would put him forward."

"So what of the Lady Pariasa? Why would she —"

"The Hierophant was old, and soon to die. My guess is, she will marry the new Hierophant, Scriddle. That, I imagine, is part of her deal with him. That way she keeps her power. It's all very simple, really. Of course, that's only my theory. I could command Scriddle to tell me the truth, but I'd rather not ask. It's better that I don't know. They call it credible deniability in human circles, I believe."

Poison watched him for a time. His cruel eyes, the sharp set of his handsome features, the deep red of his hair. She hated him; oh, how she hated him.

"Why are you telling me any of this?" she asked.

"As a sign of good faith. To help you believe me. I may be guilty of opportunism, but I *am* innocent of murdering the Hierophant. And because I have a deal to offer you."

Poison did not react. He put down his goblet and got to his feet, then paced over to the other side of the room. With a wave of his hand, the air seemed to shimmer and solidify, to swirl and thicken until it took on a shape. Poison caught her breath.

She was about Poison's age, wearing an elegant black dress, with her dark-blonde hair tied back in a braid. Pretty — prettier than Poison, anyway — but not overly so, and aided by artful make-up and mascara. She stood with her eyes downcast, her hands, clad in long, black gloves, clasped before her. She looked so familiar, a face from her past that Poison could not quite place.

"Who is she?"

"Why, Poison! For shame. Don't you recognize your own sister?"

Poison's legs went weak, and all the strength drained out of her. Now she saw. Those eyes, that nose — the resemblance was there. It seemed so obvious now, only she had been unable to think of her sister as anything but the child who had slept in the crib in her room. This girl was older, an adolescent — those tiny bones lengthened, the puppy fat gone, the innocence fled. Mere weeks had passed by Poison's human chronometer, but time had fractured over and over as she skipped between Realms. Her little sister had caught up a dozen years or so somewhere in the interim.

Poison felt tears start to her eyes and wiped them away

angrily. Twelve years, stolen from her. Twelve years when she should have been with Azalea, watching her grow, playing with her, helping her through the trials of growing up. Of all her family, Azalea was the only one Poison identified with, and secretly she had hoped she would have a companion in her sister, someone to share her loneliness with. All that had been taken from her by Aelthar. This had been the ace up his sleeve the whole time.

"She is not here," Aelthar said, his voice cold. "She cannot see us. You cannot touch her, or talk to her."

Poison could not take her eyes off the apparition of her sister. It was uncanny how much she *did* recognize her, now. "*Why?*" she breathed. "Why did you take her?"

Aelthar gave a short burst of laughter. "Why do we take *any* human babies? For breeding, of course. So that I could create for myself the perfect replacement for the Hierophant. We take them as children, and watch them grow, determining whether they have suitable qualities. Some we give back soon after we take them. Some we never give back. Those we breed from, selecting and strengthening those characteristics that would make a good Hierophant. Scriddle is the product of a long, long line of experiments. He is eminently qualified, you see: loyal to his Lord, intelligent, ruthless, learned enough to take on the post. Oh, don't worry — your sister hasn't been . . . used yet. Maybe she won't have to be, now."

Poison turned a glare of pure malice on to the Phaerie Lord, who met it with amusement. "All this . . . all this so you can wipe us out."

"Destroy humankind?" he laughed. "You imagine *that* is why I wanted Scriddle as Hierophant? You flatter yourself. Humankind is too insignificant for me to trouble with right now. All I'm concerned about is ensuring that the Hierophant is on my side. You see, you made some good guesses. The Lady

Pariasa really *did* know what the Hierophant was writing, and it was going to be very unpleasant for us. She told Scriddle, who told me. But it was Scriddle who acted, not I. For the good of the phaerie folk."

"You think that makes you *innocent*?" Poison cried. Then, ashamed that her anger had slipped her reins, she drew herself back into an icy shell. "Tell me what you offer."

"This isn't your fight, Poison," Aelthar said, tilting his head and studying Azalea. "You only came here to get Azalea back. I would not have taken her if I could have imagined that her sister would prove to be such a plague. It was entirely random, you know; don't feel hard done by. Any human child would do. I just needed a womb."

"You'll give me her back?" said Poison, her voice empty.

"If you retract what you said before the Lords and Ladies," he replied. "And then go back home, and never bother me again."

Poison frowned. "Why will that make any difference to you?"

"Many of my peers have become . . . awkward in the face of your accusation. If you tell them you were lying, then they will stop their protests."

Poison studied him carefully. She had learned by now not to trust a thing the Phaerie Lord said. This certainly did not correspond with what Fleet had told her. If she believed Fleet, then Aelthar could seize power whether the others liked it or not, and Poison's testimony either way would not make a jot of difference.

"I will have to think on this," she said.

"Poison. This is your sister," Aelthar pointed out.

"Is it?" Poison replied. "Or just an illusion? If I agree to this, you can be sure that I will have my sister back by my side before I say a word in your defence. Your kind are more treacherous than the worst of the marsh snakes."

Aelthar's face twisted in anger, and she saw she had struck a blow. "Go, then. I will be here when you return. But know this, human. If you do not agree to my terms, I will not only keep your sister, I will ensure that the remainder of her life is spent in excruciating torture!"

Poison stood, as calmly as she could. "I will be back," she said, and left.

❦

Peppercorn rushed to hug her when she returned to Fleet's chambers, sheer relief showing on her face. Poison barely felt the embrace.

"Oh, we thought you wouldn't come back!" she cried.

Bram, who had also gotten to his feet, studied her dazed expression. "What is it, Poison? What did he say?"

"He offered me my sister back," she said, over Peppercorn's shoulder. "If I retract what I said and go home and never bother him again."

Peppercorn released her slowly, gazing at Poison with her wide blue eyes. "What are you going to do?" she asked.

"I don't know," said Poison. She sat down in an empty chair by the fire. They were all watching her, even Andersen. "I don't know," she repeated.

Bram settled himself down in the chair next to her while she told them the rest of the details. Peppercorn was wringing her hands again. Andersen jumped onto her lap and curled up. Fleet's brow was furrowed, and he was puffing on his hookah.

She could practically *feel* their concern, their sympathy. The old Poison would have rejected that outright; now she tolerated it. It occurred to her that these were her friends, the only ones she had, in fact. She was even fond of the cat. She had been torn from a childhood of almost total alienation, and on the way she had found a few people worth hanging on to.

Among all the trials and pain, there were these four. She might not feel that she belonged to the rest of humanity, but she belonged here.

The thought might have comforted her in other times, but now it seemed as if it might tear her apart. She might get her sister back, but she knew well what could happen if the Phaerie Lord's plan succeeded. Despite what he had said, the last guardian of humanity would be gone with Scriddle in the Hierophant's office. And then there would be nothing standing between the phaeries and the whole Realm of Man.

And yet she still could not shake the sense that she *knew* her sister from somewhere, the girl in the apparition that Aelthar had shown her. She looked different then, but Poison was becoming more and more certain. Was it simply that she was recalling her sister's face, transposing it onto another memory? If only she could make sure of it; if only she could *remember.*

"It doesn't make sense," Fleet said. "Why offer her to you at all? I don't believe what he said about the other Lords opposing him."

"That's what I've been asking myself," said Poison. "What possible harm can I do him?"

"You must be able to do him *some* harm," Bram said. "Or he wouldn't be making this offer. He wants you out of the way."

"There has to be something . . ." Poison said, desperately searching her mind. "Something we're missing."

But she came up as blank as any of them.

The biggest frustration was that she could not share with them the strangest piece of the puzzle, for they had erased it from their minds. Only she remembered what had happened when she had been on the verge of death, how the story had unravelled around her. She knew, she *knew*, that she was living in a phaerie tale — and, furthermore, it was *her* tale. That had been proved to her by the way the world could not seem to continue without her.

But the Hierophant had thought that *he* was writing it, and now he was dead. So who was really behind it all? Was anyone?

Didn't you ever believe in a god, Poison? Then how is this different?

Bram had said that to her once. Maybe it was true. Maybe she would never know who or what was behind it. And maybe the author of *this* tale was like her, believing that he or she was master of his or her own destiny, plagued by doubts that it might not be true.

But in the end, it was all pointless philosophy. She was as free as she felt, as real as she felt. Her choices might be being made for her, but if she still believed that they were her choices, then what actual difference did it make? She wasn't certain enough to know that they weren't. She could second-guess herself endlessly and still never know.

And she had to choose now — between condemning her sister to a lifetime of torture, or risking the whole future of humanity.

⌘

At the back of Fleet's chambers a narrow, shadowy stairway climbed upwards, almost hidden between the fireplace and an overburdened bookshelf. It led to what Fleet called his "thinking room," a small study with yellowed maps pinned against the wall and books strewn across a desk. One wall and the roof were crafted from thick glass, laying the room open to the sight of the grim mountains that surrounded them. From here, high up on one side of the castle, the endless procession of black peaks that was the Hierophant's Realm trudged towards the horizon, smashed and battered by the endless rain and distant, flickering pulses of lightning.

It was here that Poison took herself to think. She could not make a decision like the one she faced with her friends offering advice and insight; she needed to be alone. She had chosen a heavy, musty armchair to sit in, facing out over the dark panorama. There were no lanterns burning up here; she liked the cool shadows, the ambient glow from outside, and the occasional brightness of the lightning. The crawling tears of the rain against the window shone on her narrow face, superimposing themselves onto the pale planes of her skin.

Impossible. The situation was impossible. On the one hand, if she chose to save Azalea and return home, then Aelthar would put Scriddle at the Hierophant's desk and humankind's last guardian would be gone, leaving Aelthar to exterminate the humans he despised so much. Poison knew better than to believe Aelthar's blithe assertion that he did not care enough about humanity to destroy it; phaeries were liars, and she knew Aelthar's true feelings on the subject from overhearing him in his chambers, back in his palace. Poison and Azalea would not be spared.

The other choice was just as bad. Abandon Azalea and oppose the Phaerie Lord. But what good was that? Poison seemed to have something about her that made the Phaerie Lord worry, or he would not be offering her this deal at all; yet since she had no idea what it was, how could she use it against him? Leaving Azalea to torture was awful enough, but the result would be the same in the end. Scriddle would become Hierophant, humanity would be wiped out.

If only she had the *key*, the one fact that she was missing that would make it make sense. She struggled to fit together any scenario she could imagine that would make her a threat to the Phaerie Lord, but she came up blank. So she sat in the dark, listening to the bellow of the thunder and watching the rain, and wondering at the cruelty of having to make such a choice as this.

<thiiief . . .>

The rasping whisper at first made her jump; then, an instant later, realization hit. She knew that broken voice.

Asinastra.

She leapt convulsively out of her chair, looking about wildly. The shadows cloaked the corners of the room. Suddenly, the play of light from the running water on the windows seemed to make the room swarm with movement.

<thiiief . . .>

Poison's heart lurched. She backed up against the windows, where there was a little more light. How could Asinastra have gotten in? There was only one entrance to this room, and that was through Fleet's chambers, and past Grugaroth's trolls who guarded it. Poison was suddenly acutely aware that the Hierophant's murder meant that the only protection she had was Grugaroth's threat of retribution to anyone that harmed her, and it felt like no protection at all now. This time, there would be no Amrae's Law to fall back on: it only worked once.

<wouldn't call for help> <not if I were you> <no, better not> <she'd be very dead> <dead before anyone could come> <not fast enough>

The Lady of Cobwebs' schizophrenic, overlapping sentences seemed to come from everywhere, lisping out of the walls themselves. Poison had no intention of calling for help, anyway; she doubted she could shout loud enough to penetrate the thick stone of these castle walls. Bram and the others might hear her down the stairs, but they would have to alert the trolls, and she realized only then that the stairway was far too narrow to allow a troll through.

Then Poison spied her. She was crouched atop a bookcase at the far end of the room, squeezed grotesquely between the shelves and the roof, her black eyes glittering above her rotted veil. Too late, Poison remembered what had happened last time she had met those eyes; by then she was already snared, her body going rigid with fear, locked in place by Asinastra's paralysing gaze.

<there now> <isn't that better?> Asinastra hissed, and then with a horrible, arachnid gait she scuttled down the bookshelf, her neck craning at an impossible angle to keep her eyes fixed on Poison while she clambered nimbly down to the floor. Her belly was even more swollen than it had been last time Poison saw her, pressing against the mouldering folds of her filthy white dress.

Poison watched in horror as Asinastra crawled slowly along the floor towards her, never breaking the contact between her black eyes and Poison's violet ones. Poison wanted to scream, but her muscles and lungs refused to go along with the notion. Imprisoned in her own flesh, she could only wait, terrified, as the spider crept up on its helpless prey.

<she stole from you> <from me! from me!> <took the dagger that was yours>

Asinastra drew herself up to stand in front of Poison, leaning close so that Poison could smell her dank, fetid breath.

<took the dagger that got stuck in Melcheron's back>

Lightning flashed and thunder roared, booming across the mountains. Poison was trying to shake her head, trying to make a sound, if only to explain that it wasn't what it looked like, that she had been forced into it.

<what should I do with her?> Asinastra asked herself, drawing one cracked nail down Poison's cheek. Poison felt tears of terror start to her eyes. <take her home. wrap her up. feed her to the newborn when it comes>

Poison's mind was ablaze with impotent pleas for mercy. A tear spilled over the edge of her lash and ran down her cheek.

<tears> Asinastra hissed. She turned her finger so that the single bead of saltwater ran onto its tip. <no good>

The Lady of Cobwebs stepped back a little, glaring at Poison with those depthless black pearls, her filthy hair straggling over her face. She stood hunched, with her pregnant belly disfiguring her shape further.

<she watched you, at the gathering> <yes, I watched you>

It took Poison an instant to realize that she meant the gathering where she had accused Aelthar. Had Asinastra been there all along, watching from the ceiling, hidden in the shadows?

<your fault I was accused> <but then you tell them it wasn't her> <why?> <she didn't understand>

Poison was having a hard time following the insane mutterings of the Spider Lady, but she grasped the gist. If she had been able to reply, she would have. But she was frustratingly, appallingly helpless to prevent any fate that Asinastra had in store.

<then she did> <aelthar made you> <for your sister> <made you steal from me> <you said it, he admitted it>

That's right! Poison thought desperately, willing the words into Asinastra's diseased mind. *That's right! It wasn't my fault!*

<did it for family> Asinastra rasped. She touched her grotesque belly. *<know family>*

Poison felt a tiny flicker of hope. Had Asinastra really understood?

<know who to blame> she breathed. *<won't kill you yet>*

Poison felt her insides melt in utter and complete relief, and with that the Lady of Cobwebs broke the gaze and Poison slumped to the floor, gasping.

<go now> she said. *<back to realm> <she's not welcome here> <never welcome>*

Poison did not know which of them she was referring to, but she dared to look up as Asinastra retreated, backing away into the shadows. For the first time, Poison saw that she was holding a blade in one hand: the forked dagger that had been found in Melcheron's back.

<she came for her dagger> she whispered, and then she seemed to step into the shadow and disappear, the darkness wrapping round her like a cloak, melting her into invisibility.

Poison lay on the floor in front of the rain-blasted windows, gasping amidst the roar of the storm.

༄ ⌒⌒ ༄

It was an hour later when she returned to the Phaerie Lord's chambers to give him her answer.

She could not unravel the knot in her stomach as she walked along the corridors of the castle, surrounded by the lumbering, armoured trolls, led by Grugaroth himself. Their red eyes scanned the corridors watchfully as they escorted her. Grugaroth had realized what Poison and the others had guessed: the fact that Aelthar wanted to make a deal with her meant that she had some leverage over him, and so she was still precious. Anything that might disadvantage the Phaerie Lord was good for the Troll King. Poison had made no mention to anyone of Asinastra's visit. For some reason, she felt a need to respect the Spider Lady's secrecy, and it would offend Grugaroth to know that she had slipped through his guards with ease. The others would only worry.

They came to a set of double doors, guarded by twenty stern-faced phaerie warriors: elves, by the look of them. An evil breed, narrow-faced and cold. The trolls came to a halt, glaring fiercely at their enemies, who regarded them with icy malice.

The girl has an answer for your Lord, said the Troll King, his voice like a distant earth tremor.

The elves waited just long enough to be insulting, then stepped aside.

"The Lord Aelthar awaits you within," said one of them, opening the door a little.

Poison took a deep breath to calm herself, then stepped inside.

Aelthar was not on the settee where she had first met him; he was seated in shadow against one wall, an empty goblet in his hand. A fire burned in the grate, lit not long ago. Poison could see the shine of the firelight on his eyes. She glanced about the room. There was a half-full bottle of dark red wine on the table, and another goblet.

"I have come with my answer," she said.

Almost at once Poison felt her throat close up, felt tears coming. It was so cruelly unfair to be forced into making a choice like this. Either way, she lost. Either way, she would have to live with the burden of her conscience for the rest of her life. She wanted to shout and scream at him, to ask him how he could play these evil games with her, to ask him if he enjoyed toying with her heart this way. But that would be weakness, and now was the time for strength.

"I . . ." she began, but her mouth had gone dry. To make this pact would be irrevocable. She found herself floundering for another second, another minute, in which to think her way out of it. "I would like some wine," she finished.

Aelthar did not reply, merely watched her from the darkness. Poison hesitated a moment, then went to the bottle and poured. Taking up the goblet, she raised it to her lips . . . and stopped.

Aelthar was still looking at the spot where she had been standing, not where she was now.

"Aelthar?" she said.

He made no reply.

Slowly, she put the goblet down, squinting at the shadows to make him out. The gloom made it hard to see anything. The sound of the rain hammering against the windows seemed suddenly terribly loud.

She picked up the marshwraith lantern and crept across the room, fearing a trick, fearing . . . she did not know what. There was a premonition of dread rising within her, but she did not understand it.

Then, when she was only a few feet from the motionless Phaerie Lord, she raised the lantern.

His eyes were glazed, staring emptily at the door. His skin was white and pale. His hand held the goblet limply, the last dregs of wine still inside.

The wine! she thought.

A flash of lightning and a crack of thunder blasted the castle simultaneously, and in its light Poison saw that there was something in Aelthar's mouth. She leaned closer, scarcely daring to breathe, not knowing what this might mean.

A long-legged spider scuttled out, making her yelp and jump back. It was followed by another, pushing out from between his cold lips and running over his cheek to his hairline. The first one disappeared over his chin and beneath the chestplate of his silver armour.

Poison staggered back a step. Asinastra. The Lady of Cobwebs had gotten her revenge.

The Phaerie Lord was dead.

KNIVES

POISON could not think. Her brain seemed to have seized and jammed the flow through her mind. She could only stare at the corpse in the chair, the phaerie creature that had been the object of her hatred for so long, now silent. Only an hour ago, when he had been drinking the very wine that killed him, Aelthar had seemed invincible, an obstacle that could not be surmounted. She had never considered that he would be beaten, only that she might persuade him somehow to give back what was hers.

Poison got you, one way or another, she thought.

That single moment of spite, when she had chosen to tell Asinastra who had been the one that sent her to steal the dagger, that single moment had set into motion a chain of events that resulted in the death of her enemy. The Hierophant's murder had meant there was no guardian of this Realm, no guarantee of safety. Asinastra had used that. Poison would never know how she got to him, but she had. With the patience of the spiders that she ruled, she'd lain in wait until the moment came to strike. By the time Asinastra had visited Poison in Fleet's study, Aelthar had already died. No wonder the Spider Lady was in the mood to be merciful; she had already dealt with the one she truly blamed for the theft.

Poison fought to process what this might mean, how she should react. Everything had shifted now, with Aelthar dead. Suddenly, the state of play was radically different, so different that Poison found herself floundering, trying to decide what to do next.

Her decision was made for her. She heard a voice outside the door. Scriddle.

Sudden, irrational panic seized her. If he caught her in here, with his master dead and nobody else in the room, what would he think? What would he *do*? A part of her wanted to stand there and face him, to confront him with what Asinastra had done. But that part — her courage — had exhausted itself already in making the choice between her sister and the fate of humanity . . . and all for nothing, it seemed, for now the point was moot.

She fled. Aelthar's chambers comprised several rooms, and she chose a doorway at random and ran. She was not a second too soon, for at that moment the double doors that led onto the corridor flung open.

"I don't *care* who is in there with him, this is *urgent*. Filthy trolls, clamouring around the door like beggars."

The doors slammed shut. Poison, wild-eyed, found herself in a small antechamber with another settee, cupboards, and a table. A tall set of windows looked out over the storm-blitzed mountainside, and long, velvet curtains hung down at either side. There were no other doorways except the one through which she had come. Clutching at the only hope of concealment she had, she slipped behind the curtains, enfolding herself in their vermilion embrace.

"My Lord Aelthar, forgive this intrusion, but it was important that the Lady and I spoke with you," Scriddle was saying, haste making his voice snippy. "Matters have become considerably more urgent, as you know, and I . . . *we* . . . must respectfully suggest that we move the date of my succession to . . . my Lord?"

Poison felt the awful inevitability of what was to follow.

"My Lord? Why are you sitting in shadow? My Lord?"

She heard a long silence.

He is dead, came a voice like the rustling of trees on a summer's day, and she knew it must be the Lady Pariasa.

"Dead?" Scriddle hissed. "*Dead?* He can't be *dead*! Not now! Not now!"

His voice was rising in pitch as he spoke, buoyed by purest anger and frustration.

And yet he is, replied Pariasa. *Alas, our plans are undone.*

"No!" Scriddle fairly screamed through gritted teeth.

They will hear you, Pariasa pointed out. Poison assumed she meant the men outside. *You should compose yourself, before we tell them.*

"Tell them? Tell them? No! No, not yet. Where is that girl? They said she was in here!"

Poison heard a thump of footsteps — only Scriddle's, for Pariasa glided like air — going from room to room. She thought of making a break for the doors, but she didn't dare; in this moment of indecision they were back and then the two of them came through the doorway and into the antechamber with her. Poison felt her heart stop in sympathy with her breathing. The two of them stood just a few feet away from where she was concealed, separated only by the thickness of the curtain. Thunder boomed distantly, followed by a long, flickering flash of brightness.

What are you doing, my love? Pariasa said softly. Her voice was frail and ethereal, gentle and resonant. How could a thing of such beauty be a murderess? *She is not here.*

"Then where is she? How did she ... how did she ..." he trailed off, almost choking on his rage.

She is dangerous, came the reply. *We all knew that. Aelthar thought he could get rid of her, buy her with her sister. To keep her ignorant and out of our way. It seems he was mistaken.*

Poison could barely credit what she was hearing. Dangerous? Her? How? Had Aelthar really feared her that much? He had offered to let her go home, to stay out of his way. *Why?*

"I must think," Scriddle replied hurriedly. "I must think. Once word is out that Aelthar is dead, the other Lords ... Our lives will be at risk. I have been put forward as Hierophant; you are accused of murdering the last one. Do you suppose we can walk out past a dozen trolls, past Grugaroth, if he thinks Aelthar is dead? He'd be liable to smash his way in here just to get back his cursed half brother's sword if he thought he had half a chance."

Without Aelthar, you cannot succeed in your bid to be Hierophant, Pariasa said evenly. *We must flee, my love. Let us leave while we can. We can be gone before they find him.*

"Leave?" Scriddle cried. "Leave for where? For what?"

I am still Lady of the Aeriads, Pariasa said. *Come back to the Realm of Phaerie with me.*

"And be what? Your consort? I am half human, Pariasa! Half of my blood has that vile taint of humanity. I can never hold an office of any power in the Realm of Phaerie! The only reason I was spawned was to be Hierophant! That's why we made our plans, remember? That's why I took that dagger from that stupid human girl; that's why you put it in old Melcheron's back. Aelthar didn't have to know; everyone would have blamed that spider bitch! If not for that accursed girl, it would all be going to plan."

But all that is over, came the calm reply. *For Aelthar is dead.*

"I refuse to be beaten by a *human*!" he hissed.

She is not just a human, said Pariasa. *We know that now, even if she does not.*

At that moment, a terrible thunderclap battered the room, making the panes of the windows shudder. Poison started, her nerves already wound taut. And though she made no noise, the slight movement was enough. The curtain was thrown back and she stood revealed before the murderous gaze of Scriddle, his expression as dark as the clouds that rolled overhead. There was a moment of hesitation, then she bolted for the doorway. She had barely moved an inch before Scriddle had caught her by the throat and slammed her against the wall, pinning her there, choking. His sharp teeth showed in a snarl; his round glasses were awry on his pointed nose. Pariasa watched them expressionlessly.

"You," Scriddle breathed, with unfathomable malice in his voice. "*You* did this. You've ruined everything."

Poison struggled against his grip, but it was like steel, cutting off her air inexorably. "Shouldn't ... have taken ... my sister," she croaked defiantly.

Scriddle gave a cry of anger and flung Poison against the other wall. The world seemed to go white for an instant as she hit, and then pain returned with reinforcements. She lay collapsed against the side of a desk. Something had broken inside her — a rib. She felt it sawing as she stirred. The agony was unbelievable.

"Your *sister?*" he cried in disbelief. "You stupid, misguided human fool! We gave your sister back long before you ever turned up to plague us!"

Poison's eyes were empty with incomprehension as she stared at him, her face tight with shock.

"She was unsuitable," Scriddle sneered, stepping closer. "By the time she reached adolescence, it was clear that she didn't have the qualities Aelthar needed for his breeding programme.

He sent her back. The Scarecrow dumped her in the midst of your foul Realm with no memory of what had happened, and we left her to make her own way home. Are you satisfied now? *We don't have your sister! Aelthar was lying to you!"*

It was too much, too much to take in at one time, but the force of comprehension was relentless, battering her even through the dizzying blaze of her broken rib. The phaeries had given her back. All this time, all this searching and fighting and heartache, and they had already given Azalea back?

Then it hit her. Like a jigsaw piece snapping into place, she remembered where she had seen the girl that Aelthar had shown her in the apparition.

It was the same girl that she met in Shieldtown, the traveller who was going to Gull. The girl she had given the message to, to pass on to her parents. No wonder she looked so strange, so haunted and travel-worn. Amnesiac, she had somehow managed to find her way back to her hometown. Poison had never asked her her name; that was the greatest irony of all. For if she had, the girl would have replied: *Azalea.*

A single question, and Poison's journey would have been complete without ever leaving her own Realm. No Lamprey, no Bone Witch, no Phaerie Lord or Hierophant. If the coin had fallen the other way, if she had thought to ask, if she had only thought to *ask!* Or if only Azalea had recognized her, remembered her elder sister, even though she had last seen her twelve years before when she was a child. Or even if Azalea had asked why Poison was sending a message to Hew and Snapdragon, instead of giving her that bland, incurious stare. Did Azalea know then that they were her parents? Would she have said anything if she did?

But how could Poison have guessed, how could either of them have guessed, when neither could have imagined then that while one week had passed in the Realm of Man since

Azalea was stolen away from her crib, twelve *years* had gone by in the Realm of Phaerie, and in that time Azalea had grown up and then been discarded.

On her quest to save her sister, she had met her along the way and not known it.

She tried to take a breath to scream, partly to bring Grugaroth and his trolls running, mostly to vent her inconsolable grief and rage at the injustice of it all; but she could draw no air, it seemed, and her throat could barely make a sound after being crushed in Scriddle's fingers. Scriddle loomed over her, his face red with rage and sweating. There was a knife in his hand, a long, curving knife with a wicked blade. Poison was too swamped in pain and sorrow to feel anything else; she regarded it dispassionately, for there was no room for fear in her.

My love, Pariasa said, appearing at his shoulder in a silent swirl of silver and gold. *You must not.*

"Why not?" Scriddle hissed. "You think I'll let her live, after what she's done to us?"

You have to, Pariasa said. *Remember the book?*

"You've got . . . Melcheron's book?" Poison whispered hoarsely. Of course. They might have searched Aelthar's and Pariasa's rooms, but not Scriddle's.

"Be silent!" Scriddle cried, pointing down at her with his knife.

You must not kill her, Pariasa begged him. *It would be bad for all of us.*

Poison fought to clear the fog in her head. This was important. There was something happening here that she did not yet understand, and her life depended on figuring it out. Why was it that they thought she was dangerous? Why not kill her and be done with it? And what did it have to do with Melcheron's book?

"Why not kill her?" Scriddle hissed, echoing her own

thoughts. He cupped her chin in his free hand and lifted her up, so that she was standing against the wall. The movement made the broken rib jolt and jar, and she almost passed out. She would not have believed that pain could reach that level of intensity. Surely she must die of it, and yet she lived. "Why not kill her?" Scriddle said again, his face inches from hers. "After all, the last one died without much of a fuss."

And there it was. The final clue had been afforded her. The last tumbler of the lock had been engaged, and the door to understanding swung open. Now she knew it all, from start to finish. Her tale had never been about rescuing her sister at all. That was just the spur to set her on the track. It all seemed so ridiculous, so simple, so *unfair*, that she could not stop herself from laughing. It was a low, bitter chuckle and it hurt her, for even the slightest movement made her rib stab at her insides. Blood flecked her lips, and still she laughed.

Scriddle and Pariasa watched her in disbelief.

"Is it the way of your kind to laugh at death?" Scriddle asked.

"You can't kill me," Poison said, still caught in the grip of that agonizing mirth. "You can't kill me. I'm the new Hierophant."

She knows! Pariasa said. Scriddle glared at her, then back at Poison. She saw on his face that she was right.

"It's in that book, isn't it?" she said, finding strength to speak, smiling through the tangle of her hair and the smears of red on her lips. "The book of Melcheron's life. You knew what he was writing. He was writing the story of a new apprentice, one who hated phaeries, one who would become the bane of your kind and take back our Realm from you." She laughed again. "All this . . . all this was a test. All this was my apprenticeship. That's why he left me so many clues; that's why he told me the truth, that this was all a phaerie tale. He wanted me to know, because one day I would be the one to write it."

"This is idiocy!" Scriddle cried. "A phaerie tale? Are you mad now?"

But Poison was never more sure of anything in her life. "You stole the book so that nobody would know who murdered him, but when you read it, you found a name. *My* name." Finally, the laughter died, and she grew serious. "There's an irony here, though. I never hated phaeries much until you took Azalea from me. You *made* me hate you. You turned me into what I am. Perhaps that was part of the tale. Perhaps he was moulding me as a successor." She coughed and gave a bitter sneer. "And I will take the Hierophant's quill and I will make your kind pay."

"Not if I end your life right here," Scriddle said, but uncertainty showed in his eyes.

"But you can't," she replied. "Don't you see? This is my story. That's why the Hierophant could die, but when I tried, everything unravelled. It's the story of how I become the Hierophant. The tale can do without him; it can't do without me. If you kill me, you kill yourself and everyone else. Until this tale is done, until I'm appointed Hierophant, I have to live."

"Such nonsense you humans talk," said Scriddle and stabbed her.

Poison's violet eyes went wide in surprise and disbelief. The knife had gone in low and to her side, beneath her ribs. She gaped, and blood trickled in runnels from the corner of her mouth. Her body had suddenly become numb and cold; she barely felt this new pain from the blade, for shock swamped it in ice.

He wrenched the knife free, and she shuddered. A moistness was spreading across her hip and the outside of her thigh. She looked into Scriddle's dark eyes, saw the glimmer of triumph therein. How could this be happening? She had been so sure, so sure . . .

Then Pariasa screamed. It was a high, fluting sound, terrible to the ear, for a voice so beautiful should never be distorted in fear or distress. Scriddle looked, and he saw, too. The walls seemed to be *thinning*, becoming less solid than they once were. Pariasa's eyes were fixed on her delicate hands, through which the structure of bonework beneath could nearly be seen. She staggered weakly, collapsing on to a settee. Poison shuddered in a breath. Even the air seemed fake, as if it was all dissolving into a dream.

Scriddle turned back to her, wild-eyed. "What is this? What are you doing?"

"I told you," she whispered, with a note of triumph in her voice. "You can't kill me. This is my tale."

My love, you must listen to her, Pariasa cried.

"No!" Scriddle shrieked, and he plunged the knife into Poison a second time. This one was deeper, and in her stomach. She whimpered at the impact, at the terrible piercing of the blade through her flesh. Once more the knife was pulled out, wet with her blood. She tottered and would have fallen if Scriddle had not been holding her up, for he had grabbed her by the throat again. There was no strength left in her, nothing left to resist him with. A tear slid from one violet eye, dropping to the stone floor. She fancied that it might pass through, for the floor was so wan and faded now that it was almost ghostly, and would have been incapable of supporting them if they were not so ghostly, too. Her vision glazed over, but she could still see how Scriddle's hair was falling out in clumps, how his teeth had become loose, how the knuckles stood out on his knife hand. In the background, Pariasa was levering herself weakly to her feet.

Stop! she cried. *You're killing us!*

But Scriddle had madness in his eye. "She will not beat us this way! She's a human!"

"You're ... already beaten," Poison said, managing a red smile. "Finish it. The last laugh will be mine."

Scriddle howled in fury, and he raised his knife a third time to plunge it into her. But at that moment, Pariasa launched herself towards him, a knife of her own appearing in her slender hand. With a cry she buried it in the side of Scriddle's neck. The world seemed to shudder to a halt.

I want to live, Pariasa whispered.

Scriddle's eyes went wide, and he struggled backwards, clutching at his throat. Poison slumped to the floor, no longer supported by his grip. He still kept his gaze fixed on her, as if it were she that had put the blade in him and not his lover. He tried to speak, but all that came out was a tide of blood that washed over his chin. Then his eyes rolled back in his head and he toppled backwards, crashing through a dressing table and bringing it down on top of him.

Poison struggled to raise her head. There was noise all around her now, a terrible clamour, a roaring in her ears and a crashing from outside. She saw Pariasa kneel down before her, almost a skeleton now, crystal tears falling from her alien eyes. She laid her hands on Poison's side, and on her stomach. Then the trolls were there, Grugaroth looming into the room like a thunderhead. He was saying something, but she could not understand, and she felt lighter than a feather as she floated up into blackness.

TO END THE TALE

LANTERN light filtered through her lashes in dim polygons.

Other sensations followed, like colour washes on a painting. Awareness, memory, pain. But the pain was more of an ache now. She could feel the heavy folds of a thick blanket on the skin of her arm. She was too weary to open her eyes fully, though she could tell that there were others in the room with her. She was alive. That was enough for now. At some point, she slept again.

This time, when she woke, her eyes flickered open involuntarily. She was in a small room, dark and close, the black stone walls leaning in. Lanterns stirred in their brackets. A distant storm pounded the castle. Someone was next to her; she could tell by his breathing that it was Bram. She moved her head, wincing as her bandaged ribs twinged. He was sitting there, still wearing the same hide clothes he had been when she first saw him in Gull, the same wide-brimmed hat and thick gloves. He was leaning slightly forward in his chair, his head bowed, asleep.

She smiled fondly, watching him for a while. The

cantankerous old bear had dozed off at his post. Feeling safer than she had in a long time, she decided to join him in oblivion.

The third time she woke, there was the weight of a cat on her chest. She opened her eyes and saw Andersen there, curled into a black muff on top of the blankets. He raised his head, sensing she was awake, and blinked green eyes at her; then he gave her a meow of welcome. Peppercorn was there in an instant, crying with joy and typically working herself into a fluster. Poison endured it indulgently. It was just her way.

She gathered strength rapidly under the ministrations of her friends and those Antiquarians who were well versed in the healing lore. They told her that her survival was due to Pariasa more than anyone; she had used her phaerie magick to undo much of the damage that Scriddle had done. But it was a close call, nonetheless. It was easy to guess that none of them remembered the way their world had begun to fall apart as Scriddle stabbed her; like the first time, it had fled their minds in the way of all things that a person wishes not to know. She was content to let it be.

Despite the aches and pains and weakness, it was a happy time. Poison enjoyed the company of Fleet, Peppercorn, Andersen, and Bram as she recovered. Never before had they been together simply for the fact of being together; there had always been a purpose, a quest, something urgent pushing them on or a danger to be avoided. Now, it was just them, and Poison felt again that sensation of belonging that had always eluded her in her childhood, this time unsullied by complications. Sleep sometimes brought nightmares of Scriddle, stabbing her again and again; but wakefulness was a better time than she had ever remembered, and she felt it was precious.

Fleet told her the whole story when she was strong enough to sit up in bed and drink soup; there was not much to tell that she had not already learned. He recounted how Grugaroth and the trolls had heard Pariasa's scream and overwhelmed the elven guards, arriving in time to raise the alarm. Pariasa herself had disappeared in the clamour, and had not been seen since. Melcheron's book had been found in Scriddle's chambers by the Antiquarians, though it was a hard search, and if they had not known it was there then they never would have managed to dig it from concealment. Its contents were a closely guarded secret, but Fleet knew — she could tell by the new look in his eyes. Admiration. Expectation. Hope. She didn't want to deal with those things right now. She didn't even know how to be Hierophant, let alone whether she wanted to be. It was the one dark cloud over her.

No, that was not strictly true. There was another. Azalea.

Her sister was lost to her.

ဢၜၜ

Poison had sent one of the Antiquarians to Gull to determine what had become of her father and stepmother, and to find her sister. When the report came back, it was much as she had expected and dreaded, for she was learning to accommodate the irregular flow of time between the worlds. The Realm of Man had moved on without her. The Antiquarian made his subtle enquiries and returned. He never did tell Hew or Snapdragon about their daughter Poison, that she was still alive and well. Poison had asked him not to. Better that the old wounds stayed closed.

Azalea did indeed come back to Gull, arriving there almost exactly two weeks after she had disappeared and Poison had gone after her. There was no question made of accepting her, even though she had been snatched as a young child and returned as an adolescent. Who knew the ways of phaeries? All they knew was that she was back, and the changeling was gone. The whole village celebrated. They thanked fortune for the mercy of returning this child to them, never once thinking to curse it for taking her away in the first place and stealing so many years of her life. They looked on the bright side of tragedy. That was the way in the Black Marshes.

Hew had grieved for his daughter Poison for many years, cherishing the hope that she might one day come back to him as his youngest daughter had, treasuring the last message that she had given Azalea, who now realized who it was that she had met on that day in Shieldtown. But Poison never came home, and the years went by, and sorrow can only last for so long before it must be shed or it will consume the sorrower.

All the time Snapdragon was there to support him. With Poison gone, theirs was a harmonious home once again, and she made him a good spouse. Hew's love for his wife deepened, overcoming that which he had felt for Poison and Azalea's mother, Faraway, and in time she bore him two boy-children. Hew and Snapdragon never left Gull, and they were old now, having lived a long and happy life together.

Azalea, though — she could never forget that moment when she and her elder sister had come face-to-face. She could not stop thinking of how Poison had gone out into the world looking for her, and how she might still be looking now, fruitlessly, never knowing that the object of her search was back at the place where she had started. And she, like Poison, had some of the Old Blood in her, as Fleet would say. So she left Gull on her twentieth birthday and set off in search of her sister, who had set off in search of *her* in the same way, many years before. That was the last anyone had seen of her. She could be wandering still.

❧

Time passed, though whether days or weeks Poison could not tell. Fleet kept her busy by teaching her some of the responsibilities of the post she had been appointed to. Poison was reluctant at first. She had not even considered whether she wanted to be Hierophant yet. But the pain of loss was unbearable, and she needed something to take her mind off Azalea.

She threw herself into her studies. If this whole tale had been some convoluted test of her worthiness, then she had passed it with flying colours; but the Hierophant had not counted on his own murder, and so she was still unprepared in the academic arts. Now that she responded to Fleet's lessons, he found her an incredibly adept pupil.

"For that is why only humans can become Hierophants," he told her. "We may seem the weakest and most insignificant of all the Realms, but our strength comes in other ways. We have what no other race has: imagination. Any one of us, even the lowliest, can create worlds within ourselves; we can people them with the most extraordinary creatures, the most amazing inventions, the most incredible things. We can live in those worlds ourselves, if we choose; and in our own worlds, we can be as we want to be. Imagination is as close as we will ever be to godhead, Poison, for in imagination, we can create wonders."

He was right. All those stories, all the tests that she had been through on her way here — Lamprey, the Bone Witch, Asinastra, Aelthar, and Scriddle — they had shown that she had the mettle to be what she was appointed to be. Imagination was in her blood, but she needed to learn how to craft it.

The days and weeks that followed were good ones. Poison divided her time between her schooling and spending time with her friends. The storm-lashed castle was hers, at least in the eyes of its occupants, and though she resisted, she found herself thinking of it more and more as home. The black stone corridors became familiar to her; the labyrinth of books that was the Great Library grew comforting; the rugs and hearth of her chambers (for she was given Melcheron's rooms, as was the tradition) were a welcome sanctuary. She dressed now in robes of purple and white, for there was no more need for the tough, practical clothes of the marsh. As she mastered her studies, she became more and more confident, and with that confidence came a lessening of the fear she had felt at becoming Hierophant. Though she knew that there was nobody else to take her place, that if she refused the appointment then a free-for-all would ensue between the other Lords and Ladies, she had always told herself that she could say no whenever she chose. She put off the decision as long as possible. Though there might be no guarantee that the new Hierophant would not be as bad as Scriddle if she turned down the post, she would not allow herself to be forced unwillingly into something she did not want to do, whatever the consequences.

But time has a way of stealthily deciding a person's mind without her conscious knowledge, and as she studied and procrastinated, Poison found one day that she had come to know her choice. She had allowed everyone to assume she would become Hierophant while secretly reserving her right to refuse; now, suddenly, she realized that she, too, assumed she would become Hierophant. The role had settled on her shoulders like a cloak, and it fitted perfectly. The decision was made.

Bram left them soon after. Poison begged him to stay with her, to live in the castle, and he harrumphed and blushed and muttered his apologies, but he was adamant.

"Wouldn't be anything for me to do here," he said. "I'm a simple man, Poison. I've no place around all these books. I earned myself three silver sovereigns — a long time ago, it seems — and I'm going to spend them. A house in the mountains, with nobody else around, where I can keep myself to myself. I've done my bit, I think; time to claim my reward."

Poison forced a sad smile. "*Four* sovereigns," she said. "I offered you another if you came into Maeb's house after me, remember? You refused then, but you still came. I owe you that one."

"Four sovereigns," Bram said proudly, twirling the end of his moustache. "I'll not need to do a day's work again."

"I wish you weren't going, Bram," Poison said, hugging him.

He hugged her back, and for the first time he did not seem awkward doing so. "The time has come," he said. "You don't need an old man like me around anymore."

"There'll be such a tale about you, Bram," she promised. "I'll write it myself."

Bram's eyes misted then, and he looked almost on the verge of tears. "You take care, girl," he said, and he left her then, never to return.

Peppercorn was inconsolable for a time after Bram departed, but as was her habit, her mood switched overnight on the third day and she shed her grief and was once again happy and flighty. She and Andersen had elected to stay with Poison, there in the castle. Poison was glad of it. She would rather have Peppercorn where she could see her.

It was Peppercorn who was her true solace in all of this. For though Poison's sister was gone, lost in the wilds of the world, Poison was not entirely alone. She remembered with shame how she had been willing to leave Peppercorn in the Bone Witch's house, and how it was only Bram's sense of honour and good-heartedness that had persuaded her to let Peppercorn come. Poison had gradually been becoming Peppercorn's surrogate older sister ever since. Peppercorn was as close to her as her family . . . closer, in fact, since Poison had always been somewhat alienated from her parents, and she had never really known Azalea. Peppercorn needed someone to look after her, and Poison needed someone to look after; unwittingly, the two of them had formed a bond, and in the days after Poison discovered Azalea was lost, it strengthened further. In the search for one sister, Poison had accidentally found another, for she thought of Peppercorn as a sister in all but blood now. In losing Azalea, she had gained Peppercorn. Perhaps, in the eyes of some, it was a fair trade.

❧❧❧

There was joy and sadness, but all too soon Poison found herself in the place that she had so long dreaded to go. Melcheron's chambers had become hers, but she had never set foot in the largest of them until now. That one held too many bad memories. It was the one in which she had first met him, in which he had shattered her illusions of life in a few short sentences, and in which he had been murdered by Pariasa.

She went to his desk, where they had found the last Hierophant slumped with Asinastra's knife in his back. She took a seat, and she looked down at the blank tome lying open before her. It had not been moved; nobody had dared touch it. Rain pounded the circular windows behind her. A fire crackled in the hearth. She held the quill pen in one hand, having dipped it in the water-like, transparent liquid that Melcheron had been using for ink.

She sat there for hours. Where should she start? What should she do? How could she begin to finish what Melcheron had begun, when she did not know how he had begun it, or where he had gotten to when he died?

But he was writing my tale, she said. *And who knows my tale better than me?*

She turned the pages of the tome, each one blank and empty, until she reached the very first page.

No tale can be read until it is finished, she remembered. The Hierophant thought that he was writing the tale of how his new apprentice had been plucked from the obscurity of the

Black Marshes, how she had fought her way through adversity to reach him at the castle. Perhaps, in his mind, the rest of the story had been her training and finally her succession to the post of Hierophant. But the story had changed. He had been murdered. And while the point of the tale was essentially the same, it was now going to be told in *her* way. For it had always been her tale, after all, and now it was ended, it had to be recorded.

She began to write.

Once upon a time there was a young lady who lived in a marsh, and her name was Poison.

Though she could not see the words, she knew they were there as clearly as if she could read them off the page. It seemed as good a beginning as any. She put the quill to the paper again, and the words came to her, flooding in almost as fast as she could transfer them to the page. It was as if the book had already been written, and she was merely tracing over sentences that were already there. It felt so natural, so easy, that a fierce grin spread across her face, and she hunched over the page, writing with a steadily growing fever.

She wrote, and wrote, and wrote. She remembered Fleet bringing her food and drink, which she took with one hand so that she did not have to slow down the torrent of words that gushed from her mind to the nib of the quill and onto the paper. Fleet never said anything, unwilling to disturb her. Though she learned later that she had been writing for the equivalent of two days and nights without a break, it felt like only moments to her. What Melcheron had started, she had *re*started; and when she turned the last leaf of the book, she realized with a shock that she was on her final few sentences. The amount of pages in the tome fitted her words exactly.

And so her tale came to an end. With its completion, it would be made legible for all. But it was only her *first* tale; that much she knew. What had Fleet said, back in the Great Library? *Some people have many tales.* Finishing this story was only the beginning. With the completion of this work, she would truly become the new Hierophant, and there was much to be done. The Realm of Man was still overrun by phaeries; humans still skulked in the low places and high peaks of the world, fearing to tread in their own land. All that would change. She would write them the tale of a leader, someone to take back what was theirs. Someone to make her race proud again. This was what Aelthar had feared; this was what she would do.

When the last words of the tale were written, she finished with a flourish, and as the final stroke was made, the words on the page emerged into being. The invisible lines of her quill turned black, and the story showed itself. She looked over what she had done and sighed. So much had passed, and it had come to this. In the sentences and paragraphs of that tome were her sorrow, her triumph, her heart. She had trapped them all inside those bindings. Was she, too, trapped inside some greater bindings, written by another, greater Hierophant? And was he or she trapped also in that way, and so on, into infinity?

Perhaps. Perhaps not. All she could do was deal with the reality that was presented to her. And she had much to do.

Slowly, she closed the tome and looked down at its embossed cover. There was a title there, where there had not been one before. She felt a smile tug her lips. A single word: *Poison.*

It would suffice.